The tickle at the back of Taylor's neck stood her hair on end.

She whirled around, her gaze staring into the darkness of the garden. Someone was watching her, staring from the safety of some hidden place. She gasped for air as if all the oxygen had been taken away from her.

"Who's there? Who…?" The words came out as a whisper then they died in her mouth. Her heart pounded in her chest and the sound roared in her ears. A wall of fear surrounded her. She forced her feet to move, to carry her toward the house. Her plodding steps turned into a run as she headed for the light at the kitchen door.

"Where have you been?" The words came at her from the darkness. A jolt of adrenaline raced through her body before she identified the voice as Donovan's. Then he grabbed hold of her arm and pulled her toward him.…

Dear Harlequin Intrigue Reader,

You won't be able to resist a single one of our May books. We have a lineup so shiver inducing that you may forget summer's almost here!

- *Executive Bodyguard* is the second book in Debra Webb's exciting new trilogy, THE ENFORCERS. For the thrilling conclusion, be sure you pick up *Man of Her Dreams* in June.

- Amanda Stevens concludes her MATCHMAKERS UNDERGROUND series with *Matters of Seduction*. And the Montana McCalls are back, in B.J. Daniels's *Ambushed!*

- We also have two special premiers for you. Kathleen Long debuts in Harlequin Intrigue with *Silent Warning*, a chilling thriller. And LIPSTICK LTD., our special promotion featuring sexy, sassy sleuths, kicks off with Darlene Scalera's *Straight Silver*.

- A few of your favorite Harlequin Intrigue authors have some special books you'll love. Rita Herron's *A Breath Away* is available this month from HQN Books. And, in June, Joanna Wayne's *The Gentlemen's Club* is being published by Signature Spotlight.

Harlequin Intrigue brings you the best in breathtaking romantic suspense with six fabulous books to enjoy. Please write to us—we love to hear from our readers.

Sincerely,

Denise O'Sullivan
Senior Editor
Harlequin Intrigue

THE SEDGWICK CURSE

SHAWNA DELACORTE

HARLEQUIN®

TORONTO • NEW YORK • LONDON
AMSTERDAM • PARIS • SYDNEY • HAMBURG
STOCKHOLM • ATHENS • TOKYO • MILAN • MADRID
PRAGUE • WARSAW • BUDAPEST • AUCKLAND

ISBN 0-373-22846-5

THE SEDGWICK CURSE

www.eHarlequin.com

Printed in U.S.A.

ABOUT THE AUTHOR

Although award-winning author Shawna Delacorte has lived most of her life in Los Angeles and has a background working in television production, she is currently living in Wichita, Kansas. Among her writing accomplishments she is honored to include her placement on the *USA TODAY* bestseller list. In addition to writing full-time, she teaches a fiction writing class in the Division of Continuing Education at Wichita State University. Shawna enjoys hearing from her readers and can be reached at 6505 E. Central, Box #300, Wichita, KS 67206. You may also visit her at her author page at the Harlequin Web site—www.eHarlequin.com.

Books by Shawna Delacorte

HARLEQUIN INTRIGUE
413—LOVER UNKNOWN
520—SECRET LOVER
656—IN HIS SAFEKEEPING
846—THE SEDGWICK CURSE

CAST OF CHARACTERS

Lord Donovan Sedgwick—He inherited the title upon the death of his father, James Sedgwick, though he hasn't come to grips with his father's sudden death.

Taylor MacKenzie—She presented herself at Sedgwick Manor as a writer doing research on British country festivals, a ploy to cover her real reason for traveling from Kansas to the English countryside, and specifically to the Sedgwick estate.

George Bradley—Head of staff for the Sedgwick estate, as other members of the Bradley family have been for one hundred and fifty years. There are no secrets in the Sedgwick family history or hidden places on the estate that members of the Bradley family haven't known about throughout the ages.

Michael Edgeware—The police inspector in charge of investigating the murders has known the Sedgwick family for years. Donovan's father was responsible for him being passed over for a promotion. Does he carry his resentment over to Donovan?

Jeremy Edwards—Owner of the village inn that has been in the Edwards' family for generations. Does he know something through his family history about the original murders that was never in the newspapers or part of a police report?

Alexander Sedgwick—Donovan's cousin, a playboy with a penchant for the gaming tables of London. Donovan has paid off several of Alex's gambling debts in the past.

Constance Smythe—She has her eye on Donovan as a marriage prospect and covets the status of Lady of the Manor. Could she be the rumored descendent of the illegitimate son William Sedgwick fathered over one hundred years ago and have a legal claim against the Sedgwick estate?

Byron Treadwell—Head of the village newspaper that has been in the family for generations. The Treadwells and Sedgwicks have been adversaries since the original murders committed by William Sedgwick one hundred years ago. Byron has a personal grudge against Donovan Sedgwick.

Chapter One

"What the hell—" Lord Donovan Sedgwick angrily slammed the local village newspaper on the breakfast table in disgust, brushing aside the more imposing *London Times*.

"Look at this, Bradley, right here on the front page. The explosion at the crypt happened at midnight last night, so how did Byron Treadwell get his hands on the story in time to make the morning edition of this scurrilous rag he calls a newspaper? No one asked my permission, no one interviewed me to find out what I had to say. And I know for a fact that Inspector Edgeware did not make a statement to the press. Byron had no right to take what happened last night at the family cemetery on the private grounds of the estate and sensationalize it all over the front page with his lurid speculations. And he's done it again—splashed his *fictionalized* version of the family curse all over the front page."

Donovan took another sip of his morning coffee as he tried to calm his anger. The Treadwells and the Sedgwicks had been at odds for a little over one hundred years, starting with the night Donovan's great-grandfather, Lord William Sedgwick, had murdered two people in a fit of complete madness.

The Treadwell newspaper had sensationalized the

crime, the trial, the execution and the sealing of Lord William Sedgwick's body inside the specially built crypt. Then the newspaper had turned its attention to the resulting curse that had been placed on the Sedgwick family, and the story of the curse continued to appear in the newspaper for several months following the interment of Lord William's body. The curse had been uttered exactly one hundred years to the day before the midnight explosion at the crypt.

Donovan allowed a frown to wrinkle across his forehead as he recalled the movement in the bushes at the cemetery following the explosion. A wave of disgust surged through him. It would be just the kind of thing Byron Treadwell would do—stage a sensational incident such as blowing open the crypt himself on the hundredth anniversary of Lord William's burial so he could sell more newspapers and publicly embarrass the Sedgwick family in the bargain, especially with the annual festival held on the grounds of the Sedgwick estate only two weeks away.

"This telegram arrived for you an hour ago, sir." Bradley handed it to him, then waited to see if there would be a response he would need to deal with. The tall, dark-haired man of forty-five maintained his normal, stoic manner. He showed no outward reaction to yet another of the moody outbursts Donovan had displayed following the untimely death of his father, Lord James Sedgwick, two months ago.

"Damn! It's that writer—Taylor MacKenzie. I completely forgot about him. He's from the United States. He corresponded with my father for about a month. He's researching some kind of book on British country festivals and is interested in our annual event—how it originally came about, the changes through the years…that kind of thing. Dad told him he could stay here for the two weeks prior to the festival. According to this telegram he flies into London late this afternoon and plans to drive straight away from the airport to the Cotswolds. He should arrive here sometime this evening."

Donovan's jaw tightened into a hard line of determination. He didn't have time for this and he certainly didn't have the desire to deal with some stranger in the house. "Put him in the second-floor corner room of the old wing. That should give him a feel for the history of the place." He mumbled under his breath, the words not really meant for Bradley's ears, "It'll also keep him out of my hair. I'm in no mood to put up with some nosy writer from the States."

He glanced out the window toward the family cemetery. The yellow crime-scene tape marked off the area of investigation around the crypt. Several police constables combed the grounds for any clue as to exactly what had happened. A little tremor of apprehension darted through his body. "Not with whatever it is that's going on out there."

"Yes, sir. I'll see that the room is prepared."

As Bradley turned to leave, Donovan stopped him. "I talked to Alex yesterday. He'll be here sometime this afternoon. For the past five months Constance has been doing her usual efficient job of organizing this year's festival, but Alex volunteered to give me a hand with the last-minute details and I'm happy to let him do it."

Donovan had been pleased when his first cousin, Alexander Sedgwick, had phoned. He and Alex were very close despite the vast differences in their lifestyles and the six-year gap in their ages, Alex's twenty-seven years compared with Donovan's thirty-three years. When they were children, Donovan had been annoyed at the way his young cousin would tag along, and it seemed as if Alex and his family were at the manor house every weekend. But as they grew older, the two men had developed a much closer bond.

He looked forward to Alex's visit and help with the festival if for no other reason than to distance himself from working so closely with Constance. Constance Smythe was a tireless worker, but she always made him uneasy. She was too willing to take on any chore, too quick to volunteer for any committee or project the village was involved with…much too anxious to find excuses to be at the manor house.

THE MOOD WAS RELAXED, a far cry from the stress that had been pushing at Donovan all day. After dinner he and Alex had gone to the snooker room where the two evenly matched players resumed their ongoing personal tournament, a contest that had started almost ten years ago. They played for two hours before Donovan returned his cue stick to the rack. He glanced at his watch. It was only nine o'clock even though it felt much later.

Donovan stifled a yawn. "I didn't get much sleep last night. I think I'll retire for the evening. Apparently that writer fellow isn't going to arrive tonight."

Alex returned his cue to the rack, then picked up the bottle of ale from the table and handed it to Donovan. "Here, you still have a swallow left." A sly grin turned the corners of his mouth. "I hate to see anything go to waste, especially good ale."

"Thanks." Donovan finished the last drink, then returned the empty bottle to the table.

Alex's manner became serious as he stared at Donovan for a moment, then spoke in carefully measured words. "Since you haven't said anything, I guess I'll just have to be brash and ask. I saw the local newspaper headlines and the police barricade at the cemetery. What's going on?"

A quick jab of anger surged through Donovan. The thought of Byron Treadwell and his sensationalist journalism still rankled. "It's very strange. At midnight last night a loud explosion woke everyone for miles around. When I went to see what happened, I found the door of Great-Grandfather William's crypt blasted off its hinges, but the sarcophagus inside appeared to be undamaged." Then a shiver of apprehension revealed his inner fears. "I don't know how or why it happened. I insisted that Inspector Edgeware take personal charge of the case, but Mike doesn't know any more about what happened than I do…at least nothing that he's conveying to me."

"So that's why you asked me to stop in the village and pick up your order at the chemist shop. You didn't want to make an appearance and be inundated with questions."

"Hopefully the furor over this will die down in a couple of days." Donovan paused for a moment to collect his thoughts as he stole a quick glance out the window. A jolt of anxiety set his nerves on edge and left his stomach tied in knots. "I'm worried, Alex. I have a terrible premonition that whatever is going on out there is far from over."

Alex tried to suppress a chuckle without much success. "You're not talking about that stupid curse thing, are you? How did that go? *To rise from the ruins—what is born of the fires of hell cannot die.* Some demented old man who was supposed to have mystical powers utters some ambiguous words as Great-Grandfather's body is being sealed in the crypt and says the curse would come to fruition in one hundred years. I could understand some ignorant and superstitious villagers in the eighteenth century buying into all this curse stuff, but not a mere hundred years ago when all this happened. And now in the twenty-first century everyone is suddenly jumping at every shadow because of some coincidental explosion that probably has some very logical explanation."

Donovan snapped out his irritation. "That's not funny, Alex." He stared out the window into the blackness of the night. Another tremor of apprehension rippled through his body, leaving him very unsettled. "Something extremely bizarre is going on and I don't have any rational explanation for it." And that included the blinding headaches that had attacked him several times in the past two months since the death of his father, like steel bands tightening around his head. They left him confused, disoriented and with memory lapses—and frightened about what it meant and what the future held.

The two men talked for a few more minutes, then Alex went to the room he had been occupying on his visits to the estate since he was a little boy. Donovan remained downstairs in the entry hall staring out a window, trying to force his eyes to see whatever it was he sensed lurking in the darkness.

The police had left a light at the site of the crypt explosion. He watched as fingers of fog crept across the ground, edging their way around the tombstones belonging to generations of the Sedgwick family—generations too numerous to count and, according to many, better left forgotten. The ground fog blanketed everything in a damp shroud just as it had that night a century ago. The light electrified the mist with an eerie spectral glow. A shudder swept through Donovan's body, causing him to hunch his shoulders as if warding off a cold wind.

"Do you require anything else, sir, before I secure the house for the night?" Bradley's last duty of the day before retiring to his quarters was to see that all the doors and windows were locked and most of the lights turned out.

"No, nothing. You go on, I'll see to the front door."

"Very well, sir. Good night."

Donovan continued to stare out the window, lost in his own thoughts and unspoken fears. He wasn't sure how much time had passed before the sound of the doorbell startled him back into reality. He opened the door to the late-night visitor.

The low, throaty voice floated toward him through the night air. "Hello. I'm Taylor MacKenzie."

"You…you're Taylor MacKenzie?" Donovan stared in disbelief at the beautiful woman standing at the front door, bathed in the soft glow of the porch light. He felt the tightening in his chest as a quick surge of heated energy darted through his reality. Something about her looked so familiar, as if he should know her, but that was impossible. No man with a spark of life in him could ever forget having met this vision who jolted his senses and nearly took his breath away. But still…he couldn't shake the strange, almost overwhelming sensation of déjà vu.

The tightening in his chest moved lower in his body as his breathing quickened. His gaze dropped to the swell of her breast, the lacy pattern of her bra faintly visible through the soft material of her shirt. Well-worn jeans encased long legs and hugged the curve of her hips without appearing too tight. He took a steadying breath in an attempt to bring his rapidly escalating yet totally inappropriate desires under control.

It had never occurred to him that the writer his father had been corresponding with was a woman. He forced his gaze away from her and toward the sports car parked in the circular drive in front of the house. She had enough suitcases piled on the luggage rack and in the storage space behind the seat to be moving in permanently.

The mysterious explosion at the crypt made the presence of a stranger in the house unwelcome. He wished that he had written to her following his father's death and withdrawn the invitation to stay at the manor house and use the family archives.

He did not have time in his life for this unexpected woman, or the desire that flooded his body, certainly not until he came to terms with his father's premature death and resolved the problem of what had happened at the crypt. He was glad he had decided to put the writer in a bedroom far away from his own suite of rooms. Hopefully it would keep temptation at bay for the duration of her visit. And there was no doubt in his mind that she represented temptation of the most primal kind—temptation combined with some strange indefinable allure that left him puzzled and a bit rattled.

A touch of hesitation surrounded her words, matching the confused expression on her face. "And you're Lord Sedgwick?" She extended her hand and offered a pleasant albeit businesslike smile. "It's a pleasure to meet you. I certainly appreciate your hospitality and cooperation in opening your home and the family archives. It will be a great help to me in my research. Although I must admit that I had pictured you as being older."

The title had led her to make the assumption about his age. This man was much younger than she had anticipated, not that much older than her thirty years. His hair, a soft shade of brown, was thick and full. It was long enough to hang over his shirt collar in back and cover his ears. She had an almost irresistible impulse to run her fingers through it. The front dangled across his forehead in a disorganized manner that made him look little-boy innocent and very sexy at the same time—a dangerous combination, but one that she found very compelling. He appeared to be about six foot two—tall, even compared to her five-seven.

His piercing blue eyes held a haunted look as if they had witnessed all the horrors of a thousand centuries. He seemed to be staring right through her. He was a total stranger, yet somehow she sensed something about him, something very familiar and at the same time unsettling. Something that left her decidedly uneasy as it put her nerves on edge and her senses on alert.

Something she didn't understand.

Donovan made no effort to respond to the woman's out-stretched hand. He simply stood there staring. Her short, windblown hair framed her face in a wild profusion of bright copper. Her large emerald eyes were wide with in-nocence while still holding a wisdom far beyond her years. A distinct chill stabbed at his spine, a disturbing chill that somehow managed to become entwined with the very real heat of excitement that still nestled low in his body. Con-fusion clouded her face as she lowered her hand.

"This is the Sedgwick estate, isn't it? I'll admit that driving on your country roads was a little confusing for me, especially at night. I thought I'd taken all the correct turns. I realize it's late, but my telegram did say I'd be arriving tonight."

Her eyes widened as if a sudden thought had just oc-curred to her. A sense of urgency crept into her voice. "You did receive my telegram, didn't you?"

"Uh…yes, your telegram. Of course." Donovan shook the fuzziness from his brain and extended his hand toward her as he forced a smile. "I apologize for my rudeness. You took me by surprise. I'm Donovan Sedgwick. It was my father,

James Sedgwick, who you had been corresponding with. Please, come in." He stepped aside as she entered the house.

A tinge of red flushed across her cheeks indicating her embarrassment. "Oh, I'm so sorry. I should have realized that Lord Sedgwick wouldn't be answering his own door."

"The household staff have retired for the night. I happened to be in the entry hall when you rang the doorbell." A whiff of her perfume tickled his senses, drawing them even more taut. "I was expecting a man. The name Taylor led me to believe...well, I didn't realize my father had been corresponding with a woman." He noticed the hint of surprise that had quickly darted across her face. He felt it, too, the moment their hands clasped. It was an indefinable sensation—a combination of destiny, fate and desire that he found intriguing yet at the same time disturbing.

"I hope my gender won't present you with a problem." Taylor was thankful to have the sensually sparked physical contact broken. She surveyed the cavernous entry hall as she stepped into the room. A large crystal chandelier hung all the way from the top of the three-story cathedral ceiling. Richly paneled walls were lined with paintings she assumed to be the Sedgwick ancestors, and a large staircase with a hand-carved oak banister curved up to the second and third floors, supported by alabaster columns.

She shivered slightly as her gaze swept across the scene for the second time. The low lights shrouded the elegantly appointed entry hall in a dim gloominess. From what she had been able to observe upon her arrival at the estate, the gardens, grounds and buildings all seemed to be well maintained. The estate projected an image of wealth, but it still reminded her of a movie set from some old Gothic film where sinister happenings enveloped the occupants in a cloak of mystery and danger. An involuntary shiver darted up her spine. Did the rest of the house project an equally ominous feel?

"This is an interesting—" Her words stopped, her hand went to her mouth as a startled gasp escaped her throat when her gaze fell on the portrait hanging on the wall. She quickly turned to stare at Donovan, then returned her attention to the painting. Her throat tightened and her mouth went dry as she stared at the portrait. The subject of the painting stared back at her with the same eyes and features as her host, but with clothes from a century earlier. An oppressive stillness filled the entry hall. She tried to shed the sudden apprehension that settled over her, pressing down like a heavy weight.

Donovan followed her line of sight, the expression on her face saying more than words could convey. "That's my great-grandfather. His name was William." He pointed to another painting. "That one's my grandfather, Henry Sedgwick, and this one—" he indicated yet another painting "—is my father, James Sedgwick."

"Is your father here? I'd like to meet him after all our back-and-forth correspondence."

"My father died two months ago." His voice was flat, showing no emotion one way or the other.

"Oh…I'm so sorry. I didn't know." The unexpected news left her with an odd sensation, a combination of unfulfilled prophecy and destiny that totally baffled her. She tried to shake away the strange and uncomfortable feeling. "I hope my presence here won't be an inconvenience for you or an intrusion into your period of mourning."

Donovan mustered a smile and tried to project a gracious manner. "Of course not."

Taylor looked across the gallery of Sedgwick ancestors that preceded William, then the ones Donovan had identified, before returning her attention to her host. "No paint-ing of you?"

"No...not yet. I suppose it's something I'll have to do one of these days—tradition and all that." He was momen-tarily lost in thought, in a world of his own that he was un-willing to share with anyone else. Having the traditional portrait done was the last step in replacing his father as lord of the manor, a step he could not quite bring himself to take. The emotional turmoil and the circumstances con-nected to his father's death were still too painful for him.

Taylor studied Donovan as he stood there. This was not at all what she had expected. He was a very attractive, sexy and desirable man. She could not deny that he made her pulse race and her breathing quicken. The thought crossed her mind—and not for the first time since board-ing the plane for her transatlantic flight—that perhaps all of this had not been such a good idea after all. She should never have misrepresented herself, pretending to be a writer in order to gain access to the Sedgwick family archives for her own personal reasons.

At that precise moment she wished she was safely back in Wichita, Kansas, tending to her secretarial duties at the University rather than having taken a three-month leave of absence. But it was too late for that.

"Well." Donovan whirled around to face Taylor, feign-ing an affability he didn't feel. "I'm sure you must be tired. I imagine you'd like to go to your room, unpack and get settled in."

She raked her gaze across the entry hall again, the lav-ish setting in direct opposition to the ominous feeling that shoved at her reality. A tremor of apprehension darted through her body—a tremor that had a dark cloud of dan-ger and foreboding attached to it.

"I heard the doorbell and…hey, who do we have here?" The upbeat, cheerful voice came from the bottom of the staircase. "Aren't you going to introduce me to your friend?"

"Alex…" Donovan turned to face his cousin. "This is Taylor MacKenzie, the writer I told you would be staying here for the next two weeks." He returned his attention to Taylor. "Miss MacKenzie, this is my cousin, Alexander Sedgwick. Alex is here to help me get this year's festival off to a good start."

"Please, call me Taylor. Miss MacKenzie sounds so formal." She offered Donovan a dazzling smile.

"And you may call me Donovan rather than Lord Sedgwick." His words trailed off, as if his mind were on other things. "The title passed to me only two months ago. I haven't had it long enough to be comfortable with it yet." What he did not say was that he felt as if he did not really deserve the title even though it had been in the family as many centuries as the estate had. The title should still belong to his father.

"And you may call me whatever you like, as long as you promise to call me." Alex's attention and words were directed to Taylor as he extended a teasing smile followed by a quick but blatantly obvious survey of her physical assets.

She looked from Donovan to Alex, then to the painting of William Sedgwick. An uncomfortable chill swept across her skin. There was no mistaking the distinct family resemblance shared by the three men.

Alex crossed the entry hall to where Taylor stood, his outstretched hand grasping hers. "So, is this the *man* from the States who's researching a book about British country festivals?" He flashed a sexy grin as he again looked her up and down. "You certainly don't look much like a man to me. Of course, Donovan is stuck out here in the country away from London and doesn't get out much, but even he couldn't make this sort of a mistake."

She felt the heat of embarrassment return to her cheeks as she lowered her gaze. This made twice that she had been embarrassed since arriving at the estate and she hadn't even gotten past the entry hall. These two men, cousins who bore a dramatic similarity in appearance, were quite different in their demeanor. Donovan seemed very serious, a little distracted and what could even be called moody, but undeniably sexy. Alex, on the other hand, unabashedly flirted with her in an open and easy manner.

Donovan rang for Bradley, who made an immediate appearance. "This is Taylor MacKenzie. Please show Miss MacKenzie to her room and have someone bring in the luggage from her car."

He returned his attention to Taylor. "Bradley will see to your needs. Breakfast is served at eight o'clock. We'll have a chance to talk then." Again the heated desire swept through his body as he took one last look at her before turning to go to his suite of rooms in the new wing. "Good night, Taylor."

"Good night, Donovan." His abrupt attitude and departure surprised her and left her slightly unsettled. It was almost as if he was desperate to get away from her as fast as he could.

"Well, I guess that's my cue to leave. Good night, Taylor. I'll see you in the morning. Unless—" Alex flashed a wry grin as he winked at her "—there's something I can do for you tonight. I'm sure there's certain *needs* that I can handle far better than Bradley...." He allowed his voice to trail off as he openly leered at her.

She shot a quick glance at Bradley, but he showed no

reaction to Alex's words. She forced a polite chuckle, not at all sure how to interpret Alex's attitude and what he had said. "I can't think of a thing. I've had an incredibly long day and am definitely tired. I'm going to collapse in bed and get a good night's sleep." She turned her attention to the somber-looking man standing at the foot of the stairs.

"This way, Miss MacKenzie." Bradley showed Taylor to the second-floor room that had been prepared for the visiting writer. He demonstrated how to turn on the heat in the bedroom and acquainted her with the idiosyncrasies of the bathroom's ancient plumbing, then he departed. A few minutes later her luggage was delivered.

Taylor took in her surroundings. The four-poster bed dominated the well-appointed room. The furnishings were obviously antiques and looked very elegant, but not particularly comfortable. She undressed, then slipped into the large football jersey she had commandeered from her ex-fiancé a few years ago. Even though the room had been cleaned, a stuffiness clung to everything, attesting to the fact that it had not been occupied for quite some time. She opened one of the windows just enough to let in some fresh air, climbed into bed and turned off the lamp on the nightstand.

Sleep, however, eluded her. Overly tired—that was her explanation. Perhaps reading for a little while would help her fall asleep. She turned on the lamp and picked up the book she had started on the plane. She read only a couple of pages before her exhaustion won out and she succumbed to sleep.

IT WAS WELL PAST MIDNIGHT when the shadowy figure moved silently down the hallway, then entered a linen closet on the second floor of the old wing. He moved a cupboard aside, then slid back a small panel and peered into the adjoining room. The soft light from the reading lamp fell across the woman's face. Three large pillows propped up her back. A book rested in her lap. She appeared to have fallen asleep while reading.

Without even a whisper of sound, the secret door that led from the hall linen closet into the clothes closet in her bedroom swung open. The centuries-old house was filled with hidden doors and secret passages, and he knew all of them.

He stood inside the closet and watched her from behind the hanging clothes. Her long, dark lashes rested against her upper cheek. The gentle rise and fall of her breasts told him she was sleeping. She was his. She always had been and always would be…till death do them part.

He had time. It was still two weeks until the festival. It would be just as it should have been a century ago. It had been his intention that they should pledge their love to each other the night before the beginning of the festival, even though a couple of months earlier her husband had grown suspicious of his attentions toward her. But this would be different. This time there would not be any interference.

He stepped out of the closet and silently crossed the room, coming to a halt next to the bed. He reached out his hand and lightly touched her hair. What had she done to her hair? Where were the glossy raven tresses that had so captured his attention, the beautiful raven tresses that fell to her shoulders? Had his memory played tricks on him? He reached out his hand to touch her hair again just as she began to stir. He quickly withdrew as a soft moan escaped her throat and her hand moved toward her hair.

TAYLOR JERKED BOLT UPRIGHT in bed, her eyes wide open. Her heart pounded in her chest. She couldn't catch her breath. The acrid taste of adrenaline filled her mouth. She quickly glanced around, but nothing looked out of place. She was sure someone had been in the room with her. She had sensed it, felt a menacing presence that had frightened her out of her sleep. It must have been a bad dream, yet it all seemed so real.

She desperately needed some sort of rational explanation. She finally attributed the experience to exhaustion, trying to convince herself she had been overly susceptible to suggestion fueled by the ominous atmosphere of the centuries-old house and the lifetime of Sedgwick family history that surrounded her. She slid out of bed, went to the bathroom and got a drink of water.

She stopped by the large corner window on her way back to bed, pulling the drape aside to look out over the grounds. She spotted someone, a shadowy form, aimlessly wandering around the garden. She squinted in an attempt to identify the mysterious person, but to no avail.

A little tremor of anxiety moved through her body as she turned away from the window. She drew in a calming breath, held it a moment, then slowly exhaled. Her lack of sleep had caused her mind to play tricks on her. It was the only logical explanation. But still, the feeling of someone being in the room with her had seemed so real.

She decided to lock the bedroom door, but to her dismay the door turned out to have an old-type lock that required a key in order to be locked. She looked around, then grabbed a straight-backed wooden chair and propped it at an angle under the doorknob. The action made her feel a little foolish, but at that moment her instincts were screaming at her to remain alert and be very careful.

She tried to convince herself that things would make more sense in the morning after a good night's sleep. She turned off the lamp, then changed her mind. She knew it was ridiculous, but she felt she would sleep better with the light on. She switched the lamp on, then settled into bed.

Donovan stared up through the night air at the second-floor window, watching as the light went off then came on again a moment later. The blinding headache throbbed at his temples. Dark waves of confusion clouded his mind, leaving him disoriented. When and why had he gotten out of bed, dressed and left the house? What was he doing wandering around the garden in the middle of the night? Waves of apprehension washed through his body. He squeezed his eyes shut as he rubbed his temples in an attempt to force the pain away and make some sense of what had happened.

He had been experiencing the same symptoms his father had complained of for about three months prior to his death. There were the sudden headaches followed by disorientation, confusion and memory lapses.

Then two months ago James Sedgwick had committed suicide.

Had his father suspected he was going mad and killed himself before it became complete? While he still had some conscious control over his actions? Was the same thing now happening to Donovan? Was he himself going mad? Had the curse imposed on the family by his great-grandfather's brutal crimes finally come to fruition with the opening of the crypt?

Had he now become the recipient of the Sedgwick curse?

A cold jolt of fear assaulted his senses. It was a frightening puzzle and somehow he had to figure it out before he lost his ability to reason. And Taylor MacKenzie... something about her was so familiar. Somehow there had to be a connection, but what could it possibly be?

Donovan returned to his private living quarters in the

new wing. He poured a glass of water from the carafe he kept on his nightstand, took one of the tablets the doctor had prescribed for his sudden attack of blinding headaches, then fell on top of his bed. He closed his eyes and tried to force sleep in order to ease his confusion and drive away the pain. After tossing and turning for what seemed like an eternity, he finally fell into a troubled sleep.

Dark visions and strange dreams plagued him. The malevolent countenance of his great-grandfather's face appeared before him, then disappeared again. He caught fleeting glimpses of his father. He had a sense of a woman's face, an image from long ago, but it never quite came into focus. The images swirled around in evil black clouds that seemed to hide something even more sinister than they revealed.

Chapter Two

"Yes? Come in," Taylor responded to the knock at her bedroom door. She had just finished dressing and was making the bed before going downstairs for breakfast.

The door opened and a middle-aged woman entered. As soon as she saw what was happening, she rushed toward Taylor. "Oh, miss. Please don't do that. I'll see to your room for you. Is there anything special that you require?"

"No, nothing at all. I hope I won't be too much of an added burden to you." Maid service—this was certainly more than she had anticipated.

"Breakfast is being served in the informal dining room. It's on the ground floor, miss, to the right at the bottom of the stairs."

"Thank you." Taylor left the bedroom and followed the directions. Donovan and Alex were already seated at the table. Both men rose to their feet when she entered the room.

It was Donovan who spoke first. "I trust you found everything you needed. Did you sleep well?"

"Yes, I'm all settled in. It's a lovely room." Her strange dream about someone being in her room, *if* it had been a dream, flashed through her mind. No, she had not slept well at all. "I'm sure I'll be very comfortable."

She noted the haunted look in Donovan's eyes and the drawn lines on his face. It did not stop the pull of his sexual magnetism, of the very disruptive and baffling effect he had on her senses.

She quickly turned her attention to Alex. Unlike Donovan, no stress showed on his face. "Good morning."

There was no mistaking the glint in Alex's eyes as he allowed his gaze to wander across her features. "Well, international travel must agree with you. You look even better than last night."

Breakfast passed in an amiable manner. The conversation was casual, albeit superficial. Alex did most of the talking. The only truly uncomfortable moment came when he asked Taylor the titles of her other books. She sidestepped the issue by saying her writing credits were primarily magazine articles.

As soon as everyone had finished with their coffee, Donovan rose from his chair. He had tried to keep from staring at Taylor during breakfast, but he had been unable to keep his eyes off her. He hoped she hadn't noticed. He forced a casualness to his words that he did not feel. "If you like, I'll show you around the house and the grounds, then you can get started on your research."

"I don't want to intrude on your time, but I'd certainly appreciate the tour."

"I have some pressing business to take care of first." He glanced at his watch. "I'll meet you here in about an hour, if that's convenient for you."

"That will be perfect." She extended a gracious smile and forced an outer calm. Her inner jitters were another story, the result of the way he had been staring at her all through breakfast combined with the intense and unexpected attraction she felt toward him. She had never experienced that type of intensity, not even with her ex-fiancé. The potent combination proved impossible to dismiss.

Alex's voice intruded into her thoughts as he spoke to Donovan. "You don't need me for any of this. I promised Constance Smythe we would get together this morning and go over what she's done so far for the festival."

Donovan shot a warning look toward Alex. "I'd appreciate it if you did that at her house and not here."

"No problem. I'll go over there and get a status report. Then I have some personal business to take care of."

Alex grasped Taylor's hand and brought it to his lips, kissing the back of it in a courtly manner. "I'm sorry I won't be here to keep you company until Donovan is available to give you the tour."

A twinge of something jabbed at Donovan as he watched Alex's all-too-obvious manner and easy flirting with Taylor. He wasn't sure he really wanted to put an exact word to the feeling. Could it be jealousy? He didn't want to admit that the instant attraction he felt for her had gotten under his skin.

Donovan fought to keep the irritation out of his voice. "Don't you have someplace to be, Alex?"

Alex crossed the room to the door. He gave Taylor one last libidinous glance and an easy smile. "I'll see you at dinner tonight."

Alex hurried to his car and drove the five minutes to Constance's house. He gave two quick raps on the front door, then opened it and walked in without waiting to be invited. "Connie? Are you ready to get to work?" His familiarity said they were much more than casual acquaintances.

Constance emerged from the back room. Her blond hair hung to her shoulders, her makeup perfectly applied. She glanced around, then her gaze landed on Alex. She tightened the sash of her silk robe. "You're alone?"

Alex studied her for a moment. She claimed to be thirty-one, but he knew she was closer to forty. She'd maintained a youthful appearance and an appealing body, especially for an *older* woman—older compared to his twenty-seven years. In fact, there were a lot of other things he knew about Constance that he was sure no one else knew.

He looked around, feigning a hint of confusion about what she might have been searching for when she entered the room. "You were expecting Donovan to be with me? Or perhaps you were hoping for Donovan by himself." He reached out and tugged at the silken sash until it came loose, allowing her robe to fall open, revealing the sheer nightgown she wore.

A sly smile curled the corners of Alex's mouth as he raked his gaze over her obvious charms. "Ah, yes…I see you were hoping for Donovan solo. Well—" he removed his jacket and tossed it over the arm of the couch "—never let it be said that I failed to help out a lady in obvious distress." He tugged on the front of her robe, slowly drawing her toward him.

Connie stepped away, closed her robe, retied the sash and leveled a steady gaze at him. "You're quite the randy lad, Alex…always ready for a tumble."

Alex winked at her. "As you know from personal experience—ready, willing and *very* able."

"Well, you'll have to put all of that 'ready, willing and able' aside until another time and another place. Right now we have festival business to discuss."

"Whatever you say. Business first—" he cocked his head and shot a questioning look in her direction "—and pleasure later?" He retrieved a notebook from his jacket pocket and seated himself at her dining room table.

Constance picked up the file folder from the corner of

the table and withdrew several sheets of paper. "I've compiled a list of what needs to be done and what I've already accomplished. I think we're in good shape for this year's festival, just the last-minute details to take care of."

Alex took the list from her, but didn't bother to look at it. "You know, Connie—" he pulled her into his lap "—it's not doing you any good to set your sights on the status that being married to Lord Donovan Sedgwick would give you. After all, Donovan has rebuffed your increasingly blatant overtures in that area. Even before Uncle James died, you had decided on Donovan. I assume you believed that Uncle James's age meant that Donovan would be coming into the title sometime very soon. And by a strange quirk of fate, he came into it sooner than anyone anticipated. But even though you have decided Donovan is going to be your next husband—"

"*Next* husband?" Constance jumped to her feet and took a couple of steps away from Alex. "Whatever are you talking about? Everyone knows that I've never been married."

A sly grin turned the corners of his mouth. "Sorry, Connie…I keep forgetting about the myth you insist on perpetuating."

He emitted a soft chuckle, as if an amusing thought had just occurred to him. "But as I was saying maybe it would be more feasible if you set your sights on someone else. There are lots of men out there with titles. Of course, not many of them have such a lucrative estate to support that title as Donovan does."

She furrowed her brow in momentary concentration. "Perhaps you're right. Maybe I need to use another tactic." She gave Alex an appraising look, then leaned her face into his and placed a kiss on his lips. "But first, let's finish with the festival business. We'll have time later this morning for other pleasantries."

DONOVAN STOOD at the door of the informal dining room. He watched as Taylor poured herself a cup of coffee, then stood in front of the window staring at the gardens. He continued to be bothered by the strange sensation that he knew her from somewhere. He closed his eyes for a moment, but the image continued to swirl around in his mind. He was inexplicably drawn to her, almost as if she had cast some sort of spell over him—as if some unknown force had pulled him into a fateful liaison fraught with unknown danger.

Taylor turned toward him as he entered the room. He drank in her features—the shape of her face, the creamy texture of her skin, the set of her eyes, her slightly parted lips and the fullness of a mouth that deserved to be repeatedly kissed as often as possible. He tried to shake away the powerful urge to kiss those tempting lips as the heated desire again settled low in his body, fighting with his attempts to maintain a businesslike attitude.

"Is there something wrong?" Donovan's intense stare sent a small tremor of anxiety through her body. She was determined to track down her family history. Her grandmother had filled her in on as much as she knew, but there were still so many missing pieces. Her grandmother had been born on the Sedgwick Estate where Taylor's great-grandparents were the last of the tenant farmers to live there. Her grandmother had been sent to Canada as a small child to live with an aunt and uncle.

All Taylor knew of her great-grandparents, Clark and Emily Kincaid, was that they had been murdered by Lord William Sedgwick, a crime for which he had been swiftly convicted and then executed. She knew nothing of the details, but was determined to seek them out. Only now that she was actually at the Sedgwick Estate, standing face-to-face with the very appealing and disturbing Lord Donovan Sedgwick…

"Do I have jelly on my face or an orange juice mustache?" She forced a nervous chuckle as she moved her fingertips to the side of her mouth as if to wipe away an offending smudge.

Donovan's hand followed hers, his fingers lightly touching her hair, then brushing against her cheek. He quickly withdrew his hand and took a step backward. He hadn't realized he was staring at her so intently. "I'm sorry. It's just that…well—" he awkwardly shifted his weight from one foot to the other "—you look so familiar, as if I should know you from somewhere, but I can't quite place it. We, uh, we haven't ever met…have we?"

"No…" His eyes held her in a captive spell, as if he had literally drawn all the energy from her body. She experienced a shortness of breath. Her skin still tingled where he had touched her cheek. Her voice barely rose above a soft whisper. "I'm sure I would have remembered if we had."

"Yes, well…" He nervously cleared his throat. "Shall we go?"

She breathed a sigh of relief as he seemed to release her from the mystical hold he had on her senses. He led the way up the curving staircase, his voice becoming all business as he provided her with information on the history of the property.

"The original estate dates back to the late 1300s. Some of the structures from that time are still here. The tithe barn and the lodge house—" A shudder swept through his body at the mention of the lodge house. Thoughts of the grisly events from a century ago flashed through his mind.

He forced away the unwelcome intrusion and regained

his composure. "As I was saying, the tithe barn and lodge house date from that time along with some of the outer buildings."

"Has the estate always been in the Sedgwick family or did your family acquire it later?"

"My family has owned it since the late 1600s. It was a grant made after the monarchy was restored in 1660, following the civil war and the ten-year period of the commonwealth. We originally had six different families living on various parts of the estate as tenant farmers. They would keep a percentage of their crops and livestock with the rest going to the estate as their rent. Of course, the land holdings are not as vast as they once were and we no longer have tenant farmers, but it's still a very large estate by today's standards. We own several structures bordering the village that are no longer necessary to the day-to-day operations of the estate. Most of those buildings are leased out."

They arrived at the third floor in the central section of the house. It was like stepping into a time warp and suddenly being whisked back several centuries. A sense of foreboding settled over her. A cold shiver moved down her spine. An impression of evil seemed to haunt the stark hallways.

Their footsteps echoed as they walked along the well-worn hardwood floor. The stone walls lacked any feeling of warmth or welcome. Several suits of armor were on display along with shields and swords. Wall sconces were spaced at ten-foot intervals along the length of the long hallway. Taylor noted that they actually contained candles rather than electric lights. The large windows on the outer wall were devoid of any type of drapes or shutters thus allowing the daylight to stream in—the only thing to break the almost oppressive gloom that settled over everything.

Taylor tried to break the uncomfortable silence that had suddenly surrounded them. "This certainly is quite different from my room and the downstairs area." Another cold jolt tickled her spine.

"This central section is the oldest part of the house. Most of the original timbered structure burned in 1726 and was replaced with this sandstone manor house. A major addition was built in the early 1890s by my great-grandfather, William. That's the section where you're staying. The east wing was added and most of the house modernized following World War II. My father was responsible for the most recent upgrades including the swimming pool, the improved heating system in the main part of the house and redoing the electrical wiring and plumbing.

"The area where we are now, on the third floor, is not used for anything other than storage. There are rooms filled with relics that I suppose could rightly be on display in a museum—suits of armor, centuries-old weapons, furniture from various periods in history and even bathtubs from the time prior to indoor plumbing. But this floor doesn't even have electricity."

Donovan continued the tour of the house, showing her through the kitchen and butler's pantry, the formal dining room, which was now used only for special occasions, the snooker room, the original accounts room where the business records of the estate were kept during the time of the tenant farmers, and finally some of the other guest bedrooms. The music room and ballroom were evidence of the lavishness of parties and social gatherings of a bygone era. He did not take her into the east wing, did not show her his private living quarters or the modern offices where he conducted the current business matters of the estate. They ended the household tour in the library on the second floor.

It was a very large, paneled room with a high-beamed ceiling. The walls were lined with bookshelves. Two long reading tables occupied a prominent place in the room. Comfortable, overstuffed chairs were located near the many windows. "This is where all the family archives are kept, at least the ones that still exist. The records that used to be in the accounts room are here, too. When the original house burned, all the records went with it. However, for your purposes, these records date back prior to the festival. I'm sure you'll find everything you need..." His voice trailed off as he stared at her.

"This is very generous of you, allowing a total stranger to have access to your family records." Panic welled inside her. It felt as if the walls were closing in. As if she was about to be trapped in a centuries-old world without any means of escape. Her inner voice told her to run, to get out while she still could. Her feet were leaden, her muscles refused to function. The fear coursing through her was as much emotional as it was physical. She opened her mouth to speak, but no words came out. Then she saw him reach out toward her. Was this it? The moment her sense of reality would totally disappear?

Donovan's hand seemed to have a life of its own as he reached out and touched Taylor's hair. A tightness pulled across his chest. He was drawn to her like a moth to a flame. Her lower lip quivered slightly. He drew his fingertip lightly across it. Their gazes locked as a moment of intense heat passed between them. He was not sure exactly what he felt other than the obvious, quick surge of lust and a strong desire to pull her into his arms and take complete possession of her mouth with several passionate kisses. What was there about this woman that so inflamed his normally controlled desires? What was there about her that seemed so familiar? And so troubling?

Taylor took a step backward as she sucked in a startled gasp. She had certainly not expected him to touch her like that even though she had to silently admit to a surge of excitement when his fingertip brushed her lip. The electricity almost crackled out loud as it sizzled between them. She could not catch her breath. She didn't know which sensation was true…the excitement or the trepidation. It had been late the evening before when she presented herself at the front door of the manor house, and in the short time since, Donovan Sedgwick had somehow managed to enfold her in a magnetic web of desire tempered with confusion and apprehension. She closed her eyes and tried to force away the strange feelings that stirred inside her.

And now this. She was enfolded in more than his aura, yet she felt helpless to offer even the slightest of protests. It was Donovan who finally broke the spell binding them together with invisible ties.

"The, uh, grounds. I promised to show you the immediate grounds, too." He glanced out the window. Dark storm clouds hung low in the sky giving a menacing appearance to the countryside. The tree tops moved in the stiff breeze. "There seems to be a storm building. We'd better hurry."

"Yes…I'd like very much to see the grounds." She couldn't stop the slight huskiness that surrounded her words.

Neither made mention of the incident in the library as they walked down the stairs, then along the hallway to the side door. They exited onto a large promenade bordered by beautifully manicured gardens on a terraced hillside. She had arrived at the estate at night and hadn't realized that the manor house stood on a small bluff overlooking a long valley with a winding river flowing off to the horizon. The trees had turned their autumn reds and golds. It was a breathtaking sight that immediately filled her with a sense of calm and serenity.

"This is my favorite view." Donovan paused for a moment of quiet reverie. "In summer the sunlight lingers across the green hills and reflects golden off the river. The air is filled with the fragrance of a thousand flowers." He took a deep breath and stared out over the valley, lost in his own thoughts—thoughts that vacillated between the serenity spread out before him, the dark malevolence of the disturbing dreams that had first invaded his sleep about a month ago and the very real passion that Taylor stirred in him.

"I can see why you like it here. This is truly lovely." It was a time of quiet contemplation that she found very calming after her unsettling dream the night before and the dark, almost sinister atmosphere clinging to the centuries-old house.

Neither Taylor nor Donovan spoke for several minutes.

"Well—" he turned toward her "—shall we continue with our tour?" He took her first to the tithe barn. "This is an exceptionally large structure for a tithe barn especially for its time period, but then it was a very large estate. The barn is 132 feet by 44 feet and is the oldest building still standing on the estate. It was constructed in 1389 and goes back to the time when all of this was church property. Ten percent of everything from all the surrounding area, usually crops, was given to the church and brought here for storage, thus the name tithe barn. In fact—" he pointed to an enclosed loft room with a window overlooking the interior of the barn "—the abbot or his representative used that room to keep an eye on everything."

They stepped farther into the dimly lit interior of the large stone structure. "As you can see, it's not currently being used." The wind whistled through the window openings. Like the third floor in the oldest part of the house, she had the feeling of being transported back to another time and another place. She became acutely aware of the fact that he stood very close behind her, even imagining she could feel his breath against her hair. She ran her hand across the back of her neck in an effort to still the tiny shiver.

Taylor turned around and found herself looking up into the intensity of Donovan's blue eyes and his handsome features. She stepped backward and quickly averted her eyes, pretending a momentary interest in the uneven cobblestones that covered the floor. "This barn was already a century old before most Europeans even entertained the idea of the world being round and land existing across the ocean to the west. That makes this all that much more impressive to me." She looked around the barn again, stared up at the abbot loft, then peered farther up into the dimly lit rafters in an attempt to locate the birds she could hear. "If these walls could talk they would surely have quite a few exciting tales to tell."

"Perhaps it's just as well that they can't say anything." His mind darted to the lodge house and the horror of the story those walls could tell. His words came out in a near whisper, as if he did not want to even think them let alone say them. "This many centuries of history is bound to offer up a few dark tales of brutality…and even madness." He shoved the bothersome thoughts away and continued in a more confident manner. "After all, the Middle Ages were not a particularly gracious or genteel period."

Again the details of the murders of a century ago filled his mind along with the confusion of the strange dreams and happenings that had become part of his present. The uncertainty that had plagued him from the moment he'd laid eyes on Taylor continued to shove at his reality, intensified by his strong physical attraction to her.

Without saying anything else, Donovan placed his hand at the small of her back and gently steered her out the door of the tithe barn. His touch again sent little tingles of excitement racing through her body. They walked down the path together as he continued the tour of the estate.

"Over here are the stables. Of course, there are only a half-dozen or so horses these days, which leaves most of the stable area unused." He suddenly stopped walking and looked questioningly at her. "Do you ride?"

"Yes, I used to ride quite a bit. I've only ridden with a Western saddle, though. I've never tried an English saddle. Unfortunately, I haven't had any opportunity to ride for the past few years."

"Perhaps you could make some time during your research and I can show you the rest on the estate. It's best seen by horseback, where we're not restricted to the roads."

His question had seemed almost tentative, as if he were unsure about asking it. She offered him an engaging smile as she replied to his invitation. "I'd like that…very much."

Jerry Denton, her ex-fiancé, had owned a small two-passenger airplane. During the time Taylor had been dating him and through their subsequent engagement, he had often flown them from Kansas to Colorado where he had a friend who owned a ranch. They had spent many hours horseback riding in the mountains. In retrospect it was the only part of the relationship that held any value for her.

It had been a messy breakup and had left Taylor gunshy where men were concerned. Even though she had made a concentrated effort to avoid any type of emotional entanglement for the past three years, she could not deny that this man—Lord Donovan Sedgwick, one of a long line of Sedgwick gentry—had her senses running amok.

The one good thing that did come from the emotionally painful breakup of her engagement was the additional time she had spent with her grandmother. Those special times had fueled her desire to search out her roots. Her grandmother had died two years ago at the age of 102. Her mind had been sharp and clear until the very end.

And now Taylor was standing on the very ground where her grandmother had been born and talking to the descendent of someone who had been responsible for the death of her great-grandparents.

"Over here are the greenhouses and hothouses. The small one is for flowers and plants that are ultimately transplanted to the gardens surrounding the house. The large ones are vegetable gardens that provide us with produce almost year-round. Actually, with the vegetable gardens, grain and feed crops, livestock and poultry, the estate can be self-sufficient as far as food is concerned." He held the door open for her and they entered one of the large glass structures.

They continued the tour well into the afternoon. He carefully kept her away from the lodge house and cemetery, even though the police had taken down the yellow crime-scene tape from around the crypt. He pointed out the areas that would be utilized for the annual festival.

"The tithe barn will be used by local antique dealers. We'll erect a large tent on the south lawn for crafts people from the nearby villages to display their wares. The field adjacent to the barn will be turned into a minicarnival. The north lawn will be used for the children's competitions such as the sack race, three-legged race, tug-of-war... things like that."

For the most part, each kept the conversation on a superficial level, much as it had been during breakfast. Taylor asked some questions about specific aspects of physically setting up the festival, and Donovan provided her with the requested information. She was very impressed with everything Donovan had shown her. Even though the house gave off ominous vibes of past misdeeds, in the sunlight it was beautiful and the interior elegantly appointed. The estate seemed every bit as prosperous as she had first thought.

She gestured toward the swimming pool. "This is a very interesting juxtaposition…a fourteenth-century tithe barn next to a modern swimming pool and hot tub."

Donovan took a steadying breath. No matter how much he didn't want it to be, she made his heart pound and his pulse race. He continued to be troubled by the eerie sensation that he knew her.

Donovan had been far more discreet in his relationships with women than his cousin. Alex already had two failed marriages and a flamboyant lifestyle that included many unprofitable forays into the private casinos in London. On several occasions Donovan had paid off his cousin's gambling debts.

While Donovan had engaged in numerous quiet affairs away from the village, he had never married. But he had never before been so immediately and strongly attracted to any woman as he was to Taylor MacKenzie. It was an overwhelming and mysterious attraction he couldn't explain and didn't understand.

An attraction that frightened him as much as it fascinated him.

He took an impulsive step in Taylor's direction, brushed his fingertips against her cheek, then slowly lowered his mouth to hers. It was a fleeting kiss, barely more than a touching of the lips, but one that held all the heat and passion he felt when he had resisted the urge to kiss her earlier. He ran his fingers through her hair, then started to wrap her in his embrace.

"Taylor…I—" He let her go and took a quick step backward, putting distance between them. He immediately berated himself for his foolish and unacceptable behavior. The words felt awkward as they left his mouth. "I…I'm sorry. I didn't mean for that to happen."

Taylor's words came out as a startled whisper. "That's all right." She had to force the rest, not at all sure what to say or how to say it. "No harm done."

No harm done? Waves of confusion swept through her. She desperately needed to apply some logic to what had happened. At first a sense of relief washed through her, telling her how thankful she was that he had changed his mind and not pursued the kiss any further. It saved her from having to make a decision about whether to allow it.

There was no mistaking the ripples of excitement that accompanied her confusion or the heated desire she experienced every time Donovan looked at her. The feeling was almost surreal, as if she was being drawn into something beyond her control—something disturbingly ominous yet so enthralling that she couldn't resist the temptation. Nothing in her experience had prepared her for the strange dichotomy going on inside her at that moment.

He was not what she expected when he opened the door to her upon her arrival. Dynamic…yes. Handsome…yes, very. Incredibly sexy…most certainly. Mysterious and secretive…also true. He had a manner she could almost describe as brooding even though the couple of occasions when he displayed his dazzling smile showed an entirely different side to him. But still, the impact on her senses was anything but subtle—far more than she had believed could happen and she wasn't able to shake it away.

Donovan awkwardly shifted his weight from one foot to the other, his words carrying the hesitation and uncertainty he felt. "I should let you get started on your work, and I have some estate business to tend to. I'll see you later. If you need anything, please feel free to ask. If I'm not available, Bradley will tend to whatever you need or want."

"Thank you for the tour. It was fascinating. I think I'll go to my room and get my notes together." *And see if I can't get my composure and emotions together, as well.*

Donovan escorted Taylor inside the manor house, then watched as she ascended the staircase to the second floor. As soon as she was out of sight he returned to his suite of rooms to seek privacy and some much-needed solitude. He poured a glass of water from the carafe before sinking into the large chair. He rubbed his temples as he took several deep breaths. He desperately needed to sort things out, especially the mysterious pull she exerted on his senses whenever he was around her, which had expanded to include every time he thought about her. And those occasions seemed to be occurring with increased frequency with each passing hour.

He tried to collect his thoughts. First there was the shock of his father's death—his father's *suicide*—two months ago, a situation that still caused him great emotional pain. Then there were the blinding headaches that would strike from out of nowhere followed by periods of disorientation—the same symptoms his father had experienced before his suicide. Then came the disturbing dreams. Next came the bizarre happenings at the crypt.

And finally the appearance of this very disconcerting, yet very familiar, woman.

He could not dislodge the feeling that some sort of mysterious thread tied all of these events together. If only he could figure out what it was. Taylor's countenance continued to haunt his mind—the set of her eyes, the shape of her face, the sensual mouth...the *deliciously* sensual mouth that tasted of everything he had ever wanted. The nagging feeling that he had encountered her somewhere continued to confound him. There had to be an answer. He closed his eyes. An image began to form, a faint vision of a woman's face. He tried to bring it into focus, but it refused to completely materialize.

Donovan opened his eyes, the disturbing image having faded completely. His gaze landed on his father's trunk. His father had always kept it locked and he had never known what was in it.

When his father committed suicide he had left a note. Donovan found it the next morning when he discovered his father's body. The note was only an apology and did not shed any light on the reason the elder Sedgwick had committed suicide.

Donovan had found the key to the mysterious trunk in the nightstand next to his father's bed. He had done a cursory check of the contents following his father's funeral and had been disappointed in the routine items he found. The way his father had kept the trunk locked had led him to believe that it contained something pertinent. However, he had not inspected anything in depth.

He emitted an audible sigh of resignation, then rose from the chair and took the key from his dresser drawer. Now would be as good a time as any to do a more thorough check of the contents. Maybe upon closer inspection he would find some clue that would help him figure out why his father had committed suicide, and lead to some answers about what had been happening to him.

A cold chill made its way up his spine. A sense of foreboding seemed to permeate the very fabric of the house as if something menacing lived in the walls and stalked the hallways. He had never felt it before and had first became aware of the odd sensations about the time his father began to suffer the blinding headaches and disorientation. And now it was happening to him in the same manner. A stab of fear sliced through him.

He still did not understand what had driven his father to commit suicide. The two of them had been very close. James Sedgwick had been well over forty years old when he and Donovan's mother had married. Donovan was their only child. His mother died when he was six.

Even though his grandfather, and later his father, had sold off part of the land and had leased out some of the buildings along the main road, the estate was still quite large and diversified. Unlike many other large land holdings in England, it was not mired in financial problems. Quite the contrary. Due to intelligent and enlightened management, combined with shrewd investments and business dealings, the estate had shown an above-average return for the past several years. That was one of the reasons why his father's suicide had been so difficult to accept. Nothing about it made any sense.

When Donovan had originally looked inside the trunk he'd found some handwritten journals that he'd only skimmed, some old photographs he'd merely glanced at, and what appeared to be blueprints and architectural drawings for the addition to the manor house his great-grandfather had built. As well, there were the plans for the modernization of the estate his grandfather had completed, and finally the most recent changes his father had made.

He picked up one of the journals. It was dated one hundred years ago—the year his great-grandfather had committed two murders. The journal had his great-grandfather's name on the inside cover. It was filled with notations that revealed his obsession with Emily Kincaid and his plans to make her his mistress in spite of the fact that she was married, had a young daughter and had repeatedly turned down his advances. His plan called for Emily to give herself to him the night before the start of the festival—willingly or otherwise.

Donovan set the journal aside. The subsequent events and resulting murders had been well documented in the local village newspaper along with the Treadwells' personal bias against the Sedgwick family, a bias that did not exist in the news articles published by the *London Times*. And Byron Treadwell had maintained that personal bias since taking over as managing editor and publisher of the village newspaper.

There were two journals with his grandfather's name on them. And finally four journals with the name James Sedgwick on the inside cover, the most recent one dated just a couple of months before his suicide. There had to have been some reason for Donovan's father to have kept those specific items locked away. And some reason for him to have stopped making journal entries two months before his death. He hadn't hidden them in the trunk because they had monetary value.

One thing Donovan knew for sure was that none of the journals belonged in the library as part of the family archives, where someone else could have access to them. And that would certainly extend to Taylor MacKenzie and her research. The last thing he wanted was to see mention of the family's evil deeds in a book on British country festivals.

He picked up a large envelope and removed the photographs. He selected one of the photographs, a very old one. On the back, in his father's handwriting, were the words Emily Kincaid. He turned it over and stared at it.

It was as if someone had landed a solid punch to his body, knocking all the breath out of him. A hard lump formed in his throat and a knot tightened in his stomach. The face reached out to him, grabbing his reality and twisting it into a mystifying tangle.

The eyes were large and expressive just like Taylor's. It was the same nose and identical smile from the same sensual mouth. The hair in the photograph was long and dark, but it was Taylor's face. His attention remained riveted on the old photograph, held captive by a force that tugged at his senses and seemed to be pushing him closer to the brink of the unknown.

Who was Taylor MacKenzie? What was the real reason for her being at his house? What did she want from him?

He squeezed his eyes shut as the pounding headache struck from out of nowhere, then the darkness descended around him.

Chapter Three

"Alex phoned to say he had other plans for the evening and won't be joining us for dinner." Donovan scowled as he thought about the phone call. "I'm not sure exactly what 'other plans' means, but it no doubt has to do with a woman."

"Yes, Alex struck me as being a ladies' man and quite a flirt." Taylor noticed the quick look that darted across his features and disappeared before she could read it. She took a sip of her wine, not sure how much more of her opinion of Donovan's cousin would be appropriate for her to voice.

They kept up a casual conversation during the meal, talking mostly about movies, books and travel—things in which they had a common interest.

"Is this your first trip to England?" Was it nothing more than some bizarre coincidence that Taylor MacKenzie and Emily Kincaid looked enough alike to be twins? Donovan wanted to know more about Taylor, but wasn't sure just how much more. Where would it lead him? Would he get some much-needed answers or find out things he really didn't want to know?

"Yes, it's my first time in your country. Actually, it's my first trip outside the United States." She forced an upbeat, casual attitude she didn't feel in an attempt to perpetuate the lie she had created. "This is all so very exciting. I've been wanting to write this book for the past three years. I've done all the research I could from home and knew I had to come here to gather firsthand information and attend the festival. That's when I contacted your father and he graciously extended the invitation for me to stay here."

Everything about Donovan excited her. Just sitting across the table from him as they engaged in casual conversation sent little tremors of desire through her body. And the way he continued to stare at her did nothing to alleviate the feeling. She felt pressured to maintain the superficial line of conversation.

"Have you ever been to the States?"

"Yes, I lived there while furthering my education. I attended Harvard University where I received a master's degree in business administration."

"That's very impressive."

Even though neither of them showed outward signs of it, there was no denying the underlying current of sensuality that continued to sizzle between them, like electricity crackling along the power lines on a foggy day.

But there was more than sexual tension pulling at Taylor. A level of dark mystery infused the setting, an ominous sensation of fate and unfulfilled prophecy. Was it the atmosphere projected by the centuries-old house? The environment of what Donovan had described as the "less than genteel" history associated with its past?

Her dream last night of someone being in her room— someone frightening, almost an evil presence—seemed so real. Was it nothing more than her imagination fueled by the surroundings? Or was it the aura of Donovan himself trying to take control of her reality? She didn't know. An uneasiness crept through her body, leaving her slightly on edge yet unable to resist the allure of this mysterious, fascinating and very desirable man who made her blood rush hot and fast.

They finished their dinner and Taylor was the first to put an end to the evening. She didn't really want to give up Donovan's company, but she knew she had several bothersome incidents to work through in her mind. "I'd like to get a few things from the library, maybe take a couple of the books about the history of this area of England back to my room."

"Of course. I'll help you find what you want." Donovan escorted her upstairs and located some material he thought might interest her.

She took the books from him. Their hands touched. A potent arc of sexual energy zapped between them, as it had when they first met. The books fell from her hand, clattering to the floor.

"Oh…" The words caught in her throat as she looked up into the troubled intensity of Donovan's blue eyes. "I'm so sorry." She tried to catch her breath and regain control of her rampaging emotions. A sense of urgency coursed through her, an inner voice screaming at her, telling her not to linger—to get as far away from the house and everything connected with it as she could and as quickly as possible before it was too late.

"How…how clumsy of me." Taylor reached toward the books.

Donovan grabbed her arm and stopped her before she could bend down to retrieve them. It had been all he could do to maintain a facade of gentlemanly decorum during the evening. He could no longer contain what he had discovered. A hard surge of anxiety shot through him as he reached in his pocket for the photograph. He hesitated for a moment. Did he really want to start down this unknown path? Did he really want to know? He steeled his determination. Something very bizarre had invaded his life, and he had to figure out what it meant before it destroyed him.

He withdrew the picture and handed it to Taylor. Hopefully she wouldn't notice the slight quaver in his voice or the almost imperceptible tremble of his hand. His throat went dry, making it difficult for him to get out the words. "This is a picture of Emily Kincaid. She died one hundred years ago, here on the estate. Except for the hair color, you look enough like her to be her twin."

Another ripple of anxiety assaulted his senses. "Do you have any explanation for this?"

Taylor stared at the photograph in disbelief. A cold chill swept through her body. She had never seen a picture of her great-grandmother. It was like looking in a mirror. A shiver of trepidation assaulted her as she desperately searched for some guidance about what to say. It made no sense to claim ignorance, to say that it was some sort of coincidence. The circumstances had moved far beyond that point. She shoved down her rapidly escalating panic. Her gaze locked with his for a brief moment. His eyes were questioning, a little bit wary, very confused, but not angry.

"Uh, Emily Kincaid..." She tried to swallow the lump that seemed to fill her throat as she nervously glanced around the room seeking anything that might help. "She was my great-grandmother."

The shock sent Donovan reeling backward a couple of steps. "Your great-grandmother?" He tried to assimilate her words and their meaning. This was the great-granddaughter of the woman his great-grandfather had been obsessed with and had killed. And then he had killed

Taylor's great-grandfather when he couldn't have her. What type of strange path had his life taken? He took a calming breath in an attempt to bring rational thought to the situation. He wasn't sure what to say in response to her statement. He finally forced out some words even though he knew they were woefully inadequate and didn't actually address the situation. "So…your stated reason for being here is nothing but a lie?"

"No…that's not true." How deep was she going to dig the hole? Was it going to be so deep that she'd never be able to climb out? Should she tell him the complete truth? Everything that had happened since her arrival had only complicated matters. She wasn't sure what she was experiencing, but she knew that just being in the same room with Donovan Sedgwick nearly took her breath away. It was as exciting as it was bewildering. And the uneasiness resulting from her strange dream her only night in the house was equally frightening.

"What's not true?"

His steady gaze left her unnerved and rattled. She drew in a calming breath. "My stated reasons for being here are real. I'm researching British country festivals. I chose yours partly because my great-grandparents lived here and my grandmother was born on the estate, but mostly because your annual festival has been held for 250 years…a very long time for an event such as this to exist. I wanted to find out the reason for such a smashing success." Deeper and deeper she dug the hole. Soon she would be completely buried by her own lies.

"I see." Donovan's voice did not hold any hint of his true thoughts. He no longer accepted her claim about doing research, but chose not to make an issue of it by pursuing his suspicions at that time. He would wait and see what happened. Perhaps it was all a huge coincidence…words he desperately wanted to believe but knew he couldn't. Her true identity only went to confirm his earlier thought that somehow her presence was tied to the strange events that surrounded him. But how? And what did she really want from him?

Was it possible for Taylor to have orchestrated the explosion at the crypt? Could she have been in England earlier than she claimed? Possibly staying down the road in town, then appearing at his door as if she had just arrived? Too many questions and no answers.

Once again he felt the pull of her presence, an almost mystical sensation that defied explanation. Was it an omen of some sort? A warning? Then a totally frightening thought struck him. Had some bizarre quirk of fate cast them in the roles of their great-grandparents, leaving them to play out the same tragic sequence of events one hundred years later? Was the Sedgwick curse a reality? A surge of fear attacked his senses and refused to let go.

Was Taylor's life literally in danger because of him?

It was a notion that preyed on his mind, yet he was helpless to prevent it. He could not keep from playing with fire and tempting fate. He had managed to stop himself earlier when he had started to kiss her, restricting the moment to something that was not much more than a brief brushing of the lips. She had seemed startled, but not angry or offended. Was he now about to make a colossal mistake, one that would seal their fate? He dismissed the questions and concerns. He could no more control his actions than he could control the rising and setting of the sun.

He drew her into his embrace and held her body tightly against his. Heat and sensuality immediately flooded through him. A moment later his mouth came down on hers. It was a kiss he could not have prevented even if he'd wanted to. After only a slight hesitation he felt her arms slip around his neck, then she returned his kiss. It was everything he knew it would be and more. His passion intensified as the kiss deepened. His breathing grew ragged.

He wanted more of her. At that moment it didn't matter why she was in his house, what ulterior motive she might have or what the future had in store for them. Was this the same phenomenon his great-grandfather experienced when he was around Emily Kincaid? This nearly out-of-control desire that seemed to consume him? This *need?*

With great difficulty Donovan finally broke off the kiss. He fought to bring his breathing under control. "Taylor…" He continued to caress her shoulders and hold her in his arms, to draw on her warmth. He had managed to stop the kiss but couldn't completely let go of the physical contact. "Please don't think that I make a pass at every woman I meet. That's Alex's style, not mine. But from the moment I saw you standing at my front door…well, something about you—"

The blinding headache stabbed behind Donovan's eyes with the swiftness of lightning. He released Taylor from his hold and stumbled a couple of steps backward. He squeezed his eyes shut and clenched his jaw in an effort to ward off the pain. Like the other times, the excruciating agony struck without warning. He was barely able to force out the words. "Excuse me…I…" Then the blackness descended around him.

Taylor's hand went to her mouth in an effort to silence the gasp that tried to escape her lips. She stared in disbelief as Donovan backed away from her, his face contorted into a mask of pain. He bumped into a chair, then into a table as he frantically tried to escape. He yanked open the library door with such force that it crashed loudly against the wall, then slammed shut behind him.

Bewilderment, combined with a touch of panic, clouded Taylor's mind as she watched him stumble out of the room. What had happened? One moment he had her wrapped in his embrace and they were sharing a delicious kiss that had sent a thrill coursing through her body, and the next moment he stumbled out of the door in obvious pain. What happened and where had he gone in such a hurry?

She swallowed several times in an attempt to counter the dryness in her throat. She nervously paced around the room, pausing to look out each window she passed.

Large raindrops spattered against the glass. The sound of the wind whistled around the old window casements, signaling the onslaught of the storm. Panic welled inside her. All she could think about was getting to the relative safety of her room, climbing into bed and pulling the covers up around her. She stopped in front of the closed library door and reached out to grasp the doorknob.

The adrenaline surge shot her heartbeat into high gear as she jerked her hand back. She heard it but she did not recognize the sound—a strange whining noise intertwined with a scratching. Whatever it was, she immediately associated it with something she preferred not to encounter. The panic grew until it nearly consumed her. She desperately scanned her surroundings. Her heart pounded in her chest. She frantically sought another way out of the room, but there was no other door.

Her throat tried to close. She swallowed several times to keep it open. *I'm being ridiculous! I've let my imagination get the best of me. There's some perfectly logical explanation for everything that's happened. When I arrived*

I was exhausted. Nothing happened last night. It was only a dream fueled by this centuries-old house. And that noise...I'm sure it's something common to a house this old...maybe the plumbing...or...

She drew in a deep breath, held it for a few seconds, then slowly exhaled. She could not let her overreaction to some obscure noise send her into a state of paralyzing fear. She clenched her jaw in determination, crossed the room, then reached a somewhat unsteady hand out toward the doorknob.

She paused, took another deep breath, then yanked open the door. A startled gasp escaped her lips when she saw Bradley standing there. The strange expression on his face was quickly replaced by a stoic mask that gave nothing away.

"Miss MacKenzie? Is there something wrong?"

"How long have you been outside the door?" Her voice sounded too shrill, even to her own ear, as if she was accusing him of some less-than-honorable activity.

"I haven't been standing outside the door, miss. I just arrived. Is there a problem?"

"Problem?" She took a deep, steadying breath. "Uh, no, no problem. I thought I heard something outside the door shortly before I opened it."

"I didn't hear anything out of the ordinary, miss. I was about to inquire as to whether you wanted anything else before Mrs. Bradley closes the kitchen for the night."

"Mrs. Bradley? Your wife is the cook?"

"Yes, miss. I am head of staff over the entire estate, and my wife is the cook and heads the kitchen staff." Members of the Bradley family had occupied the position of head of staff at the Sedgwick estate for almost 150 years. There were virtually no secrets in the Sedgwick family history or forgotten hideaways in the manor house or on the estate grounds that the Bradley family did not know about.

For several generations there had been persistent rumors about the existence of an illegitimate son, the result of William Sedgwick having forced himself on one of the Bradley women. The same rumors speculated about what type of a legal claim the descendents of that illegitimate son would have on the Sedgwick estate, especially in light of the advent of DNA testing to prove such a claim.

"Is there anything you would like from the kitchen, miss?"

"No, nothing. Thank you." She tried to force her racing pulse to slow down. "I was just getting a couple of books to take back to my room." She picked up the books from where they had fallen to the floor. "Good night, Bradley."

"Good night, Miss MacKenzie."

She quickly left the library and returned to her room. The strange incidents of a few minutes earlier filled her mind—Donovan's odd behavior and the strange noise outside the library door. As she had the previous night, she hooked the chair underneath the doorknob. She settled into bed, her confused thoughts turning over and over in her mind until she finally fell into a fitful sleep.

THE SHADOWY FIGURE silently made his way through the trees and shrubbery bordering the long driveway as he moved toward the unused lodge house at the entrance gates of the estate. The rain had stopped, leaving only a fine mist to settle on the already wet ground. The sounds of laughter attracted his attention. He peered through the window. A lit candle spread a soft glow of light through the room. He saw several bottles of ale on the floor. A man and woman had spread a blanket on the floor and were engaged in an intimate embrace.

The vision blurred, the man fading from his conscious sight. The woman took on the physical characteristics so firmly entrenched in his mind. He pressed his face against the cold windowpane, his ragged breath fogging the glass, his voice a low raspy whisper. "Emily—my true love. My wife means nothing to me. You know we belong together. I knew you would come to me, here to our special place." He moved stealthily through the darkness, rounded the corner of the lodge house and silently lifted the latch that opened the door.

He stepped into the room.

"THIS IS CERTAINLY A FIRST." Alex accepted the cup of coffee the butler had poured, then seated himself next to Taylor. "I don't think I've ever made it to the breakfast table before Donovan. He's the early bird. Me…I'd sleep until noon if I thought I could get away with it."

"I don't think I've ever slept until noon in my life. I always wake up early without even setting an alarm."

Alex grabbed a piece of toast and spread some marmalade on it. "As a writer, do you feel that you're more creative early in the morning?"

It was an innocent enough question, but it set off a tickle of apprehension. The last thing she wanted to talk about was her nonexistent writing career. "Well—"

Donovan entered the informal dining room, poured himself a cup of coffee and slumped into a chair without saying a word of greeting or even acknowledging Taylor and Alex. His forehead was furrowed almost to the point of being a scowl with his jaw clenched in a tight line.

"Good morning, Donovan." Taylor tried to make her voice sound as cheerful as possible in sharp contrast to his apparent bad mood.

Donovan stared blankly at her for a moment, his mind too filled with the troublesome events of earlier that morning. At the break of dawn he had found himself wandering aimlessly through the rose garden by the duck pond, the pain throbbing at his temples. The last clear memory he had before that was waking up, glancing at the clock next to his bed and seeing that it was four o'clock in the morning. How had he gotten to the garden? And why?

He did not remember getting dressed, yet he had been wearing jeans and a black sweatshirt. The knees of his jeans had been damp and covered with mud as if he had been kneeling on the wet ground. There were scratches on the backs of his hands, but he didn't know where they had come from. None of it made any sense to him, the incident pulling at his already tautly stretched nerves.

He started to respond to Taylor's words, but was cut off by the sound of excited voices coming from the direction of the kitchen.

"Bradley?" Donovan's strained voice clearly indicated his irritation at the noisy intrusion into his private thoughts. "What's going on out there?"

Bradley appeared in the doorway followed closely by a man dressed in rugged outdoor clothing. Bradley glanced toward Taylor, then moved quickly to Donovan's chair. He lowered his voice to a whisper as he spoke. "There is a matter that requires your immediate attention, sir. Stanley—" he indicated the groundskeeper standing at the kitchen door awkwardly shifting his weight from one foot to the other "—has discovered something at the lodge house."

"The lodge house?" A jolt of apprehension hit Donovan. "There shouldn't be anything at the lodge house. It hasn't been used in a hundred years, ever since the night—" Donovan's words stopped when he got a good look at Stanley's face. It was ashen, and beads of perspiration stood on his forehead. A wild fear filled the groundskeeper's eyes as his gaze nervously darted around the room.

Donovan rose from his chair. "What is it, Stanley? What have you found?"

Stanley's voice was a frightened whisper. "I'm afraid to say, Your Lordship. I think you'd best come have a look for yourself."

Donovan stared at the groundskeeper for a moment. Confusion ran rampant through his mind, touched with a growing realization that something terrible must have happened. "Very well." Without further conversation the two men left the house.

Donovan came to an abrupt halt in front of the lodge house door. A startled gasp escaped his throat as he recoiled in horror at the sight that greeted him. The bodies of a man and woman lay on the floor. The man had been stabbed and the woman appeared to have been strangled. The look of terror frozen on the lifeless faces was something he knew would be burned into his mind forever.

Donovan's voice was less than steady. "What…what happened here? Who are these people?"

"I beg Your Lordship's pardon, but I don't rightly know. I was on me way into the village when I noticed the door standing open and…uh, I went to close it and—" he gestured toward the door "—found this…."

Donovan swallowed, trying to ease the lump in his throat and the churning in the pit of his stomach. "Have you, uh, touched anything?"

"No, Your Lordship. I went straight away to the big house to fetch Bradley."

"Very well." It took all the self-control Donovan could muster to remain outwardly calm and project an image of someone in control, even though it was far from the truth.

"You stay here, Stanley. Don't go inside and don't let anyone come close. I'll phone for the police."

Donovan turned, took several deep breaths to ward off the sick feeling rising in his throat, then started back toward the manor house. His step quickened until it became a full run. What had happened? When? Did this have something to do with his being in the rose garden? Something to do with the scratches on his hands? Could he have witnessed something he didn't remember?

A cold shudder assaulted his body. Or worse?

"WHAT'S GOING ON?" Taylor addressed her question to Alex as she joined him on the front porch. They watched as the body bags were wheeled out of the lodge house. She had seen the anxiety and trepidation on Donovan's face—something almost akin to panic—when he burst into the manor house at a full run and grabbed the phone. She had tried to talk to him, but he rushed past her without even acknowledging her presence.

"I'm…actually, I'm not sure exactly what's going on." Alex lifted his hand to shade his eyes as he stared down the driveway toward the front gates. He mumbled the words under his breath, but they were loud enough for Taylor to hear them. "This certainly isn't going to help Donovan's condition."

"His *condition?* Is something wrong?" Alex's words left her bewildered. "Has he been in bad health? He certainly didn't look well when he came back to the house to use the phone."

"Donovan's been under a lot of…well, a lot of stress lately. First there was Uncle James's death two months ago. My father died three years ago. I was never that close to him, but Donovan and his father were very close. The suicide hit him very hard. Then there was that business with the crypt the other night and all the sensationalized newspaper coverage. And now this. With the festival coming up in a little less than two weeks…well, I hope he'll be able to keep it all together without going off the deep end."

Suicide? The word grabbed her attention and held on to it. She had no idea that Donovan's father committed suicide. And the crypt. She had stopped in the village upon her arrival to ask directions to the estate and had seen the local newspaper headlines. She did not understand the full implications of what she had glimpsed on the front page, but knew that something very strange had occurred on the grounds of the estate the night before her arrival.

She went over Alex's words in her mind, his implication that perhaps Donovan was not as tightly wrapped as he might be. She flashed on the incident of his strange behavior and quick departure from the library the previous night. A little chill of apprehension settled over her. There was no way she could deny her attraction to this very complex man, an attraction that was most certainly physical.

And perhaps emotional, too?

But in spite of that, she was not sure about the wisdom of staying at the manor house to pursue her quest while continuing with the charade she had created. Her original thought had been that the Sedgwick family would never cooperate with her efforts to search out her family background since it was one of their ancestors who had murdered her great-grandparents. She had gone to a great deal of effort to create the false story about writing a book on British country festivals and then convince Lord James Sedgwick to help her research that *nonexistent* book.

But being at the estate, actually staying in the house, had produced a level of anxiety inside her from the moment she'd stepped into the entrance hall. Nothing was as it seemed. The feeling permeated the very air that surrounded her—an undefined sensation that refused to let go of her, almost as if she was being held captive by some mystical energy. It was more than just the death of James Sedgwick. More than her unexpected encounter with the new lord of the manor, Donovan Sedgwick—an encounter that left her reeling and confused yet wanting more.

She knew the most expedient thing for her to do would be to pack and leave as fast as she could. Actually doing it, however, was another matter. The sensual stirrings that grabbed her whenever she was near Donovan befuddled the situation even more. And the kiss they had shared only told her how much more of him she wanted.

She started to say something, but stopped when she saw the intense expression on Alex's face and realized his attention was totally riveted on Donovan and the man with whom Donovan was in deep conversation. She stared out over the scene in front of her. Even though the sun was out at the moment she could see dark storm clouds gathering on the horizon just as they had the day before. An omen of some sort? A little shiver of anxiety poked at her. She shook away the unwanted speculation and concentrated her attention on Donovan and the older man, wishing she could hear what they were saying.

Donovan's questions were almost a whisper. A sick feeling churned in the pit of his stomach as he fought to project a calm outer demeanor. "Who are they, Mike? Who are those people? What were they doing here? How could something like this have happened? Who could have done such a horrible thing?"

The fifty-two-year-old police inspector shifted his stocky five-foot-nine-inch frame from one foot to the other. "None of my men recognize them, and they don't have any identification. We're certain they're not from the village. My guess is they're from town. There's a car parked up the road. We're checking the registration. Hopefully it will lead us somewhere. As to why they were in your lodge house in the middle of the night…well, there is this."

He held out a plastic evidence bag containing a note. Donovan hesitated a moment, then took the bag from him. The note was handwritten and had a smear of blood on the corner. He read it aloud. "Emily, meet me at the lodge house at midnight." A sick lump formed in the pit of his stomach and tried to force itself up to his throat. It couldn't be true, but there it was—the flamboyant handwriting style of his great-grandfather, William Sedgwick.

He looked up at the inspector, his voice not as commanding as he would have liked. "Where did you get this?"

"We found it on the floor next to the woman's body. Can you shed any light on this?"

"Me? I don't know these people or anything about what's going on here." He wasn't sure why he had lied and not mentioned the handwriting. He needed time to sort out this new and disturbing turn of events without Mike Edgeware breathing down his neck.

Inspector Edgeware's face showed a hard line of grim determination. The task was not helped by the strained relationship that had existed between him and James Sedgwick for the past couple of years, an uncomfortable situation that extended to Donovan. Lord James Sedgwick had been responsible for Michael Edgeware losing out on a promotion to chief inspector. If he could solve the double homicide rapidly and efficiently, then the overdue promotion would soon be his. And how odd that the case to provide the promotion denied by Lord James Sedgwick would happen on the grounds of the Sedgwick estate.

"First the crypt and now this. Any comment you'd like to make to the press, Lord Sedgwick?" The sarcasm in the voice cut through Donovan as he whirled around and faced Byron Treadwell.

Donovan fixed the unwelcome intruder with a pointed stare, there being no question of the animosity he felt toward his lifelong nemesis. "Perhaps it would be more constructive if Inspector Edgeware found out exactly how much *you* know about all of this. Has it been a slow news week that needed a little something extra to boost sales?" He allowed a moment for the full impact of his insinuation to sink in before continuing. "I have nothing to say to you, Treadwell, other than to tell you that you're trespassing on private property. If you're not gone in sixty seconds I'll have you arrested."

Donovan could not hold his distaste for Byron Treadwell in check any longer. The words rushed out in an angry hiss. "Now, get out of here, you bastard!"

It had been twelve years since the incident at the pub when the pretty barmaid had rebuffed Byron's advances in favor of pursuing Donovan even though Donovan had not given her any encouragement and had no personal interest in her. Byron had blamed him for using his family position of power and wealth to steal her away. The incident still rankled Byron, and he had used every occasion to make his unhappiness known.

"In that case, Your Lordship, I'll just have to go to press with what I have." Byron slowly closed his notepad and put it back in his jacket pocket. The self-satisfied smirk that covered his face said more than his words. He had gotten the desired rise out of Donovan.

Byron turned to face Mike Edgeware. "Do you have a statement for the press, Inspector?"

"No comment at this time." Donovan was not the only one who found Byron Treadwell irritating. Inspector Edgeware had crossed swords with the Treadwell newspaper on numerous occasions. It was only a small village newspaper, but Byron used it almost as a weapon in propagating his views.

Mike was sure there was some sort of an information leak in the police department. It was the only logical explanation he could come up with for details of crime scenes making it into print so quickly, details that the police had not released—such as the story about the explosion at the crypt. Mike Edgeware had no idea how Byron Treadwell had gotten all the details, let alone in time to make an early edition of the newspaper that same morning.

Byron could not resist one final parting shot. "What happened there, Your Lordship?" He gestured toward the scratches on Donovan's hands. "Run into a little mishap of some sort?"

Donovan quickly jammed his hands into his jeans pockets and glared at Byron. He wished he had an answer for that question. He wished he knew what had happened.

As soon as Donovan was sure Byron had left the estate, he turned toward Inspector Edgeware. "Make sure you keep me apprised of everything you turn up in your investigation." It was not a request. It was an order issued by someone of rank, privilege and wealth. He returned to the manor house, immediately spotting Taylor and Alex standing on the porch.

It was Alex who spoke first. His expressionless face hid whatever was going on inside his head. "Do you need me here for anything? If not, I'll be running along." Without bothering to wait for an answer, he pulled his keys from his pocket and headed toward his car parked in the drive in front of the house.

Taylor tentatively ventured her question to Donovan as she gestured toward the lodge house. "I'm not sure exactly what's going on, but is there anything I can do to help?"

"No!" He hadn't intended to snap at her like that. His first impulse was to keep her as far away as possible from anything that could do her harm even though he didn't know what that anything might be. He gathered his composure and softened his tone of voice.

"No, things are under control. This is normally a very quiet country village. Anything requiring the attention of the police usually occurs ten miles down the road in town." Donovan straightened and assumed a more controlled manner, not wanting to give her a chance to ask any more questions.

Taylor hesitated, not sure of the propriety, then cautiously continued. "That small house at the entrance gates, the one where they just removed the, uh, bodies. Does someone live there?"

Donovan's whole being jumped to sharp attention. A defensive edge surrounded his words. "Bodies? What makes you say that?"

"I didn't mean to be so blunt, but when you see the place crawling with police and body bags being taken out of a building on gurneys, it's only logical to assume that those bags actually contain bodies." There was no mistaking the pain she glimpsed in his eyes before he turned away. There was also no mistaking the emotional jab of pain she felt in connection with the mysterious circumstances that had him so upset.

"No. No one lives there. The lodge house hasn't been used for the past hundred years, ever since…" His voice trailed off and he did not finish his sentence. He studied her face, took in each and every feature. A nagging feeling welled inside him, an uncomfortable sensation telling him that she might be in physical danger if she continued to stay at the manor house. He reached out and touched her cheek, then briefly cupped her face in his hands. The moment of physical contact helped calm his shattered nerves. He slowly pulled her into his arms and held her, reveling in the sense of closeness and comfort, something that had long been missing from his life.

Yes, indeed. She was definitely a very real temptation. She had been in his house less than forty-eight hours, yet he was having trouble keeping his hands off her. He had to put some distance between them and quickly. He abruptly let her go and walked away, calling over his shoulder as his pace quickened. "I have lots of work to do, and I'm sure you want to get started on your research."

Somewhere in his mind lurked a frightening thought. Could the Sedgwick curse be real? Was it possible that the evil spirit of his great-grandfather had passed on to him? Could he be going mad just as his great-grandfather had? What was happening to him was very similar to what his father had experienced before committing suicide. Could his father have realized he was going mad and killed himself rather than suffer the indignity and bring embarrassment to the family?

And what of Taylor MacKenzie's presence.... Even stronger than his fear for his sanity was his fear that she might be in danger. Layer upon layer, Donovan's anxiety level steadily increased.

Chapter Four

Taylor stared at Donovan's retreating form. Once again he had exhibited very strange behavior culminating in an unexpected and hasty retreat. This time, however, he didn't seem to be in the extreme pain he had demonstrated as he left the library last night. She continued to watch as he hurried around the corner of the house. She closed her eyes for a moment as she touched her cheek where his fingers had brushed against her skin. She could still feel the heat of his skin against hers and the taste of the sensual kiss they had shared the evening before. The little tremor that shot through her body only confirmed what she did not want to acknowledge. It told her how very much she was attracted to this complex man despite the mysterious circumstances that seemed to surround them. Donovan caused her heart to pound a little harder and her pulse to race a little faster.

The horror of her great-grandparents' murders had happened one hundred years ago. There was no way Donovan could be held responsible for the actions of his great-grandfather. She knew it intellectually, but her gut instincts weren't quite as clear on the subject. Where Donovan Sedgwick was concerned, her gut instincts were in a state of total disarray.

She attempted to shrug away the feeling of uncertainty as she looked up at the darkening sky. She could smell the rain in the air. What had earlier been a gentle breeze had now become a stiff one. She needed to return to the house. *The house*…something about the house gave off sinister vibrations. She'd felt them the very evening she'd arrived, before she'd ventured beyond the entry hall. Being inside *the house* had her nerves on edge.

She shook her head. No—it was a ridiculous notion. People gave off vibrations, not inanimate objects. The atmosphere had gotten to her, causing her imagination to run amok. She needed to rein it in so she could proceed with her original plan. She wanted to locate any journals, diaries or books that were available on the Sedgwick family history. Hopefully she would also be able to find the tenant farmer account records from the two-year period of time between her grandmother's birth and her great-grandparents' murders.

Donovan had previously shown her the general area where information on the festival could be found. Hopefully she would be able to find what she was really looking for without needing to ask for help. She would not have time to do much of an in-depth search. She had an appointment in two hours with Byron Treadwell to go through the newspaper files.

She also wanted to speak with the descendents of Seth Edwards who were still in the area. Seth had been responsible for seeing that her grandmother was sent to safety in Canada. Taylor hoped Seth's descendents would have family information handed down through the generations that would help her get at the truth. She stared out across the landscape at the approaching storm, then shifted her gaze to what she thought were the library windows.

A strong wave of apprehension tried to grab her attention, but she refused to allow it. A stronger surge of trepidation immediately followed, rejecting her efforts to shove it aside. Had she been too quick and too eager to dismiss a possible warning from her subconscious? Could she actually be in physical danger?

And if so, from whom? A cold shiver assaulted her senses. Or perhaps she should be asking from *what*?

Taylor went back inside the house and directly to the library. The richly appointed room didn't appear sinister in any way, but that did not lessen the tickle of apprehension that continued to pull at her nerves. She kept a close check on the time as she started a methodical search of the library shelves. After almost two hours she still had not found what she was looking for. She would have to continue at another time.

She hurried to the newspaper office, arriving just in time for her appointment.

"It's certainly nice of you to allow me access to all the back issues of the newspaper, Mr. Treadwell."

"Please call me Byron. And may I call you Taylor?"

"Of course." She glanced out the window. The rain had started to spatter her windshield as she drove from the estate to the newspaper office. It now fell in a steady downpour with no signs of letting up.

"This will certainly be helpful to me in my research of the history of the festival. Lord Sedgwick was kind enough to offer me the use of the archive material in the estate's library, but I imagine the village newspaper accounting would give me more of a local flavor than just a listing of facts."

She noticed the quick narrowing of his eyes before he hid his thoughts and feelings behind a benign mask, but he could not keep the sarcasm out of his voice. "Well, that was certainly gracious of His Lordship." His eyes narrowed again as he stared at her for a moment. "Are you staying at the Sedgwick manor house?"

"Well…yes, I am." There was something about him that made her uncomfortable. She could not quite put her finger on it—an attitude, the look in his eyes, the tone of his voice—something. He stood a little more than six feet tall with dark hair and an athletic build. He looked to be about forty, but she suspected he was older.

An errant thought entered her mind. If someone wrote down a description of Byron Treadwell it would be eerily similar to a description of Bradley, Alex and Donovan, with the exception of the ages. All four men were over six feet tall with similar builds and dark hair. If any one of them was seen from a distance on a dark night, could someone say for sure which one of them it was?

She quickly dismissed the thought that had tried to form, and returned to the business at hand. "I don't want to disturb you and take you away from your work, so if you could just show me where to find things I won't need to bother you. In fact, if I could also use your copy machine I wouldn't be cluttering up your office and disturbing your daily routine. I can make copies of pertinent things and take them with me. Of course I'll pay you for the copies."

"I wouldn't think of taking your money. I'm only too happy to cooperate with such a lovely visitor." Byron flashed a solicitous smile, but his eyes remained cold.

Taylor had the distinct feeling that he was hiding something. A little shiver tickled across the back of her neck as she turned her attention toward the card catalogue of subject files he had shown her. She had been afraid that everything would be so totally computerized she would have problems finding things on her own without revealing exactly what she was seeking.

She looked through the files for anything she could find on Clark and Emily Kincaid, her great-grandparents. She was shocked to see so many notations of articles about them. What surprised her even more was the continual mention of them every few years, right up to and including the day of her arrival. This was very perplexing. She checked through any mention of the Sedgwick family, knowing it would be a long list. Then she cross-referenced the specific dates that matched both Sedgwick and Kincaid until she had a list of back issues she wanted to see.

She stood and stretched out the kinks in her back, then glanced at her watch. It was almost six o'clock. She had been so absorbed in the task that time had gotten away from her. It appeared that everyone had gone for the day except Byron, who was still in his office. After putting everything away and gathering her belongings, she paused at his office door and knocked softly.

"Excuse me, Byron. I'm sorry to disturb you, but I wanted to let you know I was leaving."

His head jerked up in response to her voice. "I didn't realize it was so late. I was doing a final read-through of tomorrow's editorial." He rose from his chair and crossed the office toward the door. "Did you find everything you needed?"

"Yes, I believe I have an accurate list of which issues I'd like to see. Would it be okay if I came back tomorrow morning and made copies of the specific articles?"

"If the list isn't too long, perhaps I could have one of my staff do that for you."

"Oh, no. That won't be necessary." She offered a casual smile, hoping it would cover the concern his suggestion caused. She certainly did not want him to know what she was really up to. "I couldn't impose on you like that. You've already been more than helpful. Would nine o'clock in the morning be all right or would it be less disruptive to your routine if I came in the afternoon?"

"I think afternoon would be perfect. Then, after you've finished, we can have dinner together."

His invitation caught her totally by surprise. "Well, uh, I couldn't say until I check my schedule. There are several other people I want to contact. I need to see how I can arrange my time."

"In that case, why don't we have dinner right now? You don't have other plans for this evening, do you?"

"Well, no, I don't, although I'm expected back at the manor house for dinner—"

"We'll just call His Lordship and tell him to start without you." He smiled broadly as he handed her the phone.

Taylor hesitated a moment, then took it from him. She wasn't sure she was doing the most prudent thing, but there seemed to be a distinct friction between Byron and Donovan and she wanted to know more about it. Donovan wasn't in the house, so she left the message with Bradley.

"Shall we go? There's a delightful little pub at the village inn where we can get a decent meal." Byron opened the door and stepped aside for her to exit.

His words grabbed her undivided attention. The village inn…the same inn still owned by the descendents of Seth Edwards. Perhaps dinner would work out better than she had anticipated.

They were seated in a quiet corner of the pub. After placing their food order, Taylor attempted to draw Byron into a more personal conversation. "Am I correct in assuming that the newspaper has been in your family for a long time?

Your father and before that your grandfather and even your great-grandfather?"

"Yes, it's been in the Treadwell family for about 120 years, but not my direct ancestors. My mother married Colin Treadwell when I was three years old. He adopted me. I don't really know anything about my biological father other than he died before I was born. I only know my mother's side of the family back one generation before her."

"Good evening, Byron." A large, barrel-chested man in his late forties with sandy-colored hair graying at the temples stood next to the table.

Byron looked up at the sound of his name. "Jeremy…I'd like to introduce Taylor MacKenzie. She's a writer from the States, here to research the annual Sedgwick festival for a book she's writing. Taylor, this is Jeremy Edwards."

"Miss MacKenzie—" Jeremy nodded in acknowledgment "—a pleasure. I heard there was a visitor staying at the manor house."

Byron addressed his comments to Taylor. "Jeremy owns the inn. He and his daughter, Amanda, run it and the pub."

"It's nice to meet you, Mr. Edwards. Perhaps we'll run into each other again while I'm here." Perhaps…he was next on her list after Byron. What a great stroke of luck for her to have met him so that she wouldn't need to approach him cold. She now had her entry to initiate a conversation about Seth Edwards and his involvement with her great-grandparents. Dinner with Byron had not been the waste of time she had feared it would be.

"ANY NEWS YET on the identity of the murdered man and woman?" Donovan addressed his question to Mike Edgeware as the inspector exited the lodge house, closed the door and reaffixed the police crime-scene tape across the entrance.

"We traced the registration on the car parked down the lane. It belonged to a man named Kevin Nichols, age twenty-three. The keys in the dead man's pocket fit the car. We found his wallet and the woman's purse in the trunk of the car. He has been identified as the murdered man. He lived with his parents and was employed at the supermarket in town. The woman was identified as his fiancée, Jennifer Hawkins. She was twenty-one years old, also living at home with her parents. She worked at the same supermarket."

Donovan stared at the ground for a moment as he ran the names through his mind. "I don't know either of them. What were they doing on my property in the middle of the night?"

"According to a fellow employee at the supermarket, with each of them living at home and trying to save money so they could get married, they didn't have any place they could go to be alone together…to, uh, well…"

The obvious embarrassment covering the inspector's face told Donovan what the circumstances were. "So, they were using my lodge house as a meeting place to conduct their love affair?"

"Yes, so it seems. According to their friend, they were saving all their money and didn't want to pay for a hotel room and were also afraid someone would see them checking in. They chose your lodge house in particular because of the rumor that it's haunted. Apparently it was a little something that added extra excitement to their, uh…"

Donovan's anger flared. "Haunted? What next? I'm going to find out that my lodge house is everyone's favorite location to hold an orgy?" He closed his eyes and took a calming breath, but it did nothing to erase the anxiety that churned inside him. "Is this thing with my great-grandfather ever going to be put to rest?"

"What with the crypt having been blown open on the 100-year anniversary of its sealing, followed immediately by the killing of two people in the same location and in much the same manner as the original murders, I doubt it."

"Inspector Edgeware!" The excited voice belonged to the police constable running toward him. "We've found something."

Mike turned toward Donovan. "Excuse me." He quickly moved away from Donovan and consulted with the constable.

Donovan watched as the constable pointed toward the rose garden, then held up a plastic evidence bag. He was not sure, but it looked as if it contained some sort of knife. An involuntary shudder passed quickly through his body as he turned and went back to the house. The rose garden— dark images and blurry recollections swirled through his mind. Could he have witnessed something after all? He refused to allow any further thoughts or possibilities on the subject as he walked up the driveway.

As soon as he entered the house, Bradley was at his side. "Miss MacKenzie rang, sir. She is dining with Mr. Treadwell this evening."

The irritation surged thick and heavy through Donovan. "She's having dinner with Byron Treadwell? Who told her she could do that?" He didn't wait for a response from Bradley as he stormed off toward his living quarters. Once again Byron was trespassing on his property.

The shock jolted through his body. He had referred to Taylor as his property. He knew it was an absurd thought without the slightest bit of merit. He and Taylor did not have any type of understanding or even the hint of a relationship. And for him to have referred to her as *property*— his or anyone else's—well, there was no excuse for it. The rationalization, however, did nothing to lessen his irritation about Taylor and Byron having dinner together.

It was the same type of irritation he had experienced when Alex had been blatantly flirting with Taylor the night of her arrival. He did not like the notion that it might be jealousy. For starters, jealousy was wasted energy that didn't produce anything positive. But on a more personal level, if it were true, then it would mean he had developed a stronger attachment to her than just the physical. It was a situation he did not want, especially considering the bizarre circumstances surrounding him at the moment. He didn't like the implications. She was the great-granddaughter of the woman his great-grandfather had been obsessed with enough to murder.

Donovan ate dinner alone, as he had for most of the past two months. Alex had phoned with some lame excuse about grabbing a bite to eat elsewhere, which Donovan interpreted as either a card game or a new female acquaintance. He truly missed having Taylor seated across the table from him, but it was probably just as well that she had been gone for most of the day. Once again the estate had been crawling with police. He had given them as much of his time as his schedule permitted. He closed his eyes, the sight of the two bodies immediately enveloping his consciousness. A sick chill ran through him. Would the horrible vision ever fade from his memory?

TAYLOR LISTENED as the large clock in the entryway chimed twelve times, the sound echoing through the large house. She opened her bedroom door and glanced down the hallway, listening for any sound indicating someone was up and about. An eerie silence greeted her efforts. She drew in a calming breath, picked up the flashlight and cautiously ventured forth.

It had been later than she intended when she had returned to the manor house from her dinner with Byron Treadwell. A hint of disappointment had assailed her senses when she discovered everyone had retired for the night except Bradley. She had wanted an opportunity to talk to Donovan, to explain about having dinner with Byron, even though she didn't quite understand why she felt she owed him an explanation. As soon as she was in the house, Bradley finished locking up and returned to his quarters.

She glanced at her watch. Five minutes after midnight. This was her opportunity to explore the house without anyone knowing what she was doing. A moment of hesitation told her how unsettled she was with her decision. She had deceived Donovan to the point of perpetuating her lies after he had confronted her about her true identity. And now she was taking advantage of his generosity in allowing her to stay in the house by snooping behind his back. It was not a very honorable thing to do, and under normal circumstances she would never consider such an objectionable action.

But these were not normal circumstances. And something was terribly amiss. If only she could shake the uneasiness churning inside her, that constant edge that set the tiny hairs on her arms on end and left her nerves rattled. She attempted to shove away her concerns, but the best she could do was relegate them to a corner of her mind without really dismissing them.

Taylor quietly ascended the stairs to the third floor. She paused at the top of the staircase and shone her flashlight down the length of the long hallway, peering into the darkness as far as the beam of light penetrated. A cold movement of air brushed across the back of her neck. A ripple of fear made its way through her body, depositing a hard lump in her throat. She whirled around, fearful of what she would see. The only thing that greeted her was silence and an empty hallway. Another shiver jittered across her skin, electrifying her nerve endings.

Maybe she couldn't see anything, but she most certainly felt it—a sinister presence hiding somewhere in the shadows. Someone was watching her, someone who radiated menacing vibrations.

The ripple of fear she experienced at that moment came from a real person—someone made of flesh and blood. At least that's what she had to believe, otherwise the implications would be too frightening.

A sound, very soft but ever so real, reached out and grabbed her. She froze on the spot. Her heart pounded in her chest and the blood raced through her veins. Her first impulse told her to run back to her room and barricade her door. But her feet refused to move. A shortness of breath caught in her lungs. She forced her words, but they came out as a frightened whisper.

"Who's there? Come out where I can see you."

She strained to hear the noise again, to identify the sound. It seemed to be coming from down the hall, beyond the reach of her flashlight. As much as she wanted to get out of there she knew if she ran she would only be taking her fears with her, whether they were real or imagined. She tentatively took one step forward, then another as she waved the flashlight from one side of the hall to the other.

She froze in her tracks. There it was again—that sound. The blood rushed in her ears, almost drowning out the mysterious noise. She forced a tenuous calm to her rattled nerves as she tried to concentrate. The sound seemed to be a cross between shuffling feet and what she could best describe as wind whistling through an air vent. It was similar to the noise she had heard when she had been in the library. Donovan had told her the third floor had never been modernized. So what kind of air vents could there be if the heating system didn't extend to the third floor? Could it be the sound of wind against warped and worn window casements?

A little shiver accompanied another thought. Perhaps it was a secret passage of some kind.

Her insides quivered to the point where she almost visibly shook. Was she grasping at straws in a desperate attempt to explain something that didn't have a rational explanation? Surely a house as old as Sedgwick manor would have secret passages from centuries ago—movable walls, hidden rooms, sliding panels, cubbyholes large enough for someone to hide. She tried to swallow the lump in her throat, but she had no more success with that than she did in trying to quiet the churning in the pit of her stomach.

She again forced her gaze to the limits of the beam from her flashlight. Then a slight movement caught her eye, a shadowy figure disappearing around a corner. Her entire reality jumped to attention. A strange sensation of relief settled over her. She had something tangible to work with, something real. Her heart pounded, but not with fear. This time she would be able to find a clue as to what was happening, why such an ominous feeling permeated the very walls of the old house—what it meant and how it related to her search for the truth.

In a moment of hesitation she wondered if it was wise for her to pursue the shadowy figure. Was she behaving like the feisty heroine from one of those old Gothic novels who stomped her little foot in determination, then ignored the warnings and foolishly descended alone into the dark cellar where several other young women had disappeared? She quickly overruled the thought. She hurried down the hall toward the spot where the shadowy figure had disappeared. She slowed as she reached the end of the hallway, then cautiously peered around the corner, almost afraid of what she might find. To her shock she found only an alcove with a large window at the end—no doors or any apparent way out.

And it was empty.

She stood in stunned silence. She knew what she had seen. At least she *thought* she had seen it. Could her imagination have been playing tricks on her? Could the chilling Gothic atmosphere that clung to the old house have influenced the way she perceived the events? She shook her head. No, it was not an illusion, not her imagination. She saw what she saw. Someone real had been in that hallway. Someone real had rounded a corner and vanished into thin air.

And someone real was probably still there, watching her from some hidden place.

She tried to calm her erratic breathing and ease her internal shakes as she backed out of the alcove. Every nerve ending tingled, sending her the message to run, to get out as fast as she could. This time she obeyed the inner directive. She turned and raced down the hallway toward the staircase, glancing back over her shoulder every few feet. Fear followed closely behind her, nipping at her heels as if it was chasing her.

She burst through her bedroom door, shoved it closed, then leaned back against it. She gulped in a lungful of air, then another and another as she tried to slow her racing heartbeat and still her panic. Her mouth felt dry as cotton. She hooked the back of the chair under the doorknob. She knew it was an irrational act, but it somehow helped soothe her shattered nerves and made her feel safer. Well, moderately safe, anyway.

She closed her eyes and took several more deep breaths, then finally moved away from the door. She undressed and got ready for bed. Before climbing under the covers, she pulled back the edge of the drape and peered out of the window. A frown wrinkled across her forehead as she stared out across the grounds. She watched as someone walked toward the tithe barn, someone she couldn't identify in the darkness. Could it be the same figure she had seen the night she arrived, wandering around the garden? Could it be the shadowy figure she had encountered on the third floor?

Taylor burrowed into the comfort of the bed and pulled the covers up around her shoulders. A sinister atmosphere surrounded the house and the property. She had felt it the night she arrived. Then there were the bodies at the lodge house. And Donovan's strange behavior on more than one occasion, as if some unknown force had attacked him.

She closed her eyes and tried to force the thoughts from her mind, but to no avail. She spent a restless night tossing and turning as fears and possibilities swirled around in her mind, twining together into a tightly knit ball of confusion, until dawn finally arrived. She needed to talk to Donovan, to confront him. But every time she was near him her senses went astray, to be replaced with an undeniable attraction that seemed to be as much emotional as it was physical. She touched her lips, the memory of the kiss they had shared still very much alive.

Taylor showered, dressed and made her way to the informal dining room for breakfast. Both Donovan and Alex were already there. She mustered a pleasant, upbeat attitude as she acknowledged both men. "Good morning."

She went immediately to the sideboard and poured herself a cup of coffee.

Alex was the first to speak. "Good morning, Taylor. It's nice to see you. Did you sleep well?"

"I, uh, well…I was a bit restless." She felt the intensity of Donovan's gaze. She shot a quick glance in his direction, his stare sending a little tremor through her body. She tried to shake away the sensation as she responded to Alex's question. "It's probably the strange surroundings. I'm accustomed to my small apartment, not a large old house like this one—" a little shudder made its way up her spine "—with all its history."

"Perhaps it was something you ate." Donovan's voice held an edge to it, one she couldn't identify.

"I had dinner in the pub at the village inn. Everything tasted good, but I supposed there could have been something in the ingredients that disagreed with me."

"I hope you didn't have to dine alone." Alex's sly grin turned the corners of his mouth. "If I'd known you were going to be away from the house I would have been happy to keep you company."

"I, uh, I had dinner with Byron Treadwell." She saw the surprise on Alex's face and the disapproval on Donovan's. She felt a need to explain even though she knew she hadn't done anything wrong and didn't owe anyone an explanation. "He graciously allowed me access to the newspaper archives to help with my research. The afternoon got away from me and suddenly it was time for dinner. So, one thing led to another and, uh…"

"And you ended up having dinner with Byron." Donovan heard the disapproval in his voice, something he had been unable to control. If it had been anyone other than Byron… No, that wasn't true. It particularly rankled him that she had dinner with Byron, but it wouldn't have mattered who it was. He had wanted to spend the evening with her, to get to know her better—to figure out how she might fit into the ominous circumstances surrounding him.

And those circumstances had included another night of finding himself wandering the grounds without any memory of how he got there or why. Last time it was the rose garden and coincided with the murders at the lodge house. This time it was the tithe barn. Waves of anxiety had crashed through his consciousness, concerns about what he would find when he appeared in the informal dining room for breakfast. Another murder perhaps? Another unexplained event that had occurred while he'd wandered aimlessly in a state of confusion?

Or was it a state of total madness as it had been for his great-grandfather?

Donovan felt as if he had fallen into a bottomless pit. The thought frightened him. He desperately needed a strong connection with reality, some link to help him decipher fact from invalid perception. And he suspected Taylor was that link. Somehow she held the key even if she didn't know it. Should he take her into his confidence?

And if he did, would it be his final undoing?

Chapter Five

"I've got to make a quick trip into London. I should be back by this evening. Don't wait dinner on me, and tell Bradley not to wait up for me. He can go ahead and lock up at his normal time." Alex shot a wry grin in Taylor's direction. "If I don't see you tonight, I'll see you in the morning."

Donovan immediately pulled Alex aside and lowered his voice, but not so low that Taylor couldn't make out what he was saying. "What's going on here, Alex. What's so important that you suddenly need to get back to London today?"

Alex shifted his weight from one foot to the other as his gaze darted around the room. "My attorney called first thing this morning, and I need to meet with him."

"I didn't hear the phone ring. When did he call?"

"He called me on my cell phone about an hour ago." A touch of irritation entered Alex's voice. "Why all the questions?"

Donovan leveled a stern look at his cousin. "You're not in any trouble, are you? You haven't been losing money you don't have at the gaming tables again, have you?"

Alex emitted an open, easy laugh, which to Taylor sounded a little forced. "No, nothing like that. I put in a bid on a piece of property, a small vacation cottage up in the Lake District. The deal is going through and I need to sign some papers, that's all. Between meeting with my attorney, my banker and the property agent, I don't know how long it will take."

Alex departed, leaving Donovan staring after his retreating form. An uneasy feeling churned inside Taylor as he turned to face her. With Alex's departure, she was now alone with Donovan. She felt pressured to say something, to somehow ease the tension her dinner with Byron Treadwell had apparently caused.

"I, uh, I didn't mean to upset you by having dinner with Byron last night. It was just one of those things, a spontaneous situation."

"You don't owe me an explanation just because you're staying here. You're certainly free to come and go as you please. You did the courteous thing by phoning so that we knew not to wait on you. I'm the one who should be apologizing for making you feel uncomfortable. That certainly wasn't my intention."

He awkwardly shifted his weight from one foot to the other. "What do you have on your agenda for today? Is there anything I can help you with?" A ripple of excitement lodged itself just below the surface of Donovan's skin. A rush of heat settled low in his body. It was yet another sign of how she had invaded his every waking moment. Was this the same way it had been for his great-grandfather every time he was near Emily Kincaid? A little ripple of trepidation accompanied Donovan's thought. Was he falling into the same trap? Would his life repeat the same pattern as William Sedgwick's? It was a question that preyed on his grasp of reality and delved deeply into his emotions and fears.

Taylor considered his question for a moment as she

turned the possibilities over in her mind. Just how much of her real quest should she reveal? She had already confessed to her true identity. How much further should she go? How much should she take him into her confidence? "Perhaps there is something. Maybe you could help me locate some information in the library."

"Of course." He indicated the door, and the two of them walked toward the stairs. "What specifically is it that you're looking for?"

"It's a personal matter more than research for my book. Since I'm here anyway—" she paused for a moment, not sure of the best way to proceed "—I thought it might be interesting to see what type of information I could find that related to my great-grandparents…and the birth of my grandmother."

She extended a polite smile, one she hoped would look casual and nonthreatening. "Maybe some family history that you might have heard or know about?"

Donovan forced himself to continue up the stairs toward the library without displaying any outward reaction to her words, even though her request jolted him. He carefully measured his words. "I really don't know much about your great-grandparents or that part of my family history. I'm concerned with the present and the future, not the past. My father was the historian. He probably would have been able to provide you with some of the oral history that has come down, but I'm afraid he and I never really discussed it much."

He leveled a steady look at her in an attempt to judge her reaction to what he was about to say. "Perhaps if he had known who you really were, he might have discussed that facet of the family history with me, but since you didn't confide in him…" He allowed his voice to trail off, his unspoken words saying as much as if he had finished his sentence.

They continued up the stairs together, then down the hall toward the library. The scent of Taylor's perfume sent the physical attraction already pulling at Donovan into high gear. As fearful and bewildered as he was about his own mental state and as confused as he was about her possible involvement in what was happening, he couldn't stop the desire that flooded through his body whenever he thought about her. Exactly how much should he confide in her about the history of their families and how it fit together?

He reinforced his determination and gathered his composure. The entire matter was recorded history, at least most of it. It was not as if she didn't have other avenues for obtaining the facts. He wasn't preventing her from gathering information.

Then his determination began to slip. What he really wanted most was to hold her, to stroke her skin, to allow her warmth to flow to him and calm his rattled nerves. Though he believed he should maintain his distance from her, he knew it was impossible.

When they reached the library, Donovan led her to a section of shelves far away from what she had asked about. "I think most of the information about the history of the estate's business and the tenant farmers is located in this area." So much for the concept of sharing and trust. He wasn't ready to expose that much of his vulnerability, at least not yet.

Taylor watched him scan the rows of books as if he was looking for something. It was the same section she had explored the day before, and she knew there was nothing on those shelves that related to her family. Was he simply mistaken or purposely leading her away from what she wanted? She pretended to study the book titles, occasionally pulling one from the shelf and then returning it.

And all the while she felt his gaze on her as if he was using his eyes to mentally bore a hole into the very core of her existence so he could extract her deepest secrets. Was her imagination being fueled by feelings of guilt over her deceit, or was it something else? Whatever it was, she felt shaken and confused.

Donovan left her shaken and confused.

And very excited.

And wanting to know him better—much better—and on a *very* personal level.

She had never felt this type of attraction toward another man, not even her ex-fiancé. It was part physical, part emotional and all very compelling, as if she didn't have a choice in the matter—as if some force beyond her control was orchestrating her destiny.

Taylor looked up. The intensity in Donovan's blue eyes immediately grabbed her and refused to let go. Once again she felt herself being drawn in, bound to him by invisible threads made of the strongest steel—unbreakable threads that held her captive. What was this strange hold he seemed to have over her and why did it exist?

Frightened…intrigued…fascinated…wary. She no longer knew what she felt or how to interpret it. He dominated her every thought and feeling, yet he hadn't said or done anything that would explain why it was so any more than she understood why the heat of his kiss still lingered on her lips from the last time they were in the library.

A tremor of anxiety reminded her why she was there. It also resurrected the ominous vibrations that seemed to emanate from the very walls of the house, attesting to the centuries of sinister deeds hidden in the memory of the structure—*if* structures can be said to have memories.

Donovan extended his hand toward Taylor, his fingers almost touching her cheek before he withdrew. Had finding out what happened to her great-grandparents one hundred years ago been her true intention all along? Her true reason for contacting his father? He reached out toward her again, this time touching her hair and caressing her cheek. The physical contact excited him more than he thought possible. Or maybe it was something about the library.... He cupped her chin in his hand, gently lifted her face, then lowered his mouth to hers.

The second their lips touched he wrapped his arms around her and pulled her to him. It started as a simple kiss but quickly escalated to a heated need. A moment later her arms encircled his neck. Her warmth flowed to him. The physical contact again brought a calm to the dark cloud of turmoil that seemed to constantly surround him. Her earthy response excited him. He wanted so much more of her, he wanted everything. He didn't understand how he could be so consumed with her in such a short time, but he knew it was true. He had never felt so helpless in the face of adversity, almost as if some strange destiny guided his thoughts and actions.

Their kiss deepened and Taylor melted into the sensuality it conveyed. Lord Donovan Sedgwick filled her thoughts more and more with each passing minute, sometimes shoving to the background the connection between their families so that only the presence of this dynamic man remained a reality.

Something very mysterious and frightening was going on, but being in Donovan's arms temporarily erased her concerns. He made her pulse race. Was he for real or was he merely playing some kind of game with her? Toying with her feelings for some perverse reason of his own? Was anything at the Sedgwick estate real or had she been drawn into a weird vortex that deposited her in a surreal existence? As absurd as it seemed, could she possibly be falling in love with him?

Donovan reluctantly broke the kiss but refused to give up the warmth of Taylor's body pressed against his. He continued to hold her, caressing her shoulders and back as he nestled her head against his shoulder. He knew if his mouth had stayed on hers one second longer, the kiss would have turned into a serious seduction, but the last thing he wanted was to drive her away.

They remained locked in the embrace for what seemed like several minutes before Taylor finally made the move to break the physical contact. Each passing second made her want more of him, but she knew she had to keep her distance. She renewed her determination as she stepped back from him. She would complete the task she had set for herself, then return home. She simply could not permit Donovan Sedgwick to work his way any further into her life regardless of how exciting the prospect might be.

His intense stare sent a tremor through her body. His eyes weren't angry and his look wasn't threatening, but it left her with the sensation that he was again delving into the deepest recesses of her thoughts and feelings.

"I, uh, I've already taken up far too much of your time."

He pulled her into his embrace again. "I don't mind."

Little shivers of delight rippled through her body. "I don't want to be a bother—"

His mouth was on hers again. There was nothing subtle about the kiss, nothing tentative. Her breath caught in her throat as the heat of his passion infused her with a longing she couldn't ignore and knew she wouldn't be able to shove aside. If she harbored any lingering doubts about her physical desires where he was concerned, they had been completely swept away.

With great reluctance Donovan finally broke off the kiss. To have continued would have led to one place and only one—his bed. "I don't want to keep you from your schedule." It was a blatant lie, but he knew he didn't dare say what he really wanted.

"I do have an appointment with—" Taylor paused, then reworded what she had been about to say "—an appointment in the village to gather more information about the festival, sort of a local perspective." After his reaction to her having dinner with Byron the previous evening, it was probably better if she didn't mention returning to the newspaper office. A little twinge of guilt assaulted her senses. She quickly shoved it aside before it got any bigger.

Donovan glanced toward the floor before regaining eye contact with her. "Is there anything else I can help you with while I'm here?" He had mixed feelings about having directed her to the wrong section of the library. Even though the slightest physical contact with her set his desires on fire, he still didn't have things settled in his mind. He didn't know her true reason for being there.

Or why the frightening blackouts and blinding headaches had materialized from out of nowhere and continued to assault him.

"I'll just poke around the library for a bit longer if you don't mind, then I have to leave."

"That's fine. I won't be here for dinner, but we'll have more time to talk later this evening."

"That's all right. I'm..." Once again she felt herself being drawn in by his sexual magnetism and the mysterious aura that surrounded him. "I'm not sure when I'll be back. I have a busy afternoon ahead of me."

Donovan turned toward the library door. "I have several pressing matters to take care of in my office—" he managed a wry grin in an attempt to lighten the moment "—not the least of which is signing the employee payroll checks."

She immediately responded to his humor with a warm smile of her own. "I'm sure they'll appreciate that."

"I'll see you later." He reached out and gave her hand a little squeeze, then left.

Taylor collected her composure. Not only had Donovan rattled her nerves, he had clearly demonstrated the sensuality of the man that lived just below the slightly moody persona he projected.

She spent another hour searching the library shelves in an attempt to find the tenant farmer records. She had to finally abandon her search so she could meet Byron Treadwell.

She changed clothes and drove to the newspaper office. Byron greeted her warmly, but the cold look in the depth of his eyes still bothered her.

"This is certainly gracious of you, Byron. I made a list of the back issues that contain articles I want to copy. If you'll show me where to find them, I'll try to get out of your way as quickly as possible." She noted the skeptical look on his face, an expression that left her slightly unnerved. She tried to downplay the importance of what she was looking for. She extended a dazzling smile. "I promise to put everything back exactly where I found it so you won't need to clean up after me."

After settling into a small unused office, she retrieved the back issues she wanted and began making copies of the various articles. She skimmed them but did not study them in depth. She would do that in the privacy of her room where she wouldn't be disturbed.

She found the articles about the original crime, the subsequent trial and execution of William Sedgwick, his threats against some of the villagers and a curse uttered by some old hermit, the suicide of Donovan's father, the explosion that opened the crypt and the most recent news about the murders of the man and woman at the lodge house. And in between those specific events she found numerous articles that brought up everything again but did not provide any new information—articles that seemed to have no purpose other than to stir up controversy about the Sedgwick family. Could that be the reason for the animosity Donovan displayed toward any mention of Byron Treadwell?

It was almost five o'clock when she replaced the last of the back issues on the shelves and tucked the copies she had made into her large shoulder bag. "I think I have everything I need, Byron. Again, thank you so much for letting me rummage through your files."

"It was my pleasure." He glanced at his watch. "Why don't we cap off the workday with dinner?"

"Thank you for the invitation, but I won't be able to accept your kind offer." She winced inwardly at the words she had chosen to use. They sounded much too flowery—and too forced, as if she were trying too hard to be gracious. "I'm expected back at the manor house." She emitted a nervous chuckle. "Lord Sedgwick is going to go through the family archives with me and I don't want to pass up that opportunity."

It was a blatant lie, but Byron made her uncomfortable. There was something sleazy about him, something she couldn't define beyond the fact that it rubbed her the wrong way.

"Well, then…perhaps some other time."

Taylor returned to the manor house and went straight to her room. She secured the copies in a dresser drawer underneath some of her clothes. She felt foolish but somehow compelled to hide what she had been doing.

She changed clothes and proceeded to the informal dining room. Neither Donovan nor Alex were there, and the table had been set for one. Dinner was served by someone she had never seen before. Bradley was nowhere in sight. The atmosphere felt strange, almost as if something menacing loomed on the horizon, something that threatened to invade what was left of her composure.

Taylor ate quickly, then headed back to her room. She wanted to spend the rest of the evening going over the newspaper articles in detail. She paused at the foot of the stairs. So much swirled around inside her head, so many things she wanted to clarify—not the least of which was whether she might have a shot at a relationship with Lord Donovan Sedgwick. A relationship had not been at the top of her list. In fact, it hadn't been on her list at all, but Donovan occupied more and more of her thoughts with each passing day.

Perhaps a walk around the grounds in the cool night air would help clear her mind. So far, nothing else had worked.

She went out the side door, walked across the terrace, then strolled along the garden path. A little tickle of apprehension picked at her consciousness. She paused and took a minute to look around—lots of foliage, dark places where a person could conceal oneself and watch. A nervous jitter shot through her body. She had allowed the atmosphere surrounding the house to get to her again.

She shoved away her apprehension, took in a deep breath of fresh air and continued with her stroll. As she approached the greenhouse she became aware of two people inside, illuminated by the soft glow of a dim light. They appeared to be arguing. She paused, not sure what to do, then her curiosity got the best of her. She stepped closer, her presence concealed by darkness. She saw that the man was Bradley, but did not recognize the obviously angry woman with the long blond hair.

The side door to the greenhouse was ajar. A couple more steps and she might be able to hear what Bradley and the woman were saying. She strained to make out the angry words:

"This is the last time, Constance. I won't allow you to extort any more money from me. I simply don't have any more to give. I've had to do things I'm ashamed of in order to procure this payment. And I assure you that it will be the last one you'll see."

"Now, Bradley…is that any way to treat *family*—albeit a distant relative?" Constance Smythe smiled, but it was a calculating smile rather than one containing any warmth.

"I never should have allowed you to get a foothold."

"Don't be that way. You know my claim is legitimate and it can be proven if I choose to take it to court. I've researched everything very carefully. My great-grandfather was Lord William Sedgwick. The illegitimate son that resulted from his rape of Jane Bradley was my grandfather. I have a legal claim on the Sedgwick estate. I'd much rather marry into it so I can have it all rather than a token piece of it, but I have other options available to me. In fact, perhaps the most expedient thing to do would be to take this directly to Donovan. I'm sure he would—"

"Stop threatening me. Donovan is different from James Sedgwick. He won't put up with any of this. Another black mark against the family name is not as important to him as it was to his father. Donovan is concerned with far more practical matters. He doesn't feel the necessity of being bound by tradition the way his father did."

Bradley handed her a large envelope. "This is the last time, Constance. Don't come back for more."

The conversation was obviously over. Taylor hurried away before they spotted her lurking in the shadows. It was a strange conversation and she didn't understand the full ramifications, but she had garnered enough information to know that the woman was blackmailing Bradley. Should she relate what she had heard to Donovan or stay out of it? The question continued to circulate through her mind as she returned to her room.

She closed her bedroom door, then retrieved the copies of the newspaper articles from the dresser drawer. She put them in chronological order starting with the oldest one on top, then began to read everything she had brought back to the house with her. She carefully went over each article in detail, taking time to read some of them a second time.

So much information, more than she ever thought she would find. What was particularly startling to her were the articles about William Sedgwick's trial and the original murders. She had never known the reason for the murders, only that they had happened. But now she had facts. Lord William Sedgwick strangled Emily Kincaid, then stabbed her husband, Clark.

The details surrounding the crime, as reported in the newspaper, were very bizarre. It was the type of sensationalism that could just as easily be found on the front page of today's tabloid newspapers. She closed her eyes and tried to take it all in. What had started as a relatively simple, straightforward quest for information about her family history had turned into a perplexing search with many twists and turns along the way. And most baffling of all was her intense attraction to Donovan, an overwhelming sensation that had grabbed her the moment she'd seen him.

A sudden knock at her bedroom door startled her out of her thoughts. A ripple of anxiety ran through her. Could Bradley have seen her outside the greenhouse? Had he decided to confront her? She recalled the expression on his face when she had discovered him outside the library door, a sinister look that had given her a momentary chill. Another tremor assaulted her senses. Was she in danger? The fear sealed her decision to not disclose what she had overheard.

She forced out the words, her strained voice projecting a less-than-confident manner. "Yes? Who is it?"

"It's Donovan. May I come in?"

Her anxiety quickly changed to guilt. Did he know about her eavesdropping on Bradley and the mysterious woman? Was he there to ask her why she hadn't tried to find him to report what she heard? Or was her guilt running away with her imagination again? "It's late. Could it wait until tomorrow morning?"

"Please open the door. I think we need to talk…now."

Taylor hesitated a moment. His words made it a request, but his tone of voice conveyed more of an order. It also said he would not be dissuaded. She tried to swallow the nervous lump in her throat, then opened the door. Donovan stood on the other side. She glanced past him, giving a quick look up and down the hallway. He was alone. She stepped back so he could enter the room, then closed the door behind him.

He reached out for her, paused, then dropped his hand to his side. This was not the time to pull her into his arms and kiss her. He had given it a great deal of thought during the evening, even having dinner in his private suite rather than joining her, in order to not be distracted from his thoughts. He didn't know what type of relationship they had or if they even had one other than the obvious fact that he didn't seem to be able to keep his hands off her whenever they were together.

He also didn't know what was causing his blinding headaches and frightening memory lapses. He feared for her safety, but he didn't have a clue about why the danger existed or where it came from. She needed to understand what had been happening so she could be in a better position to protect herself.

Even from him, if necessary.

Or especially from him?

It was a thought that he had not been able to shake. Could the danger he felt actually emanate from him? The Sedgwick Curse coming to fruition? He took a steadying breath, then plunged into what he wanted to discuss.

"It's time we were honest with each other."

His statement caught her by surprise, and her first reaction was to defend herself from unwanted accusations regardless of how true they might be. "Honest? What do you mean? I haven't—"

He placed his fingertips against her lips to still her words. "Please, we need to move past this charade. We both know you aren't here to research a book."

She looked into the honesty of his eyes, to the sincerity of his features, both of which played heavily on her feelings of guilt. Once again the power of his masculinity and some undefined force seemed to be drawing her in. He was right. It was time for the truth.

"No." Her voice dropped to a mere whisper. "I'm not here to research a book."

He took her hand and led her to the sofa where they both

sat down. He continued to cover her hand with his, unable to relinquish the comfort of the physical contact.

"I don't know how much you know about what happened, or how much you've discovered since you've been here, but I think you should know the truth about your great-grandparents."

"I've read all the articles in the local newspaper, starting with the discovery of their bodies all the way up to yesterday's murders of the man and woman."

"I suspected that was what you were doing with Byron. So, you now have the Treadwell *biased* version of the events. I want to tell you what really happened. Part of this is oral family history and part of it comes from my great-grandfather's journal as he set it down in his own handwriting. I have his notations leading up to the murders and his thoughts following the murders and throughout the trial."

She jerked to attention. "You have journals written by your great-grandfather? May I see them?"

"Let me tell you about it first." He slowly laced their fingers together, then brought her hand to his lips. He was about to do something that he swore he would never do. He was about to tell someone the Sedgwick family version of what had happened so long ago, to reveal what a truly cruel man William Sedgwick had been even before he finally went over the edge into madness.

"My great-grandfather—Lord William Sedgwick— was, to put it mildly, not a very nice person. He took the title of lord of the manor very seriously. He would have been right at home in the Middle Ages. He believed that everything within his realm was his to do with as he pleased. And one of the things within his realm was the wife of one of the tenant farmers. He became obsessed with Emily Kincaid, partly because she had the audacity to refuse his unwanted advances. As time passed, his obsession became all encompassing.

"Then the night before the start of the annual festival he forcefully carried her off to the lodge house. According to his journal his intention was to seal their mutual desire for togetherness. The fact that she screamed and tried to fight him off when he abducted her didn't seem to make any difference to him. Seth Edwards went to fetch her husband and tell him what was happening. Clark hurried to the lodge house to rescue his wife, but he didn't make it in time. What was never reported in the newspaper or released to the public was that William had already raped her."

Donovan felt her muscles tense. He wanted to provide her some comfort but wasn't sure what to do. He didn't want to appear too aggressive and risk having her think he was of the same mind as his great-grandfather—that whatever he wanted was his to take. He hesitated for a moment, still unsure of the best way to proceed. He finally put his arm around her shoulder and slowly pulled her close to him. He was sure it was as difficult for her to hear his words as it was for him to say them.

"Emily had put up a frantic fight against William's assault, as evidenced by the many scratches on his face, arms and hands. According to his journal, when he finished she spat at him and called him an evil bastard. He became totally enraged over her harsh words, lost what was left of any control he had over his actions and strangled her. When Clark arrived a couple of minutes later, William stabbed him to death. It was only moments after he had done away with Clark that several of the villagers arrived on the scene. There was no doubt as to what had happened and who was responsible. They immediately grabbed William and turned him over to the constabulary. William took the superior attitude that as lord of the manor there was nothing they could do to him, that he had absolute authority by virtue of his title, power and wealth."

Donovan gave Taylor's shoulder a squeeze and placed a tender kiss on her forehead. "As I said, he would have been right at home in the Middle Ages." The nervousness he had felt when he knocked on her door started to diminish as he finally let go of some of the things that had been bottled up inside him from the moment he discovered her true identity.

"Even other members of the aristocracy, those he considered his peer group, could not condone what he had done. The trial was a speedy one, and his execution equally expedient. When asked if he had any last words, William threatened to come back and seek revenge on the Treadwells who had given extensive coverage to the crime in their newspaper. He also threatened Seth Edwards, the village innkeeper. It was Seth who sent your grandmother to safety in Canada to be raised by an aunt immediately following the murders. He was afraid that William's title and status would allow him to escape any retribution for his crimes, and he wanted to make sure your grandmother was somewhere safe.

"Then as William's body was sealed away in the crypt a demented old hermit placed a curse on the family, claiming that in one hundred years William would return to carry out his revenge. And, as you discovered, a mysterious explosion blew the door off the crypt on the one-hundred-year anniversary of its sealing."

"The newspaper reports seem more focused on pillorying your great-grandfather and your family than on just reporting the facts of the crimes."

Donovan clenched his jaw into a hard line. "Yes. That was when the strained relationship between the Treadwells and the Sedgwicks began. And during the ensuing years it's gone steadily downhill."

Taylor slowly nodded her head, indicating she understood what he was saying. "I guess that explains why the story seemed to resurface every twenty years or so. Kind of like making sure each generation knew all about it. That type of tactic seems considerably less than ethical."

A snort of disgust escaped Donovan's throat. "'Less than ethical'…that's putting it mildly. Byron Treadwell doesn't know the meaning of the word *ethical*."

He drew in a calming breath and tried to steady his nerves. "There's more to the ongoing saga than revealed in newspaper articles or even as part of village gossip." He wanted to tell her what had been happening to him. It was something that no one else knew, something he had not shared with another living soul—not even with the doctor when he had asked for a prescription to help his headaches. He allowed the doctor to think he was experiencing migraine headaches, but he knew it was something very different.

Yes, he wanted to tell her. But how? How did he tell someone that she might end up the object of a crazed obsession, much the same way as Emily had for William? That the danger he felt for her might actually emanate from Donovan himself? That he might be following in the footsteps of his infamous great-grandfather?

That he might have inherited the Sedgwick curse of madness?

Chapter Six

Donovan pulled Taylor's body closer to him, gathering strength and composure from her mere presence. He plunged into what he wanted to say before he could censor his words or change his mind about confiding in her. He had never totally shared his vulnerability with anyone before. It felt good to be able to tell someone what had been bottled up inside him. To have someone to share with. Was he making a mistake by placing his trust in her? Was it a mistake that could cost each of them far more than he realized? He hoped not.

"As you undoubtedly discovered in the newspaper articles, my father didn't simply die. He committed suicide. What the newspaper didn't report and what no one else knew was that for about three months prior to his death he had been plagued by blinding headaches that would attack him from out of nowhere, and strange blackouts where he couldn't remember anything that had just happened. His last memory would be of going to bed, then he would find himself somewhere else in the middle of the night with no knowledge of how he got there.

"I was aware of his headaches because sometimes I would be present when one would suddenly strike him. But the memory lapses and blackouts…" A shiver swept through his body. It was as if he was talking about himself. He sucked in a deep breath, held it for several seconds, then slowly exhaled. It did not help. "I had no idea that he was planning to commit suicide." He paused as if trying to gather his thoughts. "If I had known…maybe I…"

He leaned back and closed his eyes. His voice filled with anguish as his features took on a haunted look. "Somewhere along the way I must have missed something, some sort of clue. If only I had been able to pick up on the subtleties of what he was saying—"

"Don't do that." She placed her fingers against his lips. "Don't put yourself through guilt and bouts of *what if,* because it serves no purpose."

He emitted a sigh of resignation. "Perhaps…maybe there was something. Perhaps in his journal…"

"Did you read the entries he made in his journal?"

"No, not really. I skimmed them but haven't been able to bring myself to go through his words in detail. I barely made it through my great-grandfather's journal for the events that led up to the murder of Emily and Clark Kincaid and his thoughts about the subsequent happenings. And I only did that after I became suspicious about your true identity."

His words jabbed at her guilty feelings. "I'm sorry I deceived you like that." Her voice dropped to a near whisper. "I didn't think I'd be allowed access to your family archives if you knew who I was."

A hint of a smile tugged at the corners of his mouth. "You're probably right." The smile disappeared as he plumbed the depths of her eyes. His voice became soft and intimate. "However, I'm forced to admit I'm glad you perpetrated your deception." He touched her cheek, sending a tingle of excitement across her skin. "If you hadn't, I never would have met you." He brushed a kiss softly across her lips, sending another ripple of pleasure through her body. "My life would have felt so empty and I wouldn't have known why."

She thrilled to his words as well as the physical intimacy. She felt so warm and comfortable with just the two of them sharing personal information and concerns. It was every bit as much emotional as physical. But his attentions had nearly driven a sudden realization from her mind—almost, but not quite. His comment about being aware of his father's sudden headache attacks because he had witnessed them had triggered something in her mind. The other evening in the library, when he had behaved so strangely before hurrying out of the room—could there be a connection?

She swallowed down her sudden nervousness. "Do you mind if I ask you something?"

He stroked her hair and placed a soft kiss on her cheek. "No, I don't mind."

"Uh, the other night in the library…when you abruptly slammed out the door…" Her voice trailed off. She wasn't sure how to finish her question.

"I was about to get to that." He attempted to lighten the serious moment. "As long as I seem to be baring my soul to you, I might as well include everything." He forced a bit of a smile, but he knew it looked as weak as it felt.

He furrowed his brow in a moment of concentration as he attempted to gather his thoughts. "Ever since my father died I've been experiencing the same type of blinding headaches. It was almost as if what had been happening to him was passed on to me at his death." A quick tremor of apprehension shot through his body. He fought to maintain his composure. "At first I thought it was stress from the shock of his suicide. Then I started having strange blackout spells where I had no memory of what had just happened."

He turned toward her, cupping her face in his hands. He searched the depth of her eyes, hoping to find some understanding and maybe even some answers. "I don't know what's happening to me or why it's happening." His anxiety level jumped into high gear and he couldn't keep the anguish out of his voice. "You're the only one who knows about this. I've not mentioned it to anyone else, not even Alex or Bradley."

He placed a soft kiss on her lips, then held her tightly. "If the Sedgwick Curse is a reality…if there is madness…" He slowly shook his head to clear the confusion from his thoughts and get his emotions under control. He pulled back from her just enough to be able to see her face. "I'm concerned about your safety. I can't get away from the obvious—that everything seems to be echoing the horrible deeds of a hundred years ago. Could it be…is it possible…?"

He didn't know how to say it. He ended up blurting out the words without formulating them first. "It's almost like history repeating itself with us cast in the roles of our ancestors, left to play out the events of a century ago. Maybe the murders in the lodge house were just a warm-up." He took a calming breath. "And if by some bizarre quirk of fate that's what is happening here, then the danger could be…" He swallowed down the lump in his throat, the words the most distasteful he had ever uttered. "You could be in danger from me."

She reached out and touched the side of his face. An intense level of torment covered his features and emanated from the depths of his eyes. In spite of the ominous warning of his words, she had never felt closer to anyone than she did to Donovan at that moment. No one had ever shared that level of inner turmoil with her. He had trusted her with his deepest personal fears and shown her his vulnerability.

"I'm a part of this, too, Donovan. Our histories are irrevocably linked through a series of brutal actions, and it seems that something or someone is conspiring to see that our futures are linked to our pasts. I've seen and felt things since being here that I don't have any logical explanation for, things that truly frightened me at the time. But I believe those things were real rather than some bizarre supernatural phenomenon."

Her words caught his undivided attention. A quick jolt of adrenaline shot through him. "You've seen and felt things? Here? In the house? What things? Tell me." If she had been aware of strange happenings, then it couldn't be his mind playing tricks on him or a sign of madness taking over his reality. A wave of hopefulness washed through him, the first positive sign he'd felt since all of this began.

"Well…" Her brow wrinkled into a slight frown. "The night I arrived. The first uncomfortable sensation I had was while I was still in the entrance foyer. It felt like some sort of ominous presence in the house."

His upbeat moment quickly vanished. "That could have been me. I was the one in the entry hall with you."

"But I didn't feel it right away. It was a little later. And then that night, after I'd gone to bed…something woke me out of a sound sleep. I sensed that someone was standing next to my bed, someone who had reached out and touched me. For a moment I thought it was a dream even though it seemed so real. When I opened my eyes, no one was there. Yet the sensation had been so vivid. I tried to convince myself it was exhaustion from travel combined with the surroundings of this old house that had made me imagine the incident."

She dismissed the tremor of anxiety that accompanied her words. "I was never able to shake the feeling even though there was no logical explanation for it. I got out of bed and looked out the window. I saw someone wandering around in the gardens, but couldn't tell who it was."

Donovan's voice was a barely discernible whisper. "It was probably me. It was one of those blackouts I was talking about. I went to bed, and the next thing I was aware of was being fully dressed and outside. I had no memory of getting out of bed, dressing or going out doors. I had no idea why I was there." He searched the depth of her eyes before continuing. "I have no knowledge of being in your room that night. If someone were to ask me, I'd have to claim that I wasn't there…but do I believe that to be true?" He took a steadying breath. "I don't know."

She studied the vulnerability he had allowed himself to show—his inner self that he had been willing to share with her. "I don't think it was you in my room. Whatever it was…*whoever* it was…left me very unsettled and frightened. But I don't feel that way when I'm around you."

Donovan managed a weak smile as he squeezed her hand. "I'm very glad of that."

"There's more. Even though I knew it was wrong, last night I waited until very late so that everyone would be asleep, then I set out to explore the house." A moment of embarrassment told her how foolish and guilty she felt. "It wasn't a very nice thing to do, to take advantage of your generosity in allowing me to stay here. And I apologize."

"There's no need to apologize. What did you discover?"

"Well…I went up to the third floor. The entire time I was there I had the distinct feeling someone was watching me—the hair standing on the back of my neck, my heart pounding. I wasn't sure what to make of it other than it frightened me. Then I saw a shadowy figure move around a corner. Somehow I managed to screw up my courage and follow even though it was a stupid thing to do. But when I rounded the corner, it was a dead-end alcove with no apparent way out…and there wasn't anyone there."

She looked up at him, making eye contact and holding it. "That truly frightened me because I know I saw someone. Then there was the sensation again of being watched. It settled over me like a damp shroud. It frightened me to the point where I turned and ran back to my room." A little tremor darted up her spine as if to reinforce her memory of that night. "I'm assuming a house this large and especially one this old must have lots of secret passages and stuff like that."

"Oh, yes…" A warm smile slowly spread across his face, one that told of fond memories from happier times. "When I was a child my friends and I would play in the halls. It didn't matter where we found to hide, Bradley's father already knew the secret location. Although I know a large number of them I'm sure there are many hidden doors, secret rooms and sliding panels that I never found."

The mention of Bradley brought another incident to Taylor's mind. Should she mention what she overheard at the greenhouse? Was it really any of her business? It wasn't as if it was some type of strange mysterious happening that seemed to defy rational explanation. It was obviously nothing more than an argument between Bradley and a woman, nothing supernatural about it. And it really hadn't been any of her business, and the topic of the argument hadn't made any sense. It was embarrassing enough to admit that she had been sneaking around the house at midnight. She didn't want to compound her unacceptable behavior by admitting she had been hiding in the shadows while eaves-

dropping on a private conversation. A little chill of apprehension reminded her of the sinister look Bradley had
shown outside the library. She returned her thoughts to the
current topic of conversation.

"Isn't there any type of documentation on the house?
Something like blueprints? Maybe at the time when major
remodeling was done the construction people would have
documented what they found, or at the very least filed
plans to get a building permit?"

"Anything down in the cellars wouldn't have been
touched with the remodeling on the ground floor, and the
third floor was never remodeled." Donovan paused for a
moment, wrinkling his brow in a slight frown. "There were
some sort of blueprints in my father's trunk, but I only gave
them a quick glance."

Donovan leaned forward and placed a tender kiss on her
lips. "Thank you for talking with me tonight, for allowing
me to share my concerns with you." The emotion he felt
surrounded his words, filling them with heartfelt honesty.
"I've had so much bottled up inside me of late."

Her own emotions caught in her throat, causing her
words to falter. She took a steadying breath. "We'll work
together—"

"No! I can't allow you to be exposed to whatever danger is lurking out there." He shook his head, his voice
dropping to a whisper. "Especially if that danger ends up
coming from me."

"We're both involved in this, Donovan. We'll work *together* to figure out what's happening." It wasn't a suggestion, it was a statement of fact.

He studied the determination on her face. "You're very
strong willed, aren't you?"

"I am when it's something I feel very strongly about.

And I don't believe for even a minute that you're in any way responsible for what's happening here."

"How can you be so sure?" He sighed in resignation. "At this point I'm not sure about anything anymore."

"Do you mean what tangible proof do I have? I don't have anything concrete to show you, but I do have a very strong instinct that speaks to me, and right now it's telling me none of this is any of your doing."

They were each acutely aware of the mysterious force drawing them closer and closer together. It was almost as if the unknown danger and baffling circumstances had pushed them into an arena in which they would be forced to test each other and learn how far the boundaries of trust could be stretched. And that trust had already begun with the sharing of inner fears and concerns.

"Would it be possible for me to see your great-grand-father's journal? Maybe now?"

He glanced at his watch. "It's very late…"

"I know, but I'd like to pursue this now if it's okay with you." She smiled. "It's not like I'm going to be getting any sleep tonight anyway, not after all the things you've given me to think about."

"I don't suppose I'd be getting much sleep, either." He stood and extended his hand. "Okay, let's go to my suite. We'll explore my father's trunk and see what's there."

She took his hand and rose to her feet. A tremor of uncertainty rippled across her skin. His words about the danger possibly coming from him played through her mind. Were her instincts now trying to tell her something different from just a little while ago? Something she was choosing to ignore? Would it be a choice she would soon regret?

They descended to the ground floor and walked quietly across the house. Donovan opened the door to the wing that housed the estate's business offices and his personal living quarters. Taylor looked around in amazement. "This is incredible. It doesn't look like it even belongs in the same house. This is very modern."

"Yes, this is part of the remodeling my father did. To function efficiently in today's economic climate, an estate needs to be modern in both its management thinking and techniques as well as its offices. This estate is comparable to a combination large farm and large ranch in the States as we raise both crops and livestock. So, this is the heart of the business end where we have the computers and fax machines along with other devices necessary to a highly diversified working estate. And then there are the other business functions that do not relate to the day-to-day running of the estate such as the investments, rental properties and other holdings."

He gave her a very quick tour of the offices along with a brief explanation of the various business operations of the estate. Then he continued on down the hall toward his private living quarters. He opened the double-door entry, then stood aside so she could enter.

Taylor looked around the nicely appointed, large open area, then to the door on the other side of the room that stood ajar just enough for her to know that it led to a bedroom. It was like a separate apartment within the house and even included a small kitchenette in the corner.

"This is my private sitting room and beyond are my bedroom and bathroom. This is my personal sanctuary. A place where I can be alone with my thoughts, where I can relax and be just Donovan rather than Lord Sedgwick." He indicated a side door. "I also have a private entrance that leads directly outside to a terrace, which allows me to come and go without anyone in the house being aware."

She studied his handsome features, the chiseled good looks that could not hide the bewilderment and trauma that had surrounded him of late. "Such as leaving the house to wander in the gardens in the middle of the night?"

He pointedly stared at her. "Yes…such as that."

She heard the emotion that continued to grip his words, a wistful loneliness that touched her heart. According to what he had told her, way too much upheaval had invaded his life in the past few months. It was bad enough to have to deal with it on a personal level, but he also had to assume the reins of a large corporation that included a multi-faceted estate with many employees depending on him for their income. On top of that, there was the tradition that had to be maintained such as the annual festival. It was a lot for one man to shoulder regardless of how strong he was. And Donovan had an inner strength that was becoming more apparent to Taylor with each passing day.

"This is very nice." The room was tastefully decorated in a style different from the rest of the house. There was no question that the living quarters belonged to a man, but it did not envelop her with an overtly masculine feeling. It was very warm, relaxed and inviting, a perfect retreat from the stress and pressures of the day.

He showed her through the sitting room and into his bedroom. She immediately spotted the large antique trunk sitting next to the wall on the far side of the king-size bed. She noticed the prescription bottle next to a glass and a carafe of water on the nightstand. She pointed toward it and looked questioningly at him.

"Yes, for the headaches. It helps, but not as much as I had hoped when I asked the doctor for something to ease the pain."

Donovan opened a drawer in the nightstand and withdrew a small key. He knelt on the floor in front of the trunk and unlocked it. Taylor bent down next to him. The scent of her perfume teased his senses. Her nearness totally distracted him from the task at hand. At that moment nothing mattered more than having her in his arms again, the comfort that eased his fears. He pulled her into his embrace, and gazed longingly at her lips.

The passion that flowed between them and the sexual tension that sizzled in the air had barely been kept in check during previous intimate encounters. But now there was no danger of being interrupted. They were away from the rest of the house and the staff. It was as if they had found an island of calm in the midst of a stormy sea, a place where each felt safe to explore the physical as well as the emotional aspects of their growing relationship.

Donovan didn't know where this step would take them, but he knew he had never felt about anyone the way he felt about Taylor even though he had known her such a short time. She had a calming effect on the turmoil that had suddenly become an unwanted yet integral part of his life. She allowed him to believe things would really be all right, that there was an answer to the nightmare and they would be able to find it—together. The word *together* had a very reassuring feeling attached to it, one he didn't want to lose.

He felt as if he could accomplish anything as long as she was part of his life, that the strange events were only a temporary happening that he would be able to defeat and eventually explain. Then a dark cloud began to descend over his thoughts. There was still the possibility that he represented a threat to her. Or that she could fall prey to the same danger that seemed to be stalking him and he wouldn't be able to prevent it.

His mouth took hers and all his fears and concerns faded

into the background. Any thoughts of the trunk disappeared along with all the other concerns circulating through his mind. Taylor's addictive taste fueled his desires. He held her tighter. He brushed his tongue against hers as he intimately explored the recesses of her mouth.

Taylor slipped her arms around Donovan's neck in response to his delicious seduction. Sharing secrets, confiding in each other and extending trust had drawn her even closer to him and dramatically increased the emotional level of her desire. It was a kiss that quickly escalated into much more as passion burst into incendiary desire.

The danger surrounding them seemed to fuel the intensity of her desire, adding a new level of enticement. Perhaps their actions were not appropriate to the bizarre and ominous circumstances that seemed to be holding them in an iron grip, but possibly it was the only time and place—the only chance they would have to share what she strongly suspected was the beginnings of love. Falling in love had been the furthest thing from her mind when she boarded the flight for England. The realization of what was happening to her came as a total surprise. But if it was love, shouldn't this be a time of euphoria?

Chapter Seven

Donovan's hands slipped down Taylor's back, coming to rest on her bottom. He pulled her hips tightly against his, and she could feel his growing arousal. Her breathing quickened. Her pulse raced. She responded enthusiastically to his actions, eagerly embracing each foray. Donovan was who and what she wanted. And at that moment he was the *only* thing she wanted.

Taylor's earthy acceptance of his advances had released the desires Donovan had barely been able to keep in check. His fervor increased tenfold as his mouth fully claimed hers. He twined his fingers in her hair. He had never wanted anyone as much as he wanted her. And somewhere in the back of his mind he knew it was far more than just a sexual encounter, the meaning much deeper than any he had ever known.

The heated passion quickly exploded. The slow seduction ritual of undressing and enticing one another into the bed didn't exist. They were almost frantically eager to explore the sensual demands pulling them together. Clothes dropped away into a pile on the floor. They fell into his bed, bare skin touching bare skin along the length of their torsos. Making love with Donovan was a decision Taylor knew she would never regret.

Every place he touched sent ripples of ecstasy through her body. Her nipples hardened. Her breathing came in labored gasps and an earthy moan escaped her throat when he drew one of the taut peaks into his mouth. She skimmed her fingers across his shoulders and caressed his back.

Each became lost in the sensual explorations—learning what excited and pleased, stimulating the senses to new levels, reveling in each new tactile sensation.

It felt so right having Taylor in his bed. The creamy texture of her bare skin was everything Donovan knew it would be. He tickled his fingers up her inner thigh until he reached the moist heat of her femininity. He inserted his finger between the folds. Her soft moan of delight excited him as much as her physical response to his touch. His mouth captured hers again in a hot kiss as his hand manipulated and stimulated.

Then the convulsions claimed her, moving swiftly though her body in cataclysmic waves. She tried to catch her breath, to bring some reality to the rhapsody that had captured both her body and mind. But before she could find that reality Donovan's knee gently nudged her legs wider and he settled his body over hers.

He slowly entered her, the sensation so intense that it nearly took his breath away. Donovan paused for a moment as he buried his face in her neck. He knew he had to stop the words before they escaped—words he knew he didn't dare say aloud—words that told of his strong feelings for Taylor, the emotions coursing through his soul.

He set a smooth tempo that she immediately responded to. They moved in harmony as if they had made love together many times and knew intimately the rhythm and timing of each other's bodies. His pace quickened as the excitement built within him. A gasp escaped Taylor's mouth, then he experienced the sensation of her release. A moment later his body shuddered and the hard spasms coursed through him. He held her tightly in his arms until the spasms quieted and he was able to get his breathing under control.

Donovan stroked her hair, brushing aside some loose tendrils that clung to her damp skin. He placed a series of tender kisses across her face while holding her securely in his arms. He had never felt so complete, so at one with another person. For a little while he managed to forget the insanity surrounding him, the unknown danger that seemed to lurk around every turn. Taylor provided him an oasis in the middle of turmoil, giving him her warmth and caring.

He rolled over, bringing her with him so that her body was on top of his. He continued to caress her back and occasionally skimmed his hand across the roundness of her bottom. Everything about her was exquisite. He didn't want to ever let go. His embrace tightened.

Taylor snuggled into the warmth with her head nestled against Donovan's chest. She heard his heartbeat, absorbed the strength of his character as it radiated to her. No matter what happened over the next few days or even months and years into the future, she would never forget the magical time they had just spent together—a time that reinforced all the emotions that had been growing inside her from the moment she first met Lord Donovan Sedgwick.

His words drifted through the soft veil of utter contentment that enveloped her. "Taylor…" He placed a gentle kiss on her forehead. "Is there anything I can get for you?"

"Mmmm…not a thing."

He reached down toward the foot of the bed and pulled a blanket up until it covered them. His words tickled across her ear in a sexy whisper. "What do I need to do to get you to spend the rest of the night with me?"

She brushed a soft kiss against his chest, then raised up enough to be able to see his eyes. A slight smile tugged at the corners of her mouth. "You might try asking me."

"I can do that." A dazzling smile lit up his face as he ran his hand across her bare bottom. "Miss MacKenzie, would you do me the honor of spending the night with me?"

"It would be my pleasure, Your Lordship."

THEY WOKE EARLY the next morning, remaining in bed for a while before getting up. They talked about simple topics of enjoyment rather than discussing the dark happenings surrounding them. They touched playfully, kissed and caressed. The light moments quickly returned to the passion of the previous night. They ended up making love again, this time with a slow sensuality that further reinforced Taylor's deep feelings for Donovan. Then Donovan escorted her back to her room before any of the household staff had begun their day.

Shortly after lunch they again approached the trunk in his bedroom. He lifted the lid revealing a collection of journals, photographs, large envelopes and small boxes. Nothing immediately jumped out as being important, but Taylor knew there were several items that needed to be inspected.

There was a new feeling of closeness between them, something far more than the warm glow still clinging to them after making love. For Taylor it was an emotional bond stronger than anything she had ever felt. Regardless of Donovan's fears, concerns and uncertainties, she trusted him. Together they would discover what the mysterious force was that seemed to be interfering with their lives and literally threatening his sanity.

Donovan located his great-grandfather's journals and handed them to her. "I've gone through these. Perhaps there's something here that I missed, something that will strike your attention and have some meaning to you."

"Is it okay if I take them back to my room so I can go through them later?"

He hesitated a moment. "I'd rather you didn't. I'd feel more comfortable with them locked inside the trunk."

She accepted his answer. "I understand." Her first night in the house and the sensation of someone being in her room flashed through her mind. The hair rose on the back of her neck for just a moment, but it was enough to bring back the menacing sensation she had experienced that night. "You're right about not letting them out where someone else could come across them."

They took the various items from the trunk and separated them into categories. He stacked the journals, dividing them according to the journal's author. Then came several envelopes of photographs. They opened the envelopes and separated the photographs as best they could. Many of the pictures that Donovan didn't recognize were identified by the names written on the back, mostly in his father's handwriting.

They found the blueprints relating to the manor house from different periods of time. Each blueprint had to do with a phase of the remodeling done over the years. There were a few books about curses and inherited madness, some seeming to be a serious attempt to deal with the subject while others were more along the line of lurid speculation and sensationalism.

The small boxes each contained personal keepsakes belonging to Donovan's father, items that seemed to be of sentimental value rather than relating to what had been happening. They returned the small boxes to the trunk, but kept the other items out on the bedroom floor where they were accessible.

Taylor looked through William Sedgwick's journals while Donovan read the journals of his grandfather, Henry Sedgwick. Taylor didn't find anything new or different in William's journals than she had gleaned from the newspaper articles and from what Donovan had told her. Donovan's perusal of Henry's journals didn't give up any additional information, either.

Taylor glanced at her watch. She wanted to meet with Jeremy Edwards and his daughter, Amanda. "I have some things I want to do in the village before dinner. I shouldn't be gone long."

A quick look of concern darted across Donovan's face. "Where are you going?"

"To the village inn. I want to talk to Jeremy and Amanda. I met Jeremy the other night when I had dinner with—" She stopped midsentence, deciding it was better not to mention Byron's name.

An audible sigh of resignation escaped Donovan's throat. "I know, when you had dinner with Byron. You don't need to be afraid to mention his name in my house. It's like any vermin. Just because you don't want them near you doesn't mean you can carry on as if they didn't exist."

He reached out and took her hand in his for a moment. "Please don't stay in the village very late. It will be dark soon." He gave her hand a squeeze.

She returned the squeeze and gave him a reassuring smile. "I won't be gone long."

Taylor gathered her purse and a notebook, then left the manor house. She decided to walk to the village. The exercise would do her good and give her time to think before arriving at the inn. So much had happened in the past twenty-four hours—even less than twenty-four hours. It had been yesterday evening when Donovan had come to her room and shared his knowledge about the history of their great-grandparents with her.

And then they had made love. Her mind still reeled at the enormity of the emotional impact it had on her. But what of the future? What would happen to Donovan if they couldn't discover some rational explanation for what was happening? A shudder of trepidation worked its way up her spine. Somehow everything had to work out—it just had to.

She entered the inn and immediately spotted Jeremy Edwards. She approached him, smiled and held out her hand. "Good afternoon, Mr. Edwards. We met the other evening when I was having dinner with Byron Treadwell. I'm Taylor MacKenzie."

Jeremy returned her smile with a gracious one of his own as he accepted her handshake. "Of course, Miss MacKenzie. You're the writer researching the book. Staying at Sedgwick Manor, aren't you?"

"Well…that's only partly correct." She noted the look of uncertainty that immediately replaced his smile.

"I am staying at Sedgwick Manor, but I'm not researching a book and I'm definitely not a writer. I'd like very much to sit down with you and your daughter to discuss the real purpose of my trip here."

Jeremy's look of uncertainty quickly changed to wariness. "The *real* purpose of your trip? And what would that be? Byron didn't mention anything about some other purpose for you being here."

"Byron doesn't know. I haven't taken him into my confidence." She leveled a steady look at Jeremy. "And I hope you will keep what I'm about to tell you between us."

"You've put me in a quandary, Miss MacKenzie. I can't make a promise like that when I don't know your intentions."

She glanced around the lobby of the inn, noting the number of people coming and going, then returned her attention to Jeremy. "Could we go someplace private to discuss our business?"

He paused for a moment as if considering her suggestion, then motioned toward a young woman to come to the front desk. "Watch things for me. I'll be back shortly."

He turned toward Taylor. "Amanda is in the office working on the books. We can talk there."

She followed him to the back room. He shut the office door, introduced her to his daughter, offered her a chair, then seated himself on the couch. "Now, Miss MacKenzie, what is all this secrecy about? Why are you here if not to research a book?"

Taylor took a calming breath, then launched into the recitation she had been rehearsing on her walk to the inn. She had decided that the direct approach would be the best.

"My great-grandparents were Clark and Emily Kincaid—"

Jeremy immediately jerked to attention. There was no mistaking the look of terror that flashed across his face, an expression that sent an uneasy surge through her reality. She swallowed the discomfort and forced her rehearsed words. "The toddler your ancestor, Seth Edwards, sent to safety in Canada was my grandmother. My grandmother and I were very close and I'm here to research that part of my family history, to know what really happened and why. What I would like from you is any family history that wouldn't have appeared in newspaper articles, tales handed down through your family from those days, what the impact was on Seth after he stepped in to save my grandmother from any harm—" she paused as a moment of emotion grabbed her "—an act for which I am very grateful."

Jeremy rose from the couch, then nervously paced back and forth. "Lord Sedgwick knows who you are?"

"He didn't when I arrived, but he does now. He's given me access to the Sedgwick family archives in the library. And now I'd like to hear about any stories that have come down through your family."

"That's not possible." His gaze nervously darted around the office, looking at everything but her. "I don't know anything about it. I suggest you allow the matter to drop."

She eyed him carefully. "You seem very frightened. All of this happened a hundred years ago. What is there about it that would frighten you now? Certainly you can't believe that Donovan is somehow a threat to you. You couldn't possibly hold him in any way responsible for the actions of his great-grandfather."

Jeremy's fear came out in his words. "I assume you know about the crypt. Well, he's come back just as the curse said he would. He's here somewhere, hiding in the shadows, watching my every move. I feel his evil and I won't have anything to do with making it worse than it already is."

"But Mr. Edwards…this is the twenty-first century. Surely you don't believe in ancient curses and evil spirits."

"I only know what I feel. My daughter—" he motioned toward Amanda who sat quietly listening since Taylor had entered the office "—and I have nothing to say to you. Now I'll be asking you to leave and not talk to me of this anymore." He crossed the room, opened the office door and stood aside so she could exit. The determined set of his jaw said as far as he was concerned their conversation had come to an end.

"I wish you'd change your mind, Mr. Edwards. I need your help. This is very important to me. I promised my grandmother…"

He stared straight ahead, not even acknowledging her words. Disappointment sank into Taylor as she rose from the chair and walked toward the door. She went over his words in her mind, his comment that he felt the evil. A cold shiver darted across her skin. She understood what he meant. She had felt it, too. But it had been at Sedgwick Manor and on the grounds of the estate. That was where William Sedgwick lived and where the murders had been committed. What could Jeremy have possibly encountered in the village or at the inn that would have produced the same fearful reactions? It was a new puzzle piece, but she didn't know what to do with it or how it fit.

The Treadwells were the other family singled out by William Sedgwick before his execution. Byron had not made any mention of a similar type experience. Of course, Byron didn't know her true identity or her real purpose in going through the newspaper archives. Perhaps she should approach him with the truth.

She paused at the office door and turned to face Jeremy. "If you change your mind, please call me at the manor. I can assure you that I'll keep our conversation confidential." When he didn't acknowledge her comments, she left the office. She stepped outside onto the sidewalk, then paused to get her bearings.

"Miss MacKenzie." Taylor turned at the sound of her name. She spotted Amanda peeking around the corner of the building from a side alley, motioning toward her. She looked around to see who might be watching, then hurried down the alley toward Amanda.

"I'm sorry Poppa was so rude to you. Something terrible has been bothering him ever since the night of the explosion and he won't tell me what it is."

"Do you know anything about all of this? Any family history that would not be recorded anywhere?"

"Not too much. Poppa has always been kind of secretive about what happened." The young woman paused, as if deciding whether or not to continue. "Poppa has these *feelings* about things…I don't know how to describe them."

"Do you mean psychic impressions?"

"Maybe, I'm not sure."

A quick jolt of excitement charged through Taylor. Perhaps Jeremy Edwards was the key to unraveling the ominous threat that had settled over everything and held Donovan in its grip. "Amanda…do you think you could persuade your father to talk to me?"

"I can try. I think it will be good for him to get whatever it is that frightens him out into the open. Things aren't as scary in the light as they are when they're locked away in the dark."

"That's very true." Taylor smiled at the young woman. "Thank you for your help. I'll come back tomorrow afternoon. Would two o'clock be a good time?"

"Maybe two-thirty would be better. We will have finished with the noon meal in the pub by then. Poppa will have some free time."

Taylor extended a warm smile. "I'll see you tomorrow."

She looked up and down the street. As long as she was in the village, there were a couple of things she needed. She wrinkled her brow in concentration as she tried to come up with the British equivalent of a drugstore. Then the word popped into her mind. Chemist. That was it. She needed to find the chemist shop.

She saw the sign in the next block. She hurried down

the street, ever mindful of the darkening sky and the approach of night. After making her purchases, she walked back toward the estate.

As soon as she entered the front door of the manor house Donovan was at her side, his entire demeanor projecting his agitated state of distress.

"Where have you been?" His anxiety came through loud and clear in his tone of voice as well as in his words. "I thought I said I didn't want you wandering around at night by yourself...especially outside the house."

She looked at him curiously, bristling slightly at his words. "I understand that this is your house and as a guest I have an obligation to adhere to the *house rules,* but I didn't realize you were issuing an order." Her voice trailed off as the emotion invaded her words. "After last night, I thought...well, I sort of assumed..."

His attitude softened a little. "It wasn't an order, please don't think that. It's just..." He pulled her into his embrace and held her close. He took a calming breath. "I don't want you involved in the bizarre happenings and potential danger that has invaded my life."

Regardless of their discussion about working together to discover what was happening, the impact of their lovemaking had turned Donovan's life upside down in a way he had never believed possible. The emotional attachment he felt for Taylor had increased a hundredfold and had become impossible for him to ignore or deny.

Taylor furrowed her brow in confusion. "I thought we agreed to work together—"

"I've given it some more thought while you were gone this afternoon. I don't want you involved." He placed a soft kiss on her lips as his voice dropped to an emotional whisper. "I won't take a chance on you getting hurt."

"You can't shut me out on the grounds that I might somehow get hurt. Our family histories have tied us together, and whatever is going on here is related to that. I'm just as much a part of this as you are." She placed her hand against his cheek. "And I say we'll do this together."

He emitted a sigh of resignation, then tendered a bit of a smile. He brushed a gentle kiss on her forehead. "As I said last night, strong willed—and stubborn."

She tried, but could not suppress the slight grin that tugged at the corners of her mouth. "You'd better get used to it because I don't have any plans to change."

TAYLOR CAUTIOUSLY OPENED her bedroom door and glanced up and down the hallway. The clock in the entry hall downstairs struck one o'clock in the morning. She and Donovan had wanted to spend the night together, but could not find a subtle way to do so without alerting the household to their actions. Bradley had seemed to be involved in several household matters that kept him moving from room to room. And even Alex displayed a restlessness, drifting back and forth between the snooker room and the kitchen until late in the evening.

A pang of guilt assaulted her as she stepped out into the hall. She wanted to take another look around the manor house without anyone knowing what she was doing. A slight frown wrinkled across her brow. Snooping…that's what she was doing. There wasn't really any other word for it. And worse yet, she was doing it behind Donovan's back—not a very honorable thing to do in light of their new relationship, their agreement to pursue matters together and her thoughts about trust.

She shoved aside the bothersome concerns and started down the hallway toward the stairs. She had already looked around a good portion of the second floor. Besides her room, that's where the library was. She thought about the third floor again and an immediate cold chill ran up her back at the memory of the shadowy figure and the sensation of fear it had produced. There was a wing on the ground floor that she hadn't been in yet, even during the daytime. It seemed that there were always household staff present.

And then there was also whatever lay below—however many levels existed beneath the ground floor of the centuries-old house.

The image popped into her mind again—the old Gothic movie with the feisty heroine venturing downstairs into the darkened bowels of the gloomy mansion with everyone in the audience wanting to scream at her to go back. The panicky sensation produced by her recent midnight foray to the third floor invaded her mind one more time.

Was she about to be very foolish...*again?*

She paused on the landing as she debated whether to go downstairs or upstairs. Downstairs finally won out. She quietly descended to the ground floor and made her way toward the wing that extended to the back. She peeked into a couple of rooms, but didn't see anything out of the ordinary. She continued on down the hall, her steps becoming slower and more tentative as she progressed.

Distress pulled at her nerves, then settled over her like a blanket. The hair stood on the back of her neck. A tremor of apprehension rippled across her skin as her breathing became shallow. She felt it again, just as she had the other night on the third floor—someone...or something...watching her.

She intellectually knew it was ridiculous; there wasn't anything tangible to fear. It was just the ever-present chill that seemed to be a part of the old house. But the discomfort continued to poke at her, increasing her panic level with each passing minute. She forced her footsteps, one in front of the other, as she continued into the gloom of the nearly darkened hallway. But no matter how much she tried, she could not shake the sensation of someone's stare focused on her back.

Taylor whirled around as she clicked on her flashlight. The beam caught a quick movement at an opened door as someone ducked into the room—a room she had earlier peered into and found empty. Her heartbeat jumped and raced. She swallowed down the panic. A quick adrenaline surge allowed her to overrule her better judgment and rush down the hall toward the room rather than away from it.

She paused at the door and took a deep breath to calm her rattled nerves. She stood to one side so she was partially hidden by the wall, then shoved the door all the way open. She cautiously reached inside and found the light switch on the wall. The sight that greeted her when the lights came on was as disturbing as the quick glimpse of the shadowy figure had been. It was a sitting room of some sort with all the appropriate furniture and accessories…and no one in sight. She had seen the shadowy figure go into the room, yet the room was devoid of any human element.

She stepped farther inside, raking her gaze slowly across everything in her line of sight. There didn't appear to be any obvious place where a person could hide—no pieces of furniture large enough to conceal someone, no apparent doors to another room or a closet. She proceeded warily across the room to the only outside wall. She checked the windows. All were locked from the inside.

An icy chill darted through her body. She couldn't explain what she had seen, but she knew her eyes weren't lying to her. It had not been her imagination. It could not be explained away as being a dream. Someone had been at the door and entered the room. There wasn't any obvious way out of the room other than by the door she had just gone through, a door that had been in her sight at all times since seeing the figure.

Now that room was empty and no matter how much she tried, she couldn't come up with a logical explanation. She quickly glanced around the room again. A ripple of panic knotted in her stomach. Anxiety jabbed at her consciousness. She again experienced the unnerving sensation of someone's eyes on her, watching from a hidden place, tracking her every move.

Preparing to do her harm?

A very real evil permeated the air around her. All the courage she had been able to muster when she entered the room deserted her. She tried to shove down the rapidly escalating panic rampaging through her body. She gulped several large breaths in hopes of calming her rattled nerves, but to no avail. Her heart pounded in her chest. She backed out of the room. Once in the hallway, she turned and dashed toward the stairs and the comfort of her room. But was that really the safe haven she hoped it would be?

Taylor leaned back against her closed bedroom door as she forced a calm to what she knew was an unreasonable case of panic. But her emotions weren't as easily convinced of that. She closed her eyes and attempted to breathe slowly and evenly until a semblance of tranquility returned.

The only logical explanation for what had just happened was a hidden door or secret sliding panel that allowed someone to escape from the closed room or at the very least hide from view. Donovan had told her that even he didn't know where all the secret rooms and hidden passages in the old house were located.

Her eyes popped open and she jerked to attention. According to Donovan's childhood memory, Bradley's father knew, and that meant Bradley probably knew about them, too.

She looked around the bedroom. The night of her arrival…someone who knew all the hidden places in the old house would know about any secret entrance into her room. What had happened had been real, not the result of exhaustion. But how could it be so? No one knew her true identity or her real reason for being there. So why would someone have been in her room? Every time Taylor thought she had a portion of the puzzle solved, a new piece presented itself and confused the matter even more.

Chapter Eight

Taylor checked her watch—almost two-thirty, the time she had told Amanda Edwards she would be at the inn. Donovan had been involved in estate business all day. She had used her time to go over the newspaper articles again and make a list of specific questions for Jeremy Edwards, something to hopefully ease him into sharing what else he knew about his family history.

She gathered her purse, a notebook and again set out on foot for the village inn. When she arrived, Amanda met her at the door.

"Poppa is not happy about you coming back today. I talked to him at length last night and he finally agreed to see you, but he wouldn't make any promises about telling you anything. He's busy right now and says he can't see you for another hour yet. Would you like to wait in the pub? It's closed until four-thirty, but I can get you something to eat or drink if you'd like."

"I don't want to put you to that trouble. I'll just take a walk around the village and return in an hour."

Taylor strolled leisurely along the narrow, winding road, taking the opportunity to observe the local residents and investigate some of the shops. It was a picturesque village, looking every bit as a stereotypical English country village should, right down to the thatched-roof cottages.

Then her gaze fell on a blond woman entering the chemist shop, the same woman she had seen arguing with Bradley. She glanced at her watch. She still had half an hour until her meeting with Jeremy. She crossed the street and went inside the chemist's. She wanted to know what the woman was doing and possibly discover her identity.

She pretended an interest in some magazines as she listened to the conversation between the woman and the clerk as the woman was paying for her purchases.

"Will that be all, Constance?" The clerk offered a cheery smile.

"Yes, I believe so." She handed the clerk some money.

"This face cream is a new item for us. Have you used it before?"

"I have a friend in London who recommended it."

The clerk put the purchases into a bag, then counted the change from the cash register. "How are the arrangements for the festival coming along? Do you have everything organized? It was certainly a sad bit of news about Lord James's death. How is His Lordship holding up? We haven't seen much of him since his father's funeral."

Constance extended a knowing smile, one that implied she was on intimate terms with the current Lord Sedgwick. "Donovan was, of course, distraught over the happenings. But I've been giving him my counsel and he's feeling much better now. I've been working very closely with him on this year's festival. We have a few last-minute details to settle, but everything else is complete. It looks to be the best festival yet." She glanced at her watch. "Oh, I didn't realize it was so late. I have an appointment."

Constance Smythe—so that's who the woman was. Taylor immediately flashed on Donovan's words at breakfast that first morning about Alex coordinating with her on the festival and keeping her away from him and the manor house. It was certainly a far different picture than this woman attempted to paint for the clerk. The confrontation between Constance and Bradley played through Taylor's mind again. Perhaps it was something personal relating to Constance's obvious pursuit of Donovan, something that was none of Taylor's business and better left alone.

Now that she had satisfied her curiosity about the blond woman, she left the chemist shop and walked toward the inn for her meeting with Jeremy and Amanda Edwards. Amanda showed her into the office where her father was working at the desk.

"Miss MacKenzie…my daughter thinks I should talk to you about the unusual events that have happened here in the village. I'm not convinced it's a good idea."

"Please, Mr. Edwards. I'm not here to stir up trouble or hold anyone up to ridicule. I'm not writing a book. I'm only trying to sort out my family background and fill in the blanks with the information that my grandmother didn't know. All I want is to understand what happened and why. I've read all the newspaper articles dealing with the murders and subsequent trial and I've seen the records in the library at Sedgwick Manor. What I'd like now is any personal information handed down through your family that might add to what I've already discovered. It was your ancestor, Seth Edwards, who was responsible for protecting my grandmother. There had to be some reason he immediately rushed her away to safety as soon as the murders were discovered, even before the trial and conviction. That's what I want to know about—what spurred Seth Edwards into such decisive and drastic action."

A hint of panic crossed Jeremy's face followed by a moment of obvious fear. There was no doubt in Taylor's mind that he didn't want to talk about it, and his reasons were far removed from something as simple as feeling that it was none of her business. He was obviously frightened, but of what?

She cocked her head and leveled a questioning look at him. "Is there anything you can tell me, Mr. Edwards? Any little scrap of information that will help fill in the blanks?"

Jeremy paced nervously up and down the office floor. He stopped in front of her and stared intently, as if turning something over in his mind. "I don't have any provable information or written records, just what my parents and grandparents told me."

She extended a smile calculated to instill confidence. "I'd like to hear about it."

Jeremy paused, then finally pulled up a chair and sat down facing her. "It was something William Sedgwick said when Seth and some of the other villagers arrived on the scene immediately after the murders." He paused as if unsure about how to proceed. "He said he couldn't allow any child of Emily's not fathered by him to exist."

The words shocked Taylor. "Are you saying that he literally threatened the life of an innocent toddler?"

"Yes. Lord William Sedgwick was a very evil and cruel man." Jeremy quickly glanced around as if trying to make sure no one else could hear what he was saying. "And that evil did not die with him. It continues to live today."

"Are you talking about the so-called Sedgwick Curse? What has happened to make you believe in an old superstition?"

"It's as the curse said…on the hundred-year anniversary

of the sealing of the crypt the evil spirit will be unleashed on those he sought revenge against and that's exactly what happened, with those two folk murdered at the lodge house."

"But that man and woman had no connection to the original crime. If the curse is to blame, then why were those two innocent people chosen rather than the descendents of the other villagers that William Sedgwick held a grudge against? What would be the purpose of their murders?"

"It was the location—the same place where the original murders happened. Their murders are a warning of what is to be." He rose from his chair. His voice carried all the anxiety churning inside him. "That's all I can tell you. The curse is real." With that, Jeremy Edwards left the office.

Taylor shot a curious glance at Amanda. "What do you think of all this? Do you believe in this curse, too?"

A worried look crossed the young woman's face. Her words were hesitant. "Poppa is very entrenched in his beliefs. I don't hold with the superstitions the way he does."

"Do you know any more than what he told me? What he had to say was not very much and didn't shed any new light on the situation."

"No. Poppa refused to talk about it, especially since the night of the explosion at the crypt. What I can do is tell you about some of the Sedgwick family relatives who will be at the festival. The closest relative is Alex Sedgwick. Since he's been in the village for the past few days, I assume you've already met him."

"Yes, Alex is staying at the manor house."

A soft chuckle escaped Amanda's throat. "He's very charming, likable and outgoing—quite the flirt. The local village gossip says he has a history of gambling losses and his cousin, the current Lord Sedgwick, has paid off those debts for him on numerous occasions. Rumor is that he had every opportunity for a good education. He was studying to be a scientist of some sort, then changed when he decided he wanted to be a doctor. The villagers say he didn't want to do all the studies required, so he dropped out. It's also said that he's been married at least two times. He's given me the eye on several occasions, but Poppa refuses to allow me to go with him."

"Yes, that certainly sounds like the Alex I met. Who else from the family will be there?"

Amanda filled her in on the distant relatives who usually made an appearance at the annual festival but stayed away from the estate the rest of the time, with the exception of the occasional family gatherings such as Christmas.

As Taylor wound up her conversation with Amanda, Jeremy returned. He handed his daughter a suitcase, but she didn't take it from him. "Here, you will be spending the night at your friend Millicent's house in town. She is expecting you in time for dinner."

Shock covered Amanda's face. "What are you talking about? Why are you sending me away for the night?"

"Don't argue with me, girl. It's too dangerous for you to be here. Take your suitcase, get in your car and drive into town—now!" He shoved the overnight bag into her hands.

Jeremy turned his attention to Taylor, his stern look leaving no room for discussion. "I believe your business here is finished."

"Tell me, Connie." Alex inched his body up in the bed until his back rested against the headboard. He picked up the book on the nightstand. "What are you looking for in all these genealogy books you have? Are you trying to trace your family all the way back to the Garden of Eden?"

A soft chuckle escaped his throat. "You're wanting to figure a way to get your hands on the ultimate inheritance—the entire world?"

"No…" Her response became vague and her voice trailed off. "Not that far back." She leaned her body across his and took the book from his hand, dropping it on the floor. "Genealogy is a hobby of mine. I have a few missing pieces in my family history that I wanted to check on."

She flashed a sexy smile, ran her hand down his bare torso, then placed a soft kiss on his chest. "Tell me, dear boy, just how much money does Donovan have? What is the value of the Sedgwick estate? Is it as prosperous as it appears?"

"Ah, Connie…if the prim-and-proper ladies of the village could see you now. Here you are—the president of the ladies guild, the chairperson of the historical society, the leader of what passes for local society—spending your afternoon playing sex games. Just the thought of all that money gets you hot and excited, doesn't it?"

She ruffled her fingers through his hair, then tickled her fingers across the back of his neck. "Really, dear boy… don't be so crude."

"What makes you think I know anything about Donovan's private business? True, now that Uncle James is gone, I'm the closest family member. The rest are distant relatives. But Donovan and I are first cousins, not brothers, and he doesn't take me into his confidence on business matters."

"Don't play me for a fool, Alex." She ran her foot along the edge of his calf. "I know a lot more about things than you think I do."

"Oh? Have you been researching the Sedgwick family tree? Did you find a new skeleton rattling around in the old closet?" The lascivious grin tugged at the corners of his mouth. "Sorry, luv…" He ran his hand across her bare bottom. "It's going to take a much better bribe than this for the kind of information you want."

Alex climbed out of bed and reached for his clothes. He dressed quickly. "Got to run, luv. I promised Donovan I'd have dinner at the manor house this evening and bring him up-to-date on the festival arrangements." He cupped her breast in his hand as he brushed a quick kiss on her lips. "I can truthfully report that the chairlady of the event is in fine shape and performing above and beyond the call of duty." He flashed another lascivious grin, then left the cottage.

He climbed into his car and headed toward the estate. A couple of blocks down the street he came across Taylor walking in the same direction. He braked to a stop in front of her.

"This is a pleasant surprise. May I offer you a lift? I assume you're going to the manor house."

"Alex." She flashed a warm smile. "Yes, that would be nice."

He reached across the seat and opened the door for her. As soon as she was settled, he put the car in gear and started down the road. "Are you just out for a walk or are you doing some research for your book?"

His question caught her off guard. "Well…neither, actually." She spotted the questioning glance he shot in her direction before returning his attention to the road. She felt compelled to offer some sort of an explanation about what she was doing in the village. It was apparent that Donovan hadn't informed Alex of her true identity. "I was at the inn, visiting with Jeremy Edwards."

"Oh? I didn't realize you knew anyone in the village."

"I don't. It was merely a polite duty call. He and his daughter are friends of a distant relative of mine. I promised to stop in and say hello to them while I was here."

Alex drove through the gates and up the driveway to the manor house. As soon as they got out of the car, the front door swung open and Donovan stepped out onto the front porch. She could see his agitation even though he tried to cover it up.

"Taylor…Alex…well, where did the two of you meet up?"

Alex bounded up the steps. "I found Taylor walking along the road, so I offered her a ride." He brushed by Donovan. "What's for dinner? I'm famished."

As soon as Alex had disappeared inside the house, Donovan was at Taylor's side. His tone of voice clearly conveyed his irritation. "Where have you been all afternoon?" He took a deep breath, then slowly exhaled. His words came out in a calmer manner. "I asked you not to wander about by yourself. It's almost dark out. I've been concerned about you."

She ran her fingertips across his forehead in an attempt to smooth out the frown lines. "Alex brought me back safe and sound, so as you can see I wasn't 'wandering about' by myself. I went to the inn to see Jeremy Edwards. His daughter talked him into seeing me again."

"Did you learn anything?"

"Not too much that I didn't already know, except that Jeremy Edwards is a very frightened man. He seems to have bought into this curse thing all the way."

A cool breeze ruffled through Taylor's hair, and a slight shiver darted across her skin as the last remnants of the setting sun reflected off the large windows of the entry hall. Donovan put his arm around her shoulder. "Come on. Let's go inside. It's turning chilly out here."

The rest of the evening passed without consequence, but again the household seemed restless. Donovan and Taylor managed to steal a few passionate kisses before going to their own bedrooms but were again unable to discreetly retire to his private living quarters to spend the night together.

It was nearly midnight when Taylor turned out the light on the nightstand and closed her eyes. It had been a long day, and her meeting with Jeremy Edwards had been an emotional drain on her. The genuine fear he displayed had sliced to the core of her own concerns. And his sending Amanda away for the night…well, it was almost as if he'd had some sort of premonition of danger and wanted to make sure his daughter was out of harm's way.

A twinge of apprehension made her want more than ever to be in Donovan's arms, to share his warmth. The deeper she became involved in the bewildering events surrounding Donovan, the more she was convinced that they also involved her in some baffling way—a bizarre larger plan that neither of them could see yet.

Thoughts of Donovan…speculations about the future… concerns for what the next day would bring…it all circulated through her mind until sleep finally calmed her distress.

AT THREE O'CLOCK in the morning the shadowy form made its way along the deserted village road, keeping close to the buildings to avoid being seen. The night air was cold, but it didn't phase him. A heated anger coursed through his veins, feeding his single-minded obsession.

He approached the side entrance of the inn, the locked door presenting no problem and offering no resistance. He stealthily entered the owner's quarters and moved undetected through the living room toward the bedroom area. It had been a long time, and now he would finally have the much-deserved revenge denied him so many decades ago.

His breath came in hard rushes as he quietly opened the bedroom door. Excitement built inside him, combining with the rage that fueled his every thought and action. He withdrew the knife from its sheath and stepped silently across the threshold.

DONOVAN KNOCKED at Taylor's bedroom door, then called to her. "Taylor…are you up yet?"

A moment later the door swung open. "Yes." She stepped aside so he could enter. "I was just about to go downstairs and get some coffee before breakfast was served."

"I've had a marvelous idea. The weather forecast for today is sunny and mild. I'll have Mrs. Bradley fix us a breakfast basket to take with us."

She tilted her head and extended a slightly confused smile. "Take with us? Where are we going?"

"I want to show you the rest of the estate on horseback. I'll go to the kitchen right now and have Mrs. Bradley start on our breakfast—" he did a quick perusal of the way she was dressed "—and while you're changing into some riding clothes, I'll have one of the stable hands saddle a couple of horses for us."

Taylor glanced toward the closet. "I don't have any formal riding clothes. Would jeans and a sweater be acceptable?"

He smiled, then brushed a soft kiss across her lips, "I only meant that you would probably not want to wear those nice tailored silk pants on a horseback ride. Jeans and a sweater will be fine. That's what I'll wear, too."

Then Donovan stepped fully into the room, pulled her into his arms and brought his mouth against hers as he kicked the bedroom door closed with his foot. It was the most private time they'd had together since the night they made love.

Taylor had been all he'd thought about—everything he wanted. He brushed his tongue against hers as he pulled her body tightly to him. Her arms wound around his neck. He caressed her shoulders, then slid his hands down her back and ran them intimately over her rounded hips gently urging her closer.

The heated gesture sent a tingle of excitement rippling across Taylor's skin. She ran her fingers through his thick hair. She wanted more of Donovan Sedgwick. She wanted all of him, for all time. Did that imply true love? She wasn't sure. Or maybe it was simply that she didn't want to be sure.

Taylor allowed the delicious kiss to continue for a seemingly long time before breaking the intimate connection between them. She looked up into the depths of Donovan's blue eyes. She saw his caring, his concern and emotional determination. It was as if an unspoken moment of understanding and commitment had passed between them—a moment that sent an equally determined emotion burrowing deep inside her. It was an intense connection unlike anything she had ever experienced.

A connection she reluctantly put on hold for the time being, but one she did not want to lose.

Her words came out in a breathless whisper. "I'll change my clothes and meet you at your room."

"Perfect." He placed a tender kiss on her lips before leaving her room to go to the kitchen.

Taylor changed clothes, then went downstairs. As she entered Donovan's wing of the house she was surprised to find two office employees starting their workday. She nodded a hello to them and continued to the hall that led to the double doors of Donovan's suite. She knocked softly, not sure of the proper protocol for entering his private living quarters.

Donovan opened the door. "Mrs. Bradley is having a basket packed and delivered to us at the stables."

He took her hand, and they left the house by his private side door. They strolled along the path to the stables. Another half hour and they were on their horses headed along a dirt road that circled the inside perimeter of the property. When they came to a bridge he turned off the road and they rode along the stream toward a small lake. Before long they arrived at a secluded area in a grove of trees next to a lake. He dismounted and helped her down.

Taylor drew in a deep breath to the point where she could almost taste the clean air, held it a moment, then slowly exhaled as she allowed her gaze to travel across the landscape. The autumn hues painted the trees in a profusion of color made all the more brilliant by the bright sunlight and blue sky. A soft breeze rustled through the leaves, setting a sharp counterpoint to the noisy birds.

"This is absolutely beautiful—so serene and idyllic." She turned toward him. "How fortunate you are to have a place like this to call your own."

He spread out a blanket but did not unpack the food. He took her hand and pulled her down on the ground with him. "I used to come here a lot whenever I wanted to think about things without being disturbed. It was almost like a magical place where I could clear my head of all disturbing thoughts and concerns—a private sanctuary of sorts." He cradled her in his embrace, reveling in the absolute contentment of the moment. There wasn't anything he couldn't handle as long as she was with him. All he wanted was to shut out the world so that there were only the two of them.

The loud ringing of his cell phone intruded into the quiet moment. He buried his face in the silky tresses of her hair. "Damn!" He reached for the pack he had placed on the ground next to the blanket and withdrew his phone. He was lord of the manor. He could not ignore a business emergency or shirk his responsibilities, no matter how much he wanted to be able to do just that.

"Donovan, here."

The anger and disappointment quickly faded from his face to be instantly replaced by stunned surprise as he sat up straight and listened intently to the caller. "I see. I'll be there as soon as I can." He clicked off the call and quickly scrambled to his feet.

"We have to return to the house immediately." He held out his hand to assist her. There was no mistaking the urgency in his voice or the tension carved into his features.

"What's the matter? Is something wrong?"

"Yes. That was Bradley. Inspector Edgeware is at the house." He took a deep breath and his gaze shifted away in a nervous manner before locking with hers again. "There was another murder last night...Jeremy Edwards."

"Jeremy? Dead?" She felt her eyes widen in stunned disbelief as the startling news seeped into her reality. "Murdered?" The shock robbed her of her ability to utter any more words. She recalled how agitated Jeremy had been, how blatantly frightened, so much so that he had sent Amanda away for the night. A second shock wave darted through her body. Amanda! She stared at Donovan for a moment. "What about Amanda? Is she all right?"

"Yes. She was the one who discovered his body. Apparently, she had spent the night with a friend in town and found her father when she returned to the village this morning."

A frown wrinkled his brow. He slowly shook his head as if he couldn't quite fully grasp the reality of what had happened. He stared at her for what seemed like forever before speaking again. "We need to return to the house. Inspector Edgeware is waiting to talk to me…and to you."

"Me?" A sudden jolt of trepidation shot through her. "Why does he want to talk to me?"

"He wants to know why you were there two days in a row—what your business was with Jeremy."

"How did he know I had been to see Jeremy?"

"Apparently Amanda mentioned it when he asked her about any strangers or unusual situations that had occurred."

She caught a moment of eye contact with Donovan. Their tangled family histories had transcended time and enveloped them in a modern-day lethal puzzle. She tried to quell the anxiety knotting in the pit of her stomach. "Well…I guess we'd better be going. I don't want to keep the inspector waiting any longer than necessary."

Donovan pulled her into his arms, seeking to give as much comfort as he took from the physical contact. He cradled Taylor's head against his shoulder as he placed a loving kiss on her forehead. His voice dropped to a soft whisper. "Don't worry. I'm sure the inspector just has some routine questions. It won't take very long, and I promise he won't harass you. I won't allow it."

He continued to hold her. His gaze shifted off to the horizon. Once again dark clouds gathered beyond the valley, threatening the unusually sunny day with an ominous presence. An uncomfortable sensation settled over him. A portent of dark, stormy times yet to be that had nothing to do with the weather? He tried to shake the feeling, but it refused to go away.

"We'd better return to the house. The sooner I talk to the inspector the sooner we can move on." A little tremor of anxiety darted across Taylor's skin. She had never been questioned by the police about a murder. In fact, she had never been questioned by the police about anything. She wished she felt as confident as she sounded.

They rode back to the stable at a gallop, and a few minutes later arrived at the informal dining room where Inspector Edgeware was drinking coffee and waiting for them. He rose to his feet when they entered the room.

Mike Edgeware gave a curt nod of acknowledgment in Donovan's direction. "Lord Sedgwick." He then turned his attention to Taylor. "Miss MacKenzie?"

"Yes, I'm Taylor MacKenzie."

"I need to inquire about a few matters. You're from the United States and are staying here at Sedgwick Manor?"

"Yes—I'm from Wichita, Kansas. I've been staying here since my arrival in England."

"I see." The inspector made notes as he questioned her. "What is the purpose of your visit? Are you a friend of Lord Sedgwick's?"

"Mike," Donovan interrupted the interview, his voice conveying his irritation at the way things were progressing. "What does this have to do with the murder of Jeremy Edwards?"

"I'm just trying to determine some background information." He returned his attention to Taylor. "What is the purpose of your trip to England, Miss MacKenzie?"

Taylor stole a quick glance at Donovan. She wasn't sure what to say. Should she perpetuate the lie she had initiated or should she tell the inspector the same truth she had finally confessed to Donovan? She suppressed a sigh of resignation. It was a foolish question. It wouldn't take the police very long to determine that she had never published anything in her life—that she was a secretary, not a writer. Surely there must be something in between the lie and the complete truth that would satisfy the inspector.

"Uh…well, it's sort of a vacation."

Inspector Edgeware cocked his head and leveled a skeptical look at her. "Vacation? And you booked a room here at Sedgwick Manor?"

Mike Edgeware shot a quick glance toward Donovan. "You have decided to turn the manor house into a hotel?"

Donovan bristled, but held in his anger while projecting his most authoritative manner. "A misplaced attempt at humor, Inspector? Or just a poorly thought-out effort to embarrass me as a means of getting back at my father for that incident a couple of years ago?"

An uneasiness rose inside Taylor as the two men squared off. Neither of them seemed willing to back down from what appeared to be a rapidly approaching confrontation. She needed to act quickly if she was going to be able to defuse the situation.

"When I said vacation, Inspector, I didn't mean that the entire trip was solely for tourist sightseeing activities. I'm very interested in genealogy and have been researching my family history. My ancestors came from this area. I had been corresponding with James Sedgwick. He was the one who invited me to stay at the manor house and use the family archives to help in my research. I had gone to see Jeremy Edwards because his family had lived in this area for over a century. I thought he might have some family oral history that would help me in my research."

"You've certainly had some bad luck with the timing of your trip, Miss MacKenzie."

"What do you mean, Inspector? Are you talking about that rainstorm the other night? We have far worse rainstorms in Kansas. I don't mind weather changes."

"There hasn't been a serious crime in the village in almost fifty years and that was an armed robbery. Since your arrival we have had a series of bizarre happenings. There was the explosion at the crypt, the two murders at the lodge house and now the murder of Jeremy Edwards—all coinciding with your visit. That's very strange, don't you think?"

"Well, yes…it is an odd coincidence."

"I don't believe in coincidence, Miss MacKenzie."

Donovan stepped between Inspector Edgeware and Taylor. "That's enough, Mike. You're treating Miss MacKenzie as if she was a suspect. May I remind you that the explosion happened the night before she arrived. She wasn't even in England, let alone here at the estate. And she certainly had no way of knowing the couple murdered at the lodge house. I didn't even know them, and I live here. Now, unless you have some questions for me, I think we can consider this interview concluded."

"No questions at the moment, other than to inquire where you both were at the time of the murder—"

"And exactly what time would that be?" Donovan fixed him with a hard stare. "You never said what time Jeremy was murdered."

"It figures to be about four o'clock this morning. Where were you at that time, Lord Sedgwick?"

Donovan shifted his weight from one foot to the other. Dark swirling clouds circulated through his mind. So many bewildering things had happened, he couldn't say with any certainty exactly where he had been. "I was in my bed asleep."

Mike Edgeware turned toward Taylor. "And what about you, Miss MacKenzie?"

Taylor wasn't sure what to think. She tried to ease the tension in her tautly strung nerves. The inspector's questions seemed more like an interrogation than anything else, as if she was actually a murder suspect who needed to produce an alibi. "I was, too."

"You were sleeping in Lord Sedgwick's bed, too?"

His question stunned her. "No, of course not. I was in my own—"

"That's enough!" Donovan's controlled anger spilled over into his voice. "I will not allow you to make any more insinuations of this nature. So, unless you have something pertinent—"

"I guess that will be all for now, Your Lordship." The inspector turned toward Taylor. "I'll be wanting to interview you again, Miss MacKenzie. I suggest you not leave the area without notifying me."

"I'll be here until the festival is over. Then I'll be returning to the United States." Her own words startled her. She hadn't given any conscious thought to the day when she would leave for home, when Lord Donovan Sedgwick would no longer be part of her life. The emotional stab that accompanied the realization left her with a sinking emptiness that she didn't know how to fill.

Donovan and Taylor watched as Inspector Edgeware left the house. The carefree moments by the lake had turned into low-level anxiety, the mood more serious and somber. The darkening storm clouds visible through the window carried an even more ominous feeling than they had an hour ago. A shudder moved through her body, an uncomfortable sensation that left Taylor confused and uneasy.

Chapter Nine

Following lunch in the informal dining room, Donovan excused himself saying he had business to handle. While he was busy in his office, Taylor wandered into the library as she wrestled with her rapidly growing anxieties and fears. She didn't want to worry Donovan, but the inspector's observation about the timing of the grim events coinciding with her arrival had set her nerves on edge. And his pointed statement that he didn't believe in coincidence left her truly shaken.

She stared out the library window and watched as the wind bowed the trees. The darkening sky projected a menacing aura, a sensation that matched the mood conveyed by the house. The evil presence she had associated with the manor house had become even more prevalent, as if it had been growing and expanding with each passing day—its tentacles reaching out to every nook and cranny. A cold shudder passed through her body, matching the chill that rippled across the surface of her skin.

Taylor closed her eyes for a moment in an effort to rid herself of the unwanted feelings. She opened her eyes and turned away from the window. Her pulse raced. The hair on the back of her neck stood on end. A hard jolt of fright attacked her, followed by a rapid adrenaline surge. She literally jumped as she found herself almost face-to-face with Bradley. A tickle of fear tried to take hold as she glanced toward the closed library door.

She forced a weak smile that felt unnaturally pasted on her face. "You startled me, Bradley." She shot another look at the closed door. A tremor of anxiety assaulted her senses, accompanied by a ripple of fear. "I didn't hear you come in."

"I'm sorry, miss. I didn't mean to frighten you."

"No harm done." She took a couple of steps backward in an attempt to put a little distance between them. She gestured toward the window. "I was just watching the brewing storm."

"Yes, miss. We seem to have had quite a stretch of unusual weather of late. Is there anything I can bring you?"

"No, nothing. Thank you, Bradley. I'll be fine. I think I'll get a book and go back to my room to read. That's my favorite activity on a rainy day."

"Yes, miss." Bradley turned and walked silently toward the door. He paused a moment, then opened the door and left.

Taylor collapsed into a large chair. She sighed as the relief settled over her. Had she truly been so absorbed in the approaching storm and her thoughts that she'd failed to hear him enter the library? She raked her gaze slowly around the room. Had he entered through some sort of secret passage, not realizing she was in the room? Then the thought she had tried to ignore finally forced its way into her consciousness. Or was it something more sinister than her simple lack of awareness?

Had he entered through a secret passage *because* she was alone in the room with the door closed? Alone and vulnerable? Neither choice brought her any comfort or helped settle her rattled nerves.

She grabbed a book from the nearest shelf without even bothering to look at the title. If Bradley was lurking in the hallway, he would see her doing what she had said she intended to do. She left the library carrying the book and hurried to her room. She hesitated for a moment, then hooked the back of the chair under the door handle as she had done every night, even though she knew it was a wasted gesture. There was a good chance that some sort of secret passage into her room existed, and securing the door from the hallway would not prevent a threatening force from entering. Intellectually she knew that, but blocking her bedroom door somehow made her feel better.

An involuntary chuckle escaped her throat. *I can't believe this. I'm actually standing here giving credence to that old movie cliché—the butler did it.* The light moment quickly faded as she returned to the menacing reality surrounding her.

Should she set out on her own and try to find the hidden doors on the third floor and in the first floor sitting room? Investigate without consulting Donovan? Suddenly it seemed wrong to go behind his back even though she had previously done just that. She drew in a calming breath in an attempt to settle her rattled nerves. Now wouldn't be a good time, not with the household staff going about their routine.

She looked at her surroundings. It wouldn't be snooping to explore her own room. A cold shiver invaded her senses as she recalled the way Bradley had seemingly appeared from nowhere. If she found a hidden door, what would she discover when she opened it? Did she really want to know? No. She would save the exploration for another time. She turned her thoughts elsewhere.

She looked at the book she had grabbed from the library

shelf. The irony caused her to laugh out loud, breaking the tension that had her insides tied in knots—*And Then There Were None,* written by Agatha Christie, a mystery about people being murdered at a remote location. Did she really want to read a fictional murder mystery when she was living one?

She set the book on the nightstand, then removed the large envelope containing the copies of newspaper articles from the drawer. She spent the rest of the afternoon carefully rereading every word, trying to pick up on anything she might have missed when she read them earlier. She went over the notes she had made of information she'd found in the library and gleaned from conversations with Donovan and from James Sedgwick's trunk. There had to be an answer to what was happening, something that did not involve supernatural events.

For her sake…and for Donovan's…she had to help him figure it out.

She became so absorbed in her research materials that she was oblivious to the passing of time. A knock at her bedroom door startled her back to the present. She set aside the large envelope and went to the door.

"Are you all right?" Concern showed on Donovan's face as he stepped into the room.

"Yes, I'm fine. Why?"

"I was afraid you might not be feeling well since you didn't appear for dinner."

Her eyes grew wide. "Dinner?" She glanced at her watch. "I'm sorry. I had no idea it was so late."

"Come on. I waited for you. Alex apparently has a date. He ate quickly then left."

Donovan escorted her to the informal dining room where the two of them had dinner. With servants bustling about within hearing range, the conversation remained superficial. Following dinner she put on a light jacket and they went out to the terrace to have a glass of wine. It was a comfortable time with just the two of them, yet it could not erase the apprehension that had formed into a hard lump and lodged itself in the pit of Taylor's stomach. Nor could it banish the underlying ripple of tension the bewildering circumstances had produced.

"I'm worried, Donovan. What if Inspector Edgeware seriously believes I'm somehow responsible or involved in the murders? How do I convince him I don't know anything about it?"

He placed a kiss on her forehead. "I won't let him harass you."

"What did you mean when you asked if he was attempting to get back at you for something that happened between him and your father? Did they have a run-in of some sort?"

"My father was responsible for him not receiving a promotion he thought he deserved. He's been resentful ever since. But in spite of that, underneath it all he's a good policeman and will stick with a case until he's found the answers."

"And he won't let the disagreement between him and your father cause him to form a biased opinion?"

"No…" Donovan paused for a moment as he turned the words over in his mind. "At least, I don't think so."

"I hope he finds someplace else to look other than at me. He made me very uncomfortable with his pointed questions and his manner. I've always had an image in my mind of British police being very polite and not saying or doing anything to embarrass someone. That remark he made about whose bed I was in certainly belied that idea.

I suppose that's another television-inspired concept shot down as not valid."

"I wish it *had* been my bed you were in last night." He pulled her into his arms. "It's amazing how a house this large, where you can easily get lost and where you can usually manage to avoid contact with anyone else, seems to be filled with so much activity in the evenings, right around bedtime."

Having Donovan's arms around her calmed Taylor's immediate concerns but did nothing to lessen the anxieties that had been building since the night she'd arrived. Those anxieties were compounded by her emotional involvement with Donovan, from a long line of Sedgwick aristocracy. And then there were the recent murders, for which she apparently had become a suspect.

Her thoughts began to wander in an even stranger direction. Why would she be a suspect rather than Donovan? It was his family curse, his great-grandfather, his estate and his village. *What are you thinking? That's absurd! The inspector knows Donovan, but he doesn't know me. He'd naturally have more questions for me in an attempt to learn who I am and where and how I fit into this.*

A moment of guilt told her how much the totally inappropriate thoughts upset her, even though she was the only one who knew what those thoughts were. From the moment she first set foot inside the manor house on the Sedgwick estate, everything around her had an out-of-control feeling, and it was more than her immediate attraction to Donovan that had her world turned upside down.

The ominous atmosphere that pervaded the house radiated an inexplicable environment that left her in a constant state of wariness and discomfort. It was unlike anything she had ever experienced, a sensation that she would be hard put to explain to someone else in a manner than would make any sense.

She snuggled further into Donovan's embrace, taking comfort from his warmth. "I've been going over everything I collected and all the newspaper articles I copied. There has to be an answer somewhere, some scrap of information that we've overlooked that will unlock this mystery so it makes sense."

"I think we should go through the items in my father's trunk again. We didn't thoroughly inspect everything. He kept those specific items locked away and there had to be a reason for it. Maybe tonight—"

The blinding headache struck from out of nowhere, the pain throbbing at Donovan's temples and behind his eyes. He staggered back a couple of steps, releasing his hold on her.

"Taylor…I…" He turned and walked unsteadily around the corner of the house, headed toward the side entrance into his private living quarters. His only conscious thought was to retreat to his room without running into anyone.

Taylor rushed after Donovan, put her arm around his waist to help steady him, and guided him to his suite. He leaned against her, thankful for her presence. He had shouldered the burden of the blinding headaches and periods of disorientation and blackouts by himself—bewildered and afraid to confide in anyone what had been happening. But he had shared his deepest fears with Taylor and now had someone he could lean on. He wasn't alone anymore. Just that bit of rational thought helped ease the pain. His mind began to clear, the confusion starting to lift, as if he had been able to mentally force it away.

Donovan sat on the edge of the bed. Taylor reached for the bottle of pills and water carafe on his nightstand. He reached his hand out and stopped her.

"No, I seem to be coming out of it. I think I'm all right. I'm not one for taking medicine and I'd rather not if it isn't necessary."

She sat next to him. "Are you sure?"

He saw the deep concern on her face and felt the tension in her body. He forced as much of a smile as he could muster. "Yes, I'm sure. The pain is easing and I remember everything that happened during the attack." He took her hand in his. "Maybe whatever this is has run its course and is going away." He said the words, but he did not believe them.

She stared at him for a moment, turning what he had said over in her mind. "What if—uh, I mean...well, this probably sounds weird, but what if it isn't something like a virus or illness of some sort. What if—" She frowned as she pursed her lips. It was a stupid thought.

"What if...what?" He brought her hand to his lips, then held it against his chest. She felt his heartbeat, strong and steady.

"Well, what if someone is doing this to you? What if someone is somehow making these attacks happen?"

He turned until he faced her fully, a quizzical expression covering his features. "But how could that happen? And who would do such a thing?"

"I don't know. But it's something to consider."

He shook his head as he furrowed his brow. "I don't know..." He pulled her into his embrace, not convinced that the theory she had put forth was valid. As much as he would prefer a flesh-and-blood adversary—some tangible foe to face off against—he could not shake the fear that the Sedgwick Curse might be real. He feared that the menace originated from within himself—that Taylor's continued presence put her in jeopardy just as William Sedgwick had been the danger for Emily Kincaid. But he could not bring himself to part from her or to send her away from the estate. She was the one link he had to a world that could be the way he wanted it to be.

"I want to snoop around some more."

Her statement caught him by surprise. He sat up straight and stared at her. "Snoop around? I definitely do not like the sound of that. Where? Looking for what?"

"I want to go to the newspaper office and talk to Byron Treadwell—"

"No! I absolutely—"

She placed her fingertips at his mouth and extended a teasing smile. "I certainly hope you weren't about to say that you *forbid* it."

He did not respond to her attempt to lighten the mood. "This is not a joke, Taylor, and it's certainly not a game. People are being brutally murdered. I don't know why and I don't who is responsible. What I do know is that I don't want you drawn into this."

"You don't want me drawn into it? I seem to be implicated in this whether I want to be or not. The inspector is treating me as if I was a major suspect and told me not to leave town without checking with him first. What I want is to help you get to the bottom of this nightmare and put a stop to it."

He placed his hands on her shoulders and plumbed the depths of her emerald eyes. His words were emphatic and heartfelt. "What I want is for you to be safe."

"I'll be just fine. Everything that's happened obviously relates to the so-called Sedgwick Curse. The original murders happened in a time frame that related to the festival. It seems to me that whatever is happening here is destined to come to fruition with the festival."

"Okay…I'll accept that as a logical assumption. But that

does not mean it's safe for you to venture out on your own and start talking to people. Look what happened when you talked to Jeremy—"

He saw the immediate shock that spread across her face and the hurt that crept into her eyes. He pulled her close to him. "I didn't mean to imply…I'm not in any way trying to say that you had any responsibility in his death. I'm simply saying that it could just as easily have been you. I don't want you going out there and purposely inserting yourself in a dangerous situation or creating a set of circumstances that could turn dangerous at any moment."

"The animosity between you and Byron Treadwell is obvious, even to a newcomer like me. If he knows anything about this or has any theories about what is happening, he's certainly not going to tell you about it. And from what I've observed during my limited time around him, I don't think he's likely to tell Inspector Edgeware, either. When I had dinner with him he didn't show any reluctance in talking to me even though he knew I was staying here at the manor house. I stayed away from the subject because I wanted him to believe my story about researching a book on country festivals. But if I told him my true identity, I'm sure he would have lots to say."

"I can't forbid you from doing it, but I want to go on record as saying I'm against it."

"Your objection is noted."

He cocked his head, raised an eyebrow and shot a knowing look in her direction. "And ignored?"

She held up the empty wineglass she had carried in with her from the terrace and smiled, as much in an effort to change the subject as to lighten the mood. "Do you suppose I could have another glass of wine?"

TAYLOR OPENED HER EYES and squinted through the darkness at the clock on Donovan's nightstand until she could make out the numbers. It had been nearly midnight when they had fallen asleep after making love. The warm glow of contentment continued to cling to her senses. Donovan still had his arms wrapped around her. She placed her hands on top of his, taking pleasure in the physical contact. He stirred, tightened his hold on her, then nuzzled her neck.

His voice was thick with sleep. "What time is it?"

"It's a little after five o'clock. Probably too early to be awake. However…"

He opened his eyes and shook the fuzziness from his head. "What does 'however' mean?"

"It means I should probably take advantage of this early hour and go back to my room while everyone is still asleep."

He sat upright, stretching his arms and back in an attempt to get fully awake. "As much as I hate to have you leave, it would probably be best for your reputation." He wrapped his arms around her and placed a tender kiss on her cheek. "The household staff has worked here for many years, but that doesn't mean they don't occasionally indulge in gossip when they go into the village."

She edged toward the side of the bed, then stood up. Donovan clicked on the lamp on the nightstand, then slid across the bed and stood beside her. She gathered her clothes and quickly dressed, preparing to leave his suite of rooms.

Donovan pulled her into his embrace. He ruffled his fingers through her hair, then held her close. "I don't like sneaking around like this. It's like we were doing something wrong."

"You are lord of the manor. You must maintain a certain level of propriety…especially with everything else that's been going on around here lately."

"Ah, yes—" he emitted a sigh of resignation "—we wouldn't want to give Mike Edgeware anything more to think about than he already has."

She stepped out of his embrace, then gave his hand a little squeeze. "I'll see you at breakfast."

Donovan watched as she left his suite. He clenched his jaw in a moment of irritation. Yes, indeed. His Lordship must maintain a level of propriety…wouldn't want the household staff gossiping. He fell back into the bed and closed his eyes. He wanted to wake up every morning with Taylor in bed next to him, to know that was the way it would always be.

He stayed very still for several minutes. A myriad of thoughts swirled through his mind, meshing together so that he could no longer separate them. They seemed to mirror the way the bizarre events of the past couple of months continued to confuse his grip on reality. There had to be something tangible that would lead them to the answers they needed.

He forced himself to his feet, went to his bathroom and showered. He moved through the mechanical motions of dressing and preparing for the day, but his mind was on far more urgent matters.

His thoughts gravitated toward his father's trunk. He had given it a cursory inspection, then he and Taylor had given it a more thorough investigation. There had to be something they had overlooked, something they didn't understand the full significance of. They would go through the trunk, this time meticulously scrutinizing every item. He went into his sitting room and made some coffee, then opened the trunk and removed the items. He placed them into categories as he and Taylor had done before.

Donovan sipped his coffee as he stood staring at the stacks of journals, photographs, blueprints and architectural drawings. He slowly shook his head. Something in front of him had to hold a key to what was happening. There had to be a reason for his father locking away items that had no monetary value and in some cases not even sentimental value. He counted the number of items, noting how many there were in each stack. He started rereading his father's journals, putting them aside when he realized it was time for breakfast.

He stifled a yawn as he headed toward the informal dining room. Not enough sleep. A warm feeling of contentment reminded him of why he hadn't gotten enough sleep.

Taylor and Alex were already seated at the table. They all exchanged the pleasantries of a good morning. Donovan filled his plate from the sideboard, then seated himself next to Taylor. He glanced at her dish of fresh fruit and a toasted muffin. "Is that all you're having for breakfast?"

"I'm not really all that hungry."

Donovan turned his attention to Alex who was finishing up the piece of pastry he had taken from the basket. "You're not having any breakfast either?"

Alex downed the last of his coffee. "I sure am, but not here. I'm meeting with Constance for breakfast and another festival meeting. Everything is scheduled and in place, but we're going over the last-minute details just to make sure. I'll have a computer printout for you detailing everything." He rose from his chair and winked at Taylor. "You kids have a nice day. I'll probably see you at dinner."

Donovan and Taylor watched as Alex left the room. Donovan went to the door and continued to watch Alex walk toward the entry hall and front door. When he heard the front door close, he returned to his seat at the table.

"I checked before I arrived for breakfast. Bradley is attending to a household matter in the butler's pantry which should occupy him until this afternoon. The other staff members are either in the kitchen or other parts of the house tending to their daily routine." He reached under the table and seductively ran his hand over her denim-covered thigh. His voice became a sensual whisper. "I missed you after you went back to your own room this morning. My bed seemed cold and lonely without you."

"Mine, too." She put her hand on top of his, mostly to stop the excitement his teasing touch had created. She wanted to put their conversation on a serious level. "I think we should go through every item in your father's trunk again."

"That's what I thought, too. I took everything out of it and placed the items in stacks. I thought we could do that after breakfast. I want both of us to look at each item, read every ledger. Maybe one of us will pick up on something the other missed."

They finished eating, returned to Donovan's bedroom and went right to work. They separated the journals into two piles. Taylor read one stack and Donovan read the other, then they exchanged stacks. They had lunch in his suite as they continued to read through the journals. Several hours passed before they could finally set the journals aside.

Taylor saw the disappointment on Donovan's face. She reached out and took his hand in hers as she tendered a reassuring smile. "We'll find something. There has to be an answer to this, some logical reason for what's happening."

He stared at the stack of blueprints and architectural drawings, then looked up at her. A frown wrinkled across his forehead as if he was focusing his concentration on something.

She cocked her head and shot a quizzical look in his direction. "What's the matter? Is something wrong?"

"I understand the items we found in the trunk earlier, items of sentimental value. I understand the photographs being in the trunk, some of them sentimental and others, such as the photograph of Emily Kincaid, relating to the so-called curse. I understand the journals being in the trunk, a combination of sentiment and clues that my father wanted to preserve. What I don't understand is the blueprints and architectural drawings. These are things that would be on file with the architectural firm as well as the permit office. Why would my father have locked them away with the other things? What kind of special meaning could they have that he felt he needed to protect them in that way?"

"That's a good question. Perhaps that's where we should concentrate our efforts." She paused as she turned the information over in her mind. She wanted to make sure it made sense before sharing her thoughts with Donovan.

"This is your house. You've lived here all your life. I'm sure there are things that you simply accept because you grew up with them, but for me it isn't that straightforward."

"What type of things? What are you talking about?"

"Well…how about all those secret passages and hidden doors? There's certainly nothing in my life experience that would allow me to consider something like that as being normal. Is it possible that those blueprints and drawings might show secret rooms, passages and doors? You said you knew where some of them were, but not all." She paused, not sure how to phrase her question. She looked up and made eye contact with him. "Do you, uh, do you know about a secret door into my room?"

"Your room—" he furrowed his brow in concentration

"—no, I'm not aware of any way to enter your room other than through the door from the hallway. However, this house has over sixty rooms spread out across three floors, and that does not include what's in the cellar. There are rooms in this house that I haven't been inside in years. As far as the staff is concerned, there are those whose job functions are relegated to the ground floor, others who work solely on the floor where your room is and others whose jobs are on other parts of the estate such as the greenhouses or stables. The only thing I can vouch for is this new ground-floor wing where the offices and my private living quarters are located. This was built under my father's direction, and he had no reason to add any secret passages or rooms."

She eyed him innocently. "Since I wouldn't know what I was looking at or how it relates to this house, I don't think I'd be much help in scrutinizing the drawings and blueprints. So—" she knew he wasn't going to like what she was about to say, but it made sense to her "—why don't you spend the rest of this afternoon going over them in detail while I see what kind of information I can get out of Byron Treadwell?"

Chapter Ten

Taylor's suggestion caught Donovan totally off guard. He wasn't sure how to respond. His first impulse was to exert his authority and forbid it, but he immediately realized that was a very bad idea. For starters, his entitled authority as lord of the manor did not extend to visiting Americans. She had already displayed her independence and shown her displeasure at being told what to do. And she had been correct. He had no right to try to control her or dictate her actions.

One of the things he admired about her was her independence and self-reliance. She had presented herself at his front door under the guise of a deception. It took someone with determination and tenacity to continue with the ploy when he confronted her with the photograph of Emily Kincaid. She had very neatly modified her deception to fit the circumstances. But, in spite of that, he knew she was not an inherently dishonest person. She had set a task for herself and was resolute about seeing it through.

He thought back to what she had said about his father not granting her access to the family archives if he had known her true identity, and she had been correct in her assessment. She was determined and resourceful and had found a way around that barrier in the pursuit of her goal.

She was also a total delight to be with, a compassion-
ate and caring woman who filled his thoughts. He had
shared his most private fears with her and allowed his vul-
nerabilities to show, something he had not been able to do
with anyone else. She was a truly beautiful woman, inside
and out. She also exuded a sensuality and earthiness that
took his breath away every time he was near her. The first
time they made love had been more profound than anything
he had ever experienced. He wanted to be with her always.

His thoughts stopped there. He did not want to explore
what *always* meant, at least not while the Sedgwick Curse
continued to hang over his head and three unsolved murders
haunted his life. Until he knew what had been happening to
him and why, he had no future. He had nothing to offer her.

His words were tentative, his voice hesitant. "Taylor...
I—"

She put her fingertips to his lips, then replaced them
with her mouth. It was a quick kiss, but filled with emotion. She extended a teasing grin. "You weren't going to
say something about not allowing me—"

He returned her smile. "I wouldn't think of trying to tell
you what you could or couldn't do."

"Good. And now that we have that settled, I'm going to
the newspaper office. I'll see you for dinner." She rose from
her chair, but he caught her hand, bringing her to a halt.

"Be careful." The words were heartfelt, his expression
serious.

She gave him a reassuring smile. "Don't worry. I'll
be fine."

Taylor decided to drive rather than walk. The weather
had been so iffy. She didn't want to take the chance of getting caught in an unexpected cloudburst. She went over
what she wanted to say as she drove into the village.

She glanced at her watch as she entered the newspaper office. It was later than she had intended. She would need to get right to the point rather than easing into it if she was going to make it back to the house by dark.

She spotted Byron through his open office door. He was on the phone and appeared to be unhappy with the person he was talking to. As she drew closer she was able to make out what he was saying.

"I don't care if he is getting suspicious. There's nothing he can do without proof, and we've been very careful every step of the way—" His eyes widened in surprise when his gaze fell on her. He lowered his voice and quickly concluded his phone conversation. "We'll finish this later." Byron disconnected the call and rose from his chair.

"Taylor…this is a pleasant surprise."

His words may have been warm, but his tone of voice said otherwise. His eyes were as cold and calculating as they had been the first time they met. The little bit of conversation she overheard had aroused her curiosity. It seemed far removed from business. But did it have anything to do with Donovan? She didn't know.

"I'd appreciate it if you could give me a little of your time."

"Certainly." Byron crossed the room to the door. "Come in and sit down." He closed the office door, then returned to his chair behind his desk. He gestured toward a chair for her to sit down. "What can I do for you?"

"I have some questions about your family history and how it entwines with the Sedgwick family. I know you said you were adopted into the Treadwell family, but I was hoping you had been told about the Treadwell family history. I'm particularly interested in Richard Treadwell's relationship with Lord William Sedgwick and your obvious animosity toward Donovan."

He sat up straight in his chair. His eyes narrowed as he stared at her. "That doesn't sound to me like anything connected to the annual festival. Why would you be asking something that personal?" He leaned back in his chair again, his demeanor becoming adversarial and his voice sarcastic. "Did His Lordship put you up to this?"

"No. In fact, he didn't want me to come here at all. This is personal for me, a matter of my family history." She saw the surprise flicker through his eyes followed by a moment of confusion and knew she had been successful in grabbing his undivided attention.

"Your family history? And just who are you?"

She paused a moment, as much for the effect it would have as to gather the proper words. She glanced around as if trying to make sure no one could hear what she was about to say.

"I trust that this conversation will remain private between you and me."

He nodded his head but did not say anything. She could tell from the look in his eyes that it was not a promise he could be trusted to keep.

"Emily and Clark Kincaid were my great-grandmother and great-grandfather. My grandmother was the toddler that Seth Edwards sent to safety in Canada."

Byron let out a long, low whistle as he slowly shook his head. "I have to admit that's something I wasn't expecting." He quickly regained his composure, then asked, "Does Donovan know who you are?"

She had been prepared for that question. She had decided to give Byron just enough to make her questions viable without telling him anything about what had been going on at the manor house or giving him any information about Donovan.

"My initial correspondence was with James Sedgwick, not Donovan. It was James who invited me to stay at the manor house. I'm afraid it was a bit of a surprise for Donovan. I never told James my true identity or that my purpose in coming here was to research my family history and how it related to the Sedgwick family. He believed I was a writer researching a book about British country festivals and I didn't see any reason to tell him anything different."

"I see. And exactly what is it you want from me? And what were you looking for while you were digging through my newspaper files?"

"Before my grandmother died, I promised her I would research my family history. She knew very little of what happened to her parents, only that they had been killed on the Sedgwick Estate and she was sent to Canada. It wasn't until I found the articles in your back issues that I discovered my great-grandparents were murdered by William Sedgwick and I read about the curse. And now there are all these other bizarre things that have happened." She saw a dark moment of something dart through his eyes, then quickly disappear. Had she gone too far?

He leaned back in his chair, his outer manner seeming more relaxed. "Your story certainly makes sense."

"It's not a *story,* it's the simple truth." She was in too far to turn back now. "Well…needless to say, I want to know as much as I can about all of this—especially the Sedgwick Curse."

"Curse—there is no damn curse! It's nothing but a lot of superstitious bunk that only ignorant villagers would take seriously."

"But how do you explain the strange things that have happened? The explosion at the crypt, the murder of that man and woman at the lodge house and the murder of

Jeremy Edwards? Doesn't all of that fall in line with the tenets of the curse? Events that echo those of one hundred years ago?"

"I don't have a ready explanation for what's happened." He fixed her with a hard stare. "But perhaps your questions would be better directed toward His Lordship? I'm sure he has the answers."

"Are you saying that Donovan is somehow responsible for what's been happening? But why? What motive would he have?"

"I can't answer that, either. Perhaps that's another question you can put to His Lordship." A sneer crossed Byron's face, an expression saying far more than his words. "As I said, I don't believe in the Sedgwick Curse, but I do believe in genetics. Perhaps Donovan has inherited his great-grandfather's madness. In fact, maybe that inherited *problem* is closer at hand than one hundred years ago. After all, James Sedgwick did commit suicide."

She wrinkled her brow in a moment's concentration as she carefully measured her words. "You've made it blatantly clear that you don't like Donovan. Is that just on general principle? You have no use for the aristocracy? Or is there something personal between the two of you?"

"Well, *Miss MacKenzie*—" it was the same sarcastic tone of voice he had used when referring to Donovan, one that set her teeth on edge "—if it's something personal, then there isn't much chance that I'd be telling you about it, is there?"

She offered a condescending smile that conveyed as much as her sugar-coated words. "No, I don't suppose you would be."

She rose from her chair. "Thank you for your time. I won't keep you any longer." She walked out of his office without waiting for a response from him. When she reached the front door, she turned and caught a glimpse of Byron hurrying out the back door of the building.

Taylor climbed into her car and drove back to the manor house. Her conversation with Byron had been strange, to say the least. His reactions to some of the things she said were far more revealing than his actual words. When she reached the estate, she parked in the driveway and sat in her car for several minutes as she ran everything through her mind. She kept coming back to the image of Byron rushing out the back door of the building.

She finally climbed out of her car, paused a moment, then walked slowly along the path that led around the house and through the gardens. The sun was down and the darkness of night closed in around her as she walked across the grounds. She was vaguely aware of the need to get inside the house, but her mind was filled with too many confusing and conflicting bits of information.

Jeremy Edwards had been very frightened about the recent events and had believed in the curse. She had tried to get some information from him, but he had refused to confide in her. Jeremy had been brutally murdered.

Byron Treadwell scoffed at the curse and even implied that Donovan might somehow be responsible. Then Byron rushed out of his office at great speed. Was he as frightened as Jeremy had been and only putting up a front? Or did Byron have something to hide?

Bradley…he surely knew every secret passage and hidden room in the old manor house. Taylor vividly recalled the ominous expression on his face when she opened her bedroom door and found him standing there. Then there was the way he had seemingly appeared from out of nowhere in the library. Then her thoughts once again touched on the tired old cliché: *The butler did it.* And what about that argument he was having with Constance Smythe?

And for that matter, what about Constance Smythe? She had certainly alluded to a far different relationship with Donovan when talking to the clerk in the chemist shop than reality dictated. Alex had been spending a lot of time with Constance, or at least that was what he had been claiming. Was there more between them than just festival business?

And Inspector Edgeware…could he have taken his resentment toward James Sedgwick and extended it to Donovan? Just how dedicated was he to finding the solution to these bizarre crimes?

Taylor shook her head. She was grasping at straws in an attempt to make sense of something that didn't seem to have any logic connected to it. A soft chuckle escaped her throat in spite of the fact that she had nothing to laugh about. Trying to sort out everyone in her mind was almost like a scene from a movie where the police detective told one of his men to "round up the usual suspects." And then the surprise ending showed that none of the usual suspects was the guilty party.

A hard lump churned in the pit of her stomach. She had just gone through a mental list of the "usual suspects" and Donovan was not on that list. Could Byron have been correct about the inherited madness? She clenched her jaw in determination. No, she refused to accept that possibility. She loved Donovan and would do everything possible to help him get at the truth…whatever the truth might be.

THE SHADOWY FIGURE watched from the hidden cover of the bushes as she walked along the path, her head downcast as if pondering some deep problem. *Emily, my love. It will be*

*soon now. My work here is almost finished. We will be to-
gether as fate has decreed—we will be together for eternity.* He moved stealthily through the shrubbery, keeping
pace with her so that she remained in his sight at all times.

His breathing quickened as he continued to watch her.
She was his...body and soul. She would be his for eternity.
And anyone who tried to claim her would feel his wrath.

THE TICKLE AT THE BACK of Taylor's neck stood her hair on
end. Then a full-blown tremor of fear assaulted her senses.
She whirled around, her gaze staring into the darkness as
she sought out anything that would account for the sudden
and frightening sensation.

Someone was watching her, staring from the safety of
some hidden place. Her mouth turned dry, then her throat
closed off. She gasped for air as if all the oxygen had been
taken away from her.

"Who's there? Who..." The words came out as a whisper, then they died in her mouth. Her heart pounded in her
chest and the sound roared in her ears. Panic rose from the
depths of her being and stamped out every rational thought.
Not even the rustle of the leaves penetrated the eerie silence
and wall of fear that surrounded her.

She forced her feet to move, to carry her toward the
house. Her plodding steps turned into a run as she headed
for the light at the kitchen door.

"Where have you been?"

The words came at her from the darkness. A jolt of
adrenaline raced through her body before she identified the
voice as Donovan's. Then he grabbed hold of her arm and
pulled her toward him. Her initial reaction was to back
away. He had appeared on the scene without a sound, without her even being aware of him.

Or could it have been his presence that she felt? The presence that had frightened her? She forced her thoughts into something more palatable—something logical and rational. She didn't see anything sinister when she looked into his eyes. She saw only concern. Her anxieties began to subside. She would be safe as long as Donovan was at her side.

She tried to sound casual, as if nothing was wrong. "You startled me. I just got back from the village."

"No, you got back twenty minutes ago when your car pulled into the driveway. But you never came into the house. I've been very concerned. I finally decided to search the grounds for you."

"I'm sorry, I didn't mean to worry you. I wanted to take a few minutes to clear my head of the clutter and try to put my thoughts together. I was headed toward the kitchen door when you sort of…well—" she gave a nervous chuckle "—sort of *materialized* out of thin air."

Donovan pulled her into his arms and held her body tightly against his. "I'm just glad you're safe, that's all." He continued to hold her, reveling in the warmth of the physical contact. He finally released her. "Come on, dinner is ready." They returned to the house, hand in hand.

TAYLOR AND DONOVAN were seated at the table in the informal dining room finishing their salad when Alex came charging in. He handed a binder to Donovan, then made a courtly bow. "I hereby present Your Lordship with the final rundown on this year's festival, direct from Constance Smythe's printer."

Alex sent a leering glance at Taylor, flashed a sexy grin and winked at her. "Now maybe I'll have some free time… at least until opening day of the festival." His gaze traveled between Donovan and Taylor. "So, what have you kids been up to while I've been taking care of all the festival arrangements?" His gaze landed on Taylor. "How's the research coming along? Do you plan to take pictures of the festival to include in the book?"

It was an innocent enough question, but one that made her uncomfortable. She shot an uneasy glance toward Donovan before responding to Alex's question. "I think I'm about finished with my research. As for pictures…I'm not much of a photographer." Since Alex knew nothing about her true identity or reason for being at the estate, she felt compelled to continue the deception. "Do you perhaps have a professional covering the festival who might allow me to use some of his pictures?"

"Constance has engaged a photographer. I'm sure we can make an arrangement."

Alex took his place at the table and kept up a cheerful line of chatter throughout dinner, bringing Donovan up-to-date on the festival arrangements and some last-minute, unexpected expenses. He also made several suggestions to Taylor about events that she might want to spotlight in her book. "If there's anyone specific that you'd like to interview, let me know and I'll make those arrangements for you."

"Thank you, Alex. That's very nice of you."

"That's all right." Alex flashed his patented sexy grin. "I live for the pleasure of giving pleasure."

Donovan's muscles tensed as he listened to Alex's easy flirting and sexy innuendos. It was just Alex's way, but the fact that it was directed toward Taylor set his nerves on edge. Possessiveness? Jealousy? No, that was not his nature. But he knew he had not been himself lately. Taylor was someone very special to him. He had never felt about another woman the way he felt about her.

A dark moment entered his mind. How could he think in terms of a future with Taylor when he didn't know what the future held for him? Or if he even had a future. Again he reminded himself that until the source of the headaches could be identified and the periods of confusion and memory loss banished, he couldn't be certain of anything. He tried to put a hopeful spin on the situation. The last time a blinding headache hit him he was with Taylor. He had been able to shake it off without a blackout or memory loss. Maybe it was a good sign.

Or maybe he was only fooling himself by thinking that the confusion was beginning to clear.

His mind drifted back to what Taylor had said about someone purposely doing this to him. But who? And how? And most important—why? Was there someone out there who hated him enough to try to drive him out of his mind? Someone so desperate that the murder of three innocent people could be rationalized?

They finished dinner, then Alex headed for the snooker room. He called over his shoulder to Donovan, his voice carrying the humor that showed on his face. "I'm going to put in some extra practice. Next time we compete, you won't be so lucky."

Donovan shot a lighthearted reply to Alex's challenge. "Luck had nothing to do with it, my dear cousin. It was pure skill!" He watched Alex leave, then turned his attention to Taylor. "We need to talk about your meeting this afternoon with Byron."

"Yes. And you need to fill me in on what you found in the blueprints and drawings." She glanced around the informal dining room in an attempt to see who was within earshot. "Shall we go to your suite?"

He wrinkled his brow into a frown. "I think not. A couple of my accounting people are working late this evening in the office area. It would be better if they didn't observe the two of us going into my living quarters. Maybe we could spread everything out on the tables in the library."

"Will that be private enough? Anyone could innocently walk in, not knowing we were there."

"You're right. I'll get the blueprints and drawings and bring them to your room. We won't be bothered there." He brushed a quick kiss across her lips. "I'll see you in a bit."

A little ripple of apprehension darted across Taylor's body. If a secret door into her room did exist, then there was no guarantee that they would have the privacy they needed. She glanced around. Even though the area was well lit, it suddenly seemed gloomy and oppressive.

On her way to her bedroom, she passed the snooker room. The sounds of the snooker balls hitting against each other drew her attention. She paused for a moment as she considered sticking her head in the door and saying something to Alex, but quickly changed her mind. She didn't want to start a conversation that would be difficult to get out of without arousing his suspicions. She hurried on to her room to wait for Donovan.

The nervous tension churned in the pit of her stomach as the minutes ticked by. She had expected him to appear right away, but it had been nearly half an hour. A moment of panic rose inside her. Had he fallen prey to another of the incapacitating headaches? Was he wandering around in a black fog not knowing where he was or what he was doing? Her panic grew, filling her with dread. Should she go looking for him?

A soft knock at her bedroom door brought her rampaging fears to an abrupt halt. She opened the door to Donovan, then quickly shut it behind him. She glanced at her watch. "I was beginning to worry."

He placed a tender kiss on her lips. "I was cornered by one of my accountants and had to take care of some business. And then I took some time to fetch this." He smiled as he produced a bottle of wine and two glasses from behind his back and handed them to her. He took the corkscrew from his pocket and opened the bottle.

She sent him a teasing grin. "I see you brought everything except the blueprints and architectural drawings we were going to look at."

A sheepish expression crossed his face. "I guess my mind temporarily went to more pleasant things. I'll go get them and be right back."

Donovan left and returned a few minutes later carrying several tubes containing rolled blueprints and a large envelope that held the drawings. He removed the caps from the end of the tubes, withdrew the contents, then unrolled the plans and spread them out across her bed along with the drawings.

He turned toward Taylor and took the glass of wine from her outstretched hand. "Thank you." He took a sip, then set the glass on the table. "Before we get into these plans, I want to hear about your conversation with Byron."

"Well…where Jeremy was very frightened and believed that his own life was in danger, Byron scoffed at the curse, saying it was nothing more than a lot of mindless bunk that only ignorant people would believe in. He displayed an almost reckless arrogance in his attitude. He even went so far as to insinuate that you might be much more involved than anyone realized."

Donovan's eyes narrowed into an angry glare. "That's just the type of underhanded and unethical tactic he uses in running his newspaper. It's the same way the Treadwells have been doing things since they started that newspaper over one hundred years ago, even before the original murders."

"There was something else—" her voice became hesitant as if she wasn't sure of what she was about to say "—when I left the newspaper office today…"

"Something else?" He studied the expression of uncertainty on her face. "What is it?"

"It may not mean anything, but it struck me as odd. As I was leaving I looked back toward Byron's office and I saw him hurrying out the back door."

"Well, it was the end of the workday. Maybe your being there kept him in the office later than he planned."

"I don't think so. He seemed to be busy working on something when I arrived. And he wasn't simply leaving, he was almost running out the back door. He put up a blustery, arrogant front as he ridiculed this curse notion, then he behaved as if he couldn't get away fast enough. It just seemed so out of context compared to his words. And there was something else. It didn't register until just now. He was carrying a tube," she gestured toward the plans on the bed, "like the ones the blueprints were in."

A thoughtful look came across Donovan's face. "How very interesting."

Then a dark cloud of pain settled over him. It throbbed at his temples and pounded behind his eyes. "Taylor—"

Her voice filled with alarm. "Donovan…what is it?" She reached for him, but he stumbled backward.

He squeezed his eyes tightly shut. "The pain…my head…it's happening again."

She wrapped her arms around him. Her voice was soothing yet firm. "Fight it, Donovan. You did it before and you can do it again. Shake it off." She continued to hold him, to provide him comfort.

He focused on her voice and her words. He couldn't allow the pain and darkness to throw him into another period of confusion with the memory lapse. He concentrated, repeating in his mind each and every word she said. If he could just keep his mind focused he could beat it.

He would be able to maintain control.

Chapter Eleven

The shadowy figure hugged the darkness of the back alley as he made his way across the village. His finely honed senses sent a rush of excitement through his body. His work was almost done. Soon everything would be as it should have been one hundred years ago. Emily would be his and those who opposed him and tried to stand in his way would be gone.

He arrived at the house. A new lock on the door—no matter, it would not stop him. He stealthily entered and made his way through the dark rooms. He pulled the knife from its sheath. Very soon now. Everything would be his.

TAYLOR WOKE WITH A START. She immediately reached for Donovan, but he wasn't there. She heard the clock downstairs chiming the hour—four o'clock. She glanced toward the bathroom, but the door was open and the room was empty. Where could he have gone? Together they had again managed to ward off the darkness as it descended around him. Then they'd made love—sensual and hot, yet at the same time tender and caring. She had assumed he would stay in her room all night. She felt the sheets on his side of the bed. They were cool to the touch, no remnants of body heat clinging to the fabric.

She quickly leaped out of bed, fully alert to the disturbing thought that invaded her mind. Had he suffered another headache? Where had he gone? She had to find him, to make sure he was all right. She frantically pulled on her jeans and a sweatshirt. She jammed her feet into her shoes, then grabbed her flashlight.

She made her way down the darkened hall to the staircase. When she reached the ground floor she paused, not sure what to do or which way to go. Was everything all right—had he simply decided to return to his own room and not disturb her? On the other occasions when he'd had one of his attacks, he had ended up wandering around the grounds. She would start her search outdoors.

Taylor crossed the entry hall and opened the front door. It didn't take long for her to locate Donovan. She found him sitting on a bench on the side terrace, leaning forward with his head in his hands.

"Donovan?" She placed her hand on his shoulder. "Are you all right?" He looked up at the sound of her voice. The outdoor lighting provided just enough illumination for her to see the confusion in the depth of his blue eyes.

"Taylor?" He looked around, his gaze darting from one object to another as if trying to get his bearings. "What am I doing…" He shook his head and rubbed his temples. His forehead wrinkled into a frown. "What happened?"

"I woke up and you were gone. I came looking for you."

"What time is it?" He rose unsteadily to his feet.

"It's four-thirty. Let's go inside. We'll go to your room." He put his arm around her shoulder as they walked. It was a gesture of closeness rather than a need for support.

As soon as they were behind his closed bedroom door he pulled her into his arms and held her. He caressed her shoulders and ran his fingers through her hair. His voice was soft and filled with the emotional turmoil running through his body. "I don't know what happened. I had you in my arms and we were drifting off to sleep. The next thing I remember was sitting on the terrace, and a moment later you were there. I have no idea when I left your room."

"Was it another headache?"

His words were whispered as he continued to hold her. "I don't remember being struck with one of those headaches. It's all a blank."

"You still have a few hours until breakfast. Why don't you try to get some sleep? I'll stay with you if you like."

He finally released her from his embrace but continued to hold on to her hand. "I don't really feel tired. I'd rather go back to your room and go over those blueprints. There has to be something we missed. Will you wait here for me while I take a quick shower?"

She gave his hand a squeeze. "Of course."

After Donovan disappeared into his bathroom, Taylor wandered over to the trunk. The lid was raised and most of the things were still in stacks on the floor. She took the few remaining items out of the trunk—the small boxes containing the sentimental keepsakes. As she turned away, something caught her attention—a quick flash that she saw from the corner of her eye.

She stared at the interior of the trunk, searching along the edges until she spotted something. She was not sure what she was seeing. It was almost like a tab of some sort, very small and the same color as the inside of the trunk. It appeared to rest flat against the bottom but had somehow become bent, possibly just now when she had removed the little boxes.

A tiny ripple of understanding pricked at the back of her mind. She held her breath, almost afraid to breathe. Could this be the missing piece to the puzzle that they had been searching for? The excitement grew as the realization came into full bloom. She reached for the tab and gave it a tug.

A wave of disappointment crashed through her when nothing happened. She pursed her lips as she thought a moment, turning the possibilities over in her mind. She inspected the opposite side of the trunk bottom. The excitement returned when her fingers touched an identical tab. Once again the optimism bloomed. With trembling hands she grasped both tabs and pulled on them.

Her heart pounded with her excitement as the bottom of the trunk gave way. She lifted it out and placed it on the floor. A false bottom and a secret compartment. And better yet, there was something in that compartment. Her jubilation almost burst through her attempt at being calm and pragmatic. This had to be what James Sedgwick had so carefully guarded.

This was the ultimate prize.

She jumped to her feet and raced across the room toward the bathroom, charging through the door into a cloud of steam. She pulled open the shower door. Water splashed on the floor and on her clothes. Her total exhilaration filled the room. She stepped into the shower and threw her arms around Donovan, oblivious to the water pounding down on her.

"I found it! I found the secret we've been looking for!"

A contagious joy radiated from every part of Taylor. Donovan didn't know what to make of it. He pulled her body tight against his and held her. "What are you talking about?" Her total elation lifted his spirits. Was there an answer? Would he finally be able to put this nightmare behind him?

"The trunk…it has a false bottom and a hidden compartment. There's something in that compartment, papers of some kind and what looks like another journal. It must be what your father was so adamant about keeping hidden. What he wanted to preserve for you and you alone."

A hard jolt of reality hit him. He reached for the faucet and turned off the water. Had he heard her correctly? "A hidden compartment in the bottom of the trunk?" The joy tingled through his body, chasing away the despair he had continually fought off since his father's suicide. It filled him with the first rays of hope he had experienced since this horrible nightmare had begun.

And Taylor was there to share it with him.

Donovan grabbed a towel for himself and handed one to her. He quickly dried off, then wrapped the towel around his hips as he hurried into the bedroom. He stopped in front of the trunk and stared at what she had uncovered. His heartbeat jumped and his pulse quickened. His hand trembled slightly as he removed the journal from the secret compartment and opened it. The first page contained a notation addressed specifically to him in his father's handwriting.

Donovan, my son: Guard this journal most carefully. It contains my suspicions and my fears. Hopefully it will protect you from the same fate that has befallen me. The date he had written inside the cover was the day he had committed suicide.

Donovan leafed quickly through several pages of hastily written notations. Taylor peered over his shoulder. "What does it mean?"

He closed the journal and set it on the bed. "I don't know. I think it's going to take some time to study and decipher. It's almost as if he tried to write using some sort of code in case this particular journal fell into someone else's hands."

Taylor took the pieces of paper from the compartment

and unfolded them. They were sketches that appeared to be the layout of hallways and rooms, but nothing that said where they were located. She handed them to Donovan.

"Do you recognize where this might be?"

He stared at the sketches. "No. Well, this one looks familiar." He then held up the second sketch. "But this one is a complete mystery. It doesn't look like anything or anyplace I know. Hopefully there's something in the journal that will help us understand them."

Donovan put the journal and sketches back in the compartment and replaced the false bottom. Then he put everything back in the trunk and locked it. "There, that should do it for a little while."

Total disbelief covered her face. "Aren't you going to read through the journal?"

"Yes, but we can't do it now. The household will be up and around soon. It would be very suspicious if we didn't appear for breakfast. We'll do it tonight after everyone has gone to bed and we can be assured of privacy."

A warm glow of pleasure flowed through Donovan's body as he leaned forward and placed a tender kiss on her lips. "Besides, you're all wet. You need to get back to your room and change your clothes."

"You're right." She looked up, making eye contact with him.

He saw the same level of excitement in the depth of her eyes as he felt, an exhilaration tempered with a necessary caution. He brushed another kiss against her lips. "I'll see you at breakfast."

The tingle of excitement continued to buzz through him as he dressed and made some coffee. Optimism had not been part of his life since his father's death. He could almost taste it—the end of his nightmare was at hand.

Then a moment of darkness clouded his enthusiasm. Exactly how it would end was still a mystery. Another thought cautiously entered his mind. The end to his turmoil could also signal a beginning, a chance to explore a true relationship with Taylor. But it was still too soon to make an in-depth examination of his true feelings—feelings that frightened him almost as much as the confusion surrounding him.

He slumped into a large chair and leaned back. He needed to get everything straight in his mind. He closed his eyes. His thoughts became more scattered as some much-needed sleep settled over him.

ALEX POURED HIMSELF some more coffee, then held up the pot in Taylor's direction. He cocked his head and shot her a questioning look.

"Yes, please." She extended her empty cup for him to fill. She forced an upbeat manner despite the nervous tension that churned in the pit of her stomach. Donovan had not appeared for breakfast, and she had become increasingly worried. Everything seemed fine when she left him to return to her room. There had been a feeling of optimism, a genuine sense that everything would be all right. She had even allowed her thoughts to drift toward a possible future with a man who meant everything to her.

So, where was Donovan? A twinge of panic began to push its way to the forefront. Had something happened to him? She tried to maintain a calm outer appearance in front of Alex.

"Have you seen Donovan this morning? It's odd that he hasn't shown up for breakfast. In the time I've been here, I've noticed that he's always been very prompt."

"And I'm still very prompt—" Donovan strode into the

room as he glanced at his watch "—almost." He extended a sheepish smile. "My apologies for keeping you waiting. I'm afraid I overslept."

Alex gestured toward his half-eaten breakfast. "You didn't keep us waiting for long, at least not me."

Donovan poured himself some coffee, filled his plate and seated himself across the table from Taylor. "I guess I was more tired than I realized. After I showered and dressed, I sat in my favorite chair with a book and fell asleep."

Alex chuckled. "Sounds to me like you should have stayed in bed a little longer."

Bradley stood at the door and discreetly cleared his throat. "Excuse me, sir. Inspector Edgeware is here again and is asking to see both you and Miss MacKenzie."

A cold chill darted through Donovan's body. Another visit from Mike Edgeware, especially in his official capacity, could not be a good omen. He glanced at Taylor. The expression on her face matched his unspoken concern. He turned his attention back to Bradley. "He wants to see both of us? Did he say why?"

"No, sir. He didn't say."

Donovan gathered his composure, steeled his determination and projected his authority. "Tell the inspector we're having breakfast. He's welcome to wait in the entry hall if he chooses."

"Yes, sir." Bradley left the informal dining room.

Taylor looked questioningly at Donovan. "Why would the inspector want to see us? I thought we already settled his questions about Jeremy Edwards."

Alex straightened to attention. His gaze shifted between Taylor and Donovan. "The inspector questioned the two of you about Jeremy's death? Why? What could he possibly think you had to do with it?"

"Well—" Taylor squirmed in her chair, not quite sure how to reply to Alex's questions "—it was me the inspector questioned. I had gone to see Jeremy the day before his murder and also the day of his murder—you gave me a ride from the village back to the manor house. Since I was a stranger and had specifically gone to see him, the inspector was merely following up on the situation with some routine and totally understandable questions. I thought that was all there was to it."

She shot a furtive glance toward Donovan. She attempted to swallow the apprehension welling inside her, but without any success. "What could he want with me now? With us?"

Donovan maintained his outer calm. "I suppose we'll find out *after* we finish breakfast."

Once again Bradley appeared at the door. His usually stoic mask showed a hint of uncertainty. "It's Inspector Edgeware, sir. He says it's quite urgent. He insists on speaking with you and Miss MacKenzie immediately."

Donovan set down his coffee cup. A frown wrinkled across his forehead as he turned toward Taylor. "Do you mind interrupting your breakfast?"

"No, of course not."

Taylor and Donovan left the informal dining room. He reached out and gave her hand a little squeeze. His whispered words were intended for her ears only. "Don't worry. I'm sure whatever the inspector wants can't be as serious as Bradley made it seem. It's probably just Mike's attempt to counter my statement of having him wait. I'm sure it's nothing more than his way of trying to exert some authority in my house."

They arrived at the entry hall where they found the inspector anxiously pacing back and forth. He turned to face them, the grim expression on his face conveying the seriousness of his visit.

"All right, Mike. What is so important that you had to upset the routine of my household?"

"Byron Treadwell was murdered last night." Inspector Edgeware made no attempt to soften the news. "Someone stabbed him to death in his bed in the same manner that Jeremy Edwards was killed."

Taylor gasped as the shock spread through her. "Byron was murdered?" She looked at Donovan and saw her shock and disbelief mirrored in his features. She suspected that Byron might somehow be involved, especially after she had seen him run out the back door of the newspaper offices. But now…

"And once again, Miss MacKenzie, it seems that you visited a murder victim late in the afternoon before he was killed. I'm told that you left his office and a moment later he hurried out the back door without saying anything to his staff. We can't find anyone who saw him after he left his office. So, that means you—"

She slowly nodded her head. "Were the last person to see him alive." She had said the words and understood their implication. It was like a bad movie where the heroine kept getting in deeper and deeper and no matter what she did or didn't do, everything kept pointing in her direction. Her shock quickly turned to an ever-increasing panic.

She tried to present a controlled outer demeanor, but she had never felt more out of control than she did at that moment. "I don't know anything about his murder, Inspector. Mr. Treadwell graciously allowed me to use the newspaper files and archives for research. I had been to the newspaper offices on three separate occasions. We even had dinner together one evening."

"I see." The inspector showed no hint of what was going on in his mind as he made several notations in his notepad. He looked up, making eye contact with her. "And where were you last night?"

"I returned to the manor house in time for dinner and didn't leave. I was here all night."

"Can anyone confirm that?"

Donovan stepped between Taylor and Mike Edgeware. His anger was obvious but totally under control. "That's an impertinent question and doesn't deserve a response. Miss MacKenzie gave you her answer."

"All right, Your Lordship. Where were you last night?"

"I had dinner with Miss MacKenzie and Alex. Following dinner Alex went to the snooker room. Miss MacKenzie and I spent the evening going over some old journals of my father's."

"And then?"

Donovan glared at Mike. "*And then*…what? Exactly what are you trying to imply?"

Taylor quickly interrupted the escalating confrontation. "Lord Sedgwick is attempting to protect my reputation."

"Taylor…don't—"

She gently touched his arm in an intimate gesture. "It's all right." She turned her attention toward the inspector. "The truth is that Donovan and I spent the night together. He returned to his living quarters shortly before the household staff woke. It was about five this morning."

Mike Edgeware looked up from his notebook, a quick flash of surprise darting across his face. "I see. Then the two of you alibi each other from early last evening until five this morning. Is that correct?"

A hint of irritation crept into Taylor's voice. "You have my statement, Inspector. Is there anything else?" It hadn't been a complete lie. No matter what the circumstantial evidence might suggest, she knew in her heart that Donovan could not have been responsible for the grisly murders. She loved him, and love also included trust. They didn't know what the answers to the mystery were, but she knew in her heart what they weren't.

"I'd like to talk to Alex. Is he here?"

Donovan leveled a stare at Mike. "Yes. He's the one who was permitted to eat his breakfast while it was still hot. Are you through with us? If so, I'll send Alex out here." He had made it clear that the inspector was not invited any farther into the house than the entry hall.

Taylor and Donovan returned to the informal dining room. Alex looked up from the morning newspaper as they entered the room.

"What did the good inspector want that was so important?"

"Byron Treadwell was murdered last night. The inspector is gathering alibis. He wants to talk to you."

"Byron was murdered? I guess that explains why the *London Times* is the only paper delivered this morning." Alex shoved back from the table and stood up. "Mike is in the entry hall?" He popped the last bite of his toast into his mouth and left the room.

As soon as Alex was out of sight, Donovan pulled Taylor into his arms. "You didn't need to do that. Our personal relationship is none of Mike's business. And you shouldn't have put yourself in that sort of compromising position by lying to him."

"I didn't lie. We were together when we fell asleep and you were in your room at five this morning. It's just that I didn't make any specific mention of a few hours in between."

"But the truth is that neither one of us knows where the other was during those hours." He held her closer. His voice dropped to an anxious whisper. "And I don't know where I was."

"Wherever you were, I know in my heart that it couldn't have been at Byron Treadwell's house stabbing him to death." It was the closest she had come to revealing her true feelings. Things were happening so fast—horrible things. This was the fourth murder. A shudder moved up her spine accompanied by a wave of apprehension. Four people brutally killed with Donovan and her in the middle of it.

"We have to go over the journal and papers you found in the hidden compartment. It can't wait until tonight. It has to be the key that will unlock this madness—" The word hit him in a most vulnerable spot. *Madness.* Is that what it would turn out to be after all? Would everything come down to the Sedgwick Curse?

He held her tighter. She was his anchor, the one spot of absolute security in the middle of a nearly unbearable nightmare. And he loved her. The moment he heard her tell Mike Edgeware a lie to give him an alibi for the time of the murder, he knew he could no longer deny his love for her. But that still did not ease his mind about whether she was in danger from him. It was a fear that lived deep inside him, a fear he didn't know how to fight.

Alex returned to the informal dining room. "Well, that didn't take very long."

Donovan poured a cup of coffee, handed it to Taylor, then poured another cup for himself. "What did he ask you?"

"He wanted to know where I was. I told him I was playing snooker. That was about it." Alex furrowed his brow into a slight frown as he stared at Donovan for a moment. "He did say that all these murders seemed to be the work of a madman."

The words hit Donovan with a solid punch. He looked

at Taylor. A cold shiver ran down his back. Could she be the next victim? He recalled her words about sensing that she was being watched, believing someone had been in her room that first night—about the ominous sensation that seemed to follow her. Could he be that menacing presence? A sick churning started in the pit of his stomach and tried to move up through his chest. Was he, indeed, a madman stalking his prey?

"Or someone with a specific agenda who wanted to make it seem that a madman was on the loose in the village." Taylor's words cut into his spiraling fears. He took a sip of his coffee and tried to put his disturbing thoughts behind him.

"That's certainly an interesting theory. Mike didn't say anything about pursuing that concept. Perhaps he should." Alex glanced at his watch. "I'll mention it if I run into him, but right now I need to be on my way. I'll see you at dinner."

As soon as Alex departed, Donovan grabbed Taylor's hand. "Come on. We're going to thoroughly inspect that journal and those drawings. We have to make some sense of them and figure out what my father was trying to tell me. Time is running out."

She eyed him curiously. "What does that mean—'time is running out'?" A little tremor of apprehension presented itself. "Why would you say that?"

"It's the curse. It's history repeating itself. A man and a woman were killed in the lodge house, the location of the original murders. Then Jeremy Edwards was murdered, the descendent of the first person my great-grandfather threatened. And now Byron Treadwell has been murdered. Richard Treadwell was the other person who had specifically been threatened."

"But Byron is not a descendent of Richard Treadwell."

She saw the shock register on Donovan's face. "You didn't know? Byron was adopted as a toddler."

"What makes you think that?"

"He readily admitted it the first day we met. It would seem to me that anyone who had lived in the village for a while would have known it. He's not so old that everyone living in the village at the time would now be gone. Surely it must be common knowledge among the villagers."

Donovan shook his head in disbelief. "I didn't know it."

"Technically you don't live in the village. You live here in this stately manor house on this large estate and are a member of the aristocracy. That would certainly set you apart from the villagers."

Donovan ran her words through his mind, then his thoughts drifted to more serious concerns. *I didn't know about Byron's family background, about him not being a descendent of Richard Treadwell. I assumed Byron fit into the pattern. One more reason for me to be a prime suspect.* The thought added to his anxiety. He returned his attention to what needed to be done. "Come on. Let's get to work."

They retreated to his living quarters, emptied the trunk, then took the journal and sketches from the hidden compartment.

He started to hand the journal to her, then changed his mind and extended the sketches toward her. Before she could take them, he withdrew them from her reach. "We can't split this up. You don't know the house and property well enough for the sketches to mean anything to you, assuming they relate to the property. And there's no way you would know which parts of the journal made sense and what needed to be interpreted."

"So, what do you suggest?"

"Let's start with the journal. Maybe there's a clue in it

that will tell us what the sketches mean." He set the sketches aside.

They seated themselves side by side at the table and began on page one of the journal. For two hours they analyzed each and every sentence, trying to decipher any hidden meanings. The entries detailed James Sedgwick's battle with the painful headaches and periods where he was disoriented and had memory blackouts. The descriptions were identical to what had been happening to Donovan.

As they got closer to the end of the journal, James's writings began to speak of another person, some unnamed person always lurking in the shadows—watching everything and everyone. Someone who wanted everyone out of the way. He also made several notations about drugs, chemical and natural organic, along with speculations about being poisoned.

The last notation James Sedgwick made in the journal was a chilling one. *Hopefully I will be able to complete this journal, but I fear I will be dead by morning.*

Donovan slowly closed the journal as the shock settled over him. Then a quick jab of anger pulled away the veil of confusion that had been covering everything up until that point. For the first time since the nightmare began, something became crystal clear to him.

"My father didn't commit suicide. He was murdered—cold-blooded, calculated and vicious murder." The words were spoken softly but with an intensity that set Taylor's senses on total alert. "This isn't some wild speculation about a century-old curse. This is reality, and it started with my father's murder."

Chapter Twelve

"What?" Taylor's voice was a mere whisper. Had she heard him correctly? A strange sensation swirled around inside her, a positive energy she had not felt since arriving at the estate. They were finally on the right track to discovering the truth and putting an end to the nightmarish chaos surrounding them.

"My father was murdered." Donovan clenched his jaw into a hard line of determination. An intense anger settled over his handsome features. He had made a definitive statement, not a guess or mere speculation. "If it's the last thing I ever do, I intend to find out who murdered him."

"Shouldn't you call the police? Get in touch with Inspector Edgeware and let him know what you discovered?"

"No...not yet. There's nothing specific here. I know what it means, but Mike may not see it that way. Besides, the journal never says who my father suspected. Perhaps he didn't even know who it was, only what was happening."

He impulsively grabbed her, folding her into his embrace. "For the first time I think I can see light at the end of the tunnel. We're on the right track." Positive energy flowed through him, touching every part of his awareness. Even though the implications of what they had found were sobering and pointed to the very real life-threatening danger that surrounded him, a new level of excitement lifted his spirits to a place they hadn't been in many months—the first truly positive look he had into the future.

"One-third of the puzzle is solved. We know what is happening. All we need now is to figure out the who and the why." He brushed a soft kiss against her forehead. "You said it, only we didn't realize the full impact of the words. You wondered if someone was doing this to me. It's just like what happened to my father. Whatever was used to drug him or poison him to bring on the headaches and blackout periods is probably the same thing being given to me. But how? Something I'm ingesting? Something I'm absorbing through my skin?"

Thoughts popped into Taylor's head almost faster than she could keep up with them. The first thing they needed to do was stop what was happening to him. "We'll replace everything you use, such as soap and toothpaste. From now on you'll only drink bottled water. You'll eat all your meals out and not in the same restaurant. The only thing you'll consume in this house is whatever we purchase from the market and bring directly here to your kitchenette. It has to be prepared by one of us and eaten immediately. It's imperative that the food is not out of the sight of either you or me from the moment it's purchased until it's consumed.

"Until we find out what is being used and how it's being administered, nothing you do will be routine. We'll go right now and buy replacement toiletries. We'll make the purchases in town rather than here in the village. That way no one will see what we're doing."

"Whoa…slow down. You're getting ahead of things." Even though he knew what she had said was true, he forced his thoughts toward what they needed to be doing first.

"We need to temper the runaway emotion over what we've discovered with some pragmatism. Let's finish what we've started here. We need to look over these drawings and see if we can figure out what they are telling us."

Donovan cleared his mind of the thoughts circulating through his head and the excitement pulsing through his body. He focused his concentration on the tangible items in front of him. He spread the two sketches out on the table and pointed to the first one. "This appears to be the lower level of the house…the underground rooms and hallways."

"Do you mean the dungeon?"

A bit of a smile tugged at the corners of his mouth. "You're thinking of a castle. This is a manor house, albeit a very large one, but still a manor house. Perhaps the original structure from the late 1300s might have included something akin to a dungeon area as a necessity of those times, but this house was rebuilt in the mid 1700s after the fire destroyed most of the original house. This new structure was never a stronghold or used as a military…"

Donovan's voice trailed off and his eyes widened. His entire body seemed to stiffen. He grabbed her shoulders. She could feel the intensity surging through him. His face reflected the enthusiasm of his realization. "The house was rebuilt, but it was—"

"Built on the same foundation." Her sudden realization of what he was saying sent a wave of excitement crashing through her. "Everything below ground level would still be there and be just as it was from the original house!"

The smile spread across his face. "Exactly. Maybe there are dungeons down there and who knows what else."

He put the two sketches side by side and studied each aspect of them. "They're different. These are not two sketches of the same thing. They are sketches of two different places, one much larger than the other." He put the sketch of the smaller structure on top of the larger one, then held them up to the light so that he could see the bottom drawing through the top piece of paper.

"Look at this." He held them so she could see. "The center section of the lower level matches a lot of the other drawing. There are certain places that line up exactly, most likely major support walls. I think this smaller structure is a subterranean chamber beneath the known lower level."

"How do we get down there?"

"We don't…not until tonight after the house is quiet. We don't want anyone seeing what we're doing. There's one entrance to the lower level that I know about, the primary entrance that is known to the entire staff, but there's probably at least one hidden entrance. I'll compare these sketches with the blueprints, and with what I know exists, to see if I can figure out where a secret door or hidden staircase might be."

"And while you're doing that, I'm going into town to buy you new toiletries. In the meantime, don't drink or eat anything unless it's factory sealed. And that includes water from the faucet, unless you first take it apart to make sure nothing has been put in there to seep into the water when you turn it on."

He forced an amused chuckle. "Isn't that being a bit too cautious?" His attempt to sound unconcerned fell flat.

She gave him a knowing look that said she didn't believe his casual attitude, then brushed a quick kiss against his lips. "No. You can't assume anything. Don't let down your guard."

She went to his bedroom and returned with the water carafe from his nightstand. She poured the water into the sink, then reached into her pocket and withdrew the prescription bottle that had been next to the carafe. "And that includes taking these. If you need them for the headaches we'll get the prescription refilled and you'll keep it on you at all times."

"Don't you think you're overdoing it a bit? I admit that security here isn't all that much. My father talked about putting in an alarm system, but it never happened. I suppose it's possible that somebody could come and go from the house without anyone else knowing about it, but it doesn't seem likely that anyone would have tampered with the water system or poisoned the food or my toothpaste."

He picked up the prescription bottle, took off the cap, and poured the tablets into the palm of his hand. "These look fine. It's not as if they were capsules that could be taken apart, something added, then put back together. There isn't anything unusual looking about these tablets."

"How do you know those are the same tablets that came from the chemist shop? Someone could have emptied the bottle and refilled it with different tablets, so don't take any of these."

"If I didn't know better, I'd swear you were a general issuing orders." He pulled her into his arms. A teasing grin played across his lips. "Hasn't anyone ever explained to you that the aristocracy have rights and privileges above those of the common folk? We don't take well to being ordered about."

She returned his smile. "Ah…but you seem to forget that I'm American. We don't believe in the privileged rank of the aristocracy."

"Not even if I claim you as my own?" The words were out of his mouth before he could stop them. It was the wrong place and definitely the wrong time. They still had a very difficult task ahead of them and an unknown truth yet to be revealed. There was light at the end of the tunnel, but was it daylight or could it be an oncoming train? He quickly captured her mouth with a tender kiss that was gentle while managing to convey all the heated passion that existed between them.

With great reluctance, Taylor broke off the delicious kiss before it escalated into something very erotic. "Give me a list of what I need to buy. While you're writing that down, I'll get my purse and car keys. There isn't any reason for people to pay attention to me in town, unlike the local establishments here in the village where I'll either stand out as a stranger or be recognized as the American staying at the Sedgwick Estate."

Donovan made out a list, and a few minutes later Taylor was on her way into town.

He locked the door of his living quarters so he wouldn't be disturbed by the office or housekeeping staff. He studied both sketches and compared them to the blueprints. The known entrance to the lower level was located inside the enclosed storage area beneath the main staircase in the entry hall. The storage area didn't really have a *hidden* door, but it did appear to be part of the paneled wall so that it would blend in with the overall decor of the entry hall. However, he had not been in that storage area since he was a child.

With the help of a magnifying glass he carefully scrutinized the drawing for a similar type of marking indicating hidden stairs from the ground floor to the lower level. Each new discovery lifted his optimism a notch. Time passed quickly as he became totally absorbed in the drawings.

A knock at his door startled him out of his concentration. He glanced at his watch and was surprised to find that it had been more than two hours since Taylor left for town.

He opened the door, but instead of Taylor it was Bradley standing on the other side. A quick jab of irritation shot through him. Everyone in the house knew that a locked door meant he didn't want to be disturbed. If it was some type of an emergency, he could be reached through the in-house phone system.

"Bradley?" He heard the annoyance in his voice and immediately regretted allowing his displeasure to show. "Is there a problem?"

As always, Bradley remained impassive in his outer appearance. "There's a, uh, *gentleman* here who is very insistent on seeing you straightaway. He says it's in your best interest to see him, and refuses to leave. I must say, sir, that he has a rather unsavory appearance."

A nervous twinge immediately replaced the irritation, followed by an increasing level of apprehension. "Where is this man? What's his name?"

"He refused to give his name. He would only say that it was a financial matter involving Mr. Alex. I instructed him to wait in the entry hall."

Donovan mumbled the words under his breath. "A financial matter involving Alex? That can't be anything good." He wasn't quite sure how to respond, but the situation gave him a bad feeling. "Very well. Show him into the east wing drawing room. I'll be there in a few minutes. And Bradley…there's no need to offer him any amenities."

"Yes, sir. I understand."

Donovan watched as Bradley left, then he closed the door. He immediately put everything in the trunk, locked it and put the key in his pocket. He again locked the door to his living quarters when he left. A growing degree of irritation churned inside him. He didn't have time for any of Alex's nonsense.

Donovan stood at the door of the drawing room for a moment as he studied the man standing across the room looking out the window. He knew the type from his past dealings in straightening out Alex's gambling debts. A wave of disappointment hit him. Apparently Alex had lied about quitting the gaming tables. He flashed on Alex's urgent trip into London and his claim about seeing his solicitor regarding the purchase of a vacation cottage.

He shook his head in resignation. It obviously had been nothing more than a ruse to cover the real purpose of the trip, to deal with his most recent gambling debt—a debt this man obviously wanted Donovan to settle.

Donovan entered the room. He made no attempt to be polite or even pleasant. "I have a very busy schedule this morning. State your business—some sort of financial matter involving my cousin?"

The man extended his hand as he walked toward Donovan. "Ah, top of the morning, Your Lordship."

Donovan remained motionless, his voice carrying the authority of his position. "State your business."

"Uh, yes. It has to do with the, uh, cottage Alex wanted to purchase—"

"*Wanted* to purchase? I thought he *had* purchased it."

"Uh, not quite, Your Lordship."

"And what is your connection with Alex's desire to purchase a vacation cottage?"

"The cottage belongs to me."

"And your name is…?"

A smile crossed his face. "A thousand pardons, Your Lordship. Where are my manners? My name is Robert Fontaine. I was traveling to London on other business so thought I'd stop here to see you about this matter. A bit of an embarrassment, but it needs to be handled."

Donovan's tensed muscles began to relax. Perhaps he had been a bit quick to jump to conclusions, to assume Alex was once again running up gambling debts he couldn't pay.

"And this matter is…?"

"It's the check he gave me for good faith money to hold the property until he worked out his financing, a sort of down payment. We've signed the final papers, and the bank paid me for the amount less the check Alex had given me. Unfortunately, the check has been returned to me with a notation that there wasn't enough money in the account to pay it. Alex assured me at the time he issued the check that you would stand good for it if anything should go amiss. So…I'm here to collect my money."

"You have this check with you?" Donovan watched as the man's hand started to move toward his pocket, then hesitated. Something wasn't right. The man hardly looked like a landowner, and if Alex had written him a bad check on a legitimate business transaction, then why didn't he have his solicitor handle the matter? And how could Alex have come up with the purchase price by qualifying for a bank loan, yet not have the money to cover a good-faith check? Yes…something was definitely wrong.

"This is a bit embarrassing. I seem to have left the check in my hotel room."

"I couldn't possibly discuss this any further without seeing the check. I'll take this up with Alex when I see him this evening. Where can he reach you?"

A nervousness crept into Robert Fontaine's voice. "I'm not sure where I'll be this evening. Perhaps it would be better if I contacted you tomorrow morning."

Donovan's tone of voice said that as far as he was concerned the matter was closed. "Yes, perhaps it would be better." He pushed the button by the door and a moment later Bradley appeared.

"Show Mr. Fontaine out."

Donovan returned to his private rooms, not at all sure what to think about the strange exchange that had just occurred. Was it something of Alex's doing or was someone trying to take advantage of Alex's past track record? Hopefully Alex would have an explanation, one that rang with truth rather than another of his escapades.

Before Donovan could return to his scrutiny of the drawings and comparison to the blueprints, Taylor arrived. She had a large bag filled with the items from his list plus a few additional things. She set the bag on the counter next to the sink.

"I think I have everything." She extended a questioning glance in his direction. "Did you make any viable discoveries?"

"I certainly did." He quickly moved to her side, then looked inside the bag. He gave her a teasing grin. "It looks like you have more than everything. Did you buy the entire store?"

"Only the necessities." She shoved aside the trivial conversation and concentrated on what was important. "What did you discover? Show me."

He indicated the markings on the drawings and how they related to known places on the blueprints, starting with the main entrance to the lower level.

"As you can see on the blueprint of the entry hall, this indicates stairs, and here on the sketch are these markings in what appears to be the same location, the enclosed storage area beneath the main staircase. This is the entrance to the lower level, at least the only one I've ever known about."

He unrolled another blueprint and placed it next to the

same sketch. "But look at this. On the sketch there's another identical marking in what appears to be the study and another one out here in the greenhouse. That would indicate two more ground-level entrances to the lower level."

She looked at the blueprint and the room he had indicated, the study, which apparently held a secret entrance to the lower level. A tremor of anxiety combined with a ripple of excitement. It was the room where the shadowy figure had disappeared the night she was exploring that wing of the ground floor. Someone real had used a secret passage to disappear.

Than another thought hit her. "If there's an entrance from the greenhouse, that means someone could move from outside into the house without being concerned about locked doors or windows. Whoever knew about the secret passages could come and go as they pleased without anyone being aware of the intrusion. Which means whoever is behind this isn't necessarily someone who has open access to the house. They could come and go secretly on their own."

"That's absolutely correct."

She again flashed on the image of Bradley and Constance Smythe in the greenhouse arguing about something having to do with Donovan. "Uh, I saw… Well, I saw and overheard something a few nights ago. At the time I assumed it wasn't any of my business. I didn't mention it because…well—" she glanced at the floor when she felt the heat spread across her cheeks "—I have to admit that I was embarrassed for eavesdropping on the conversation." She regained eye contact with him. "But now I wonder if it might have something to do with all of this. Especially since it appears that there's an entrance to the house from the greenhouse."

He placed his fingertips to her lips to silence her. He extended a reassuring smile. "You're not making any sense. Tell me what you saw and heard."

Taylor told Donovan about the argument she had overheard coming from the greenhouse—what Bradley and Constance had said, the comments they had made about him and how she had interpreted those comments. "At the time I didn't know who the blond woman was, but then I saw her at the chemist shop and heard the clerk call her by name. I recognized it as that of the woman Alex was meeting with about the festival arrangements. I also recalled your reaction to her, which was totally the opposite of the impression she was giving the clerk about her relationship with you."

"From what you've said about their conversation, it sounds like she thinks she has some claim against my family." His forehead wrinkled into a scowl. "I wonder what her game is and why Bradley didn't come forth with what was happening? If she has proof, I'd think she would have had her solicitor contact my father about her claim against the estate."

"Well, maybe it doesn't have anything to do with what's been going on. I supposed it could be just a coincidence."

"I wonder. There seem to be lots of coincidences—" he stared intently at her "—including the arrival at the estate of Emily Kincaid's great-granddaughter the day after the explosion occurred at the crypt." Donovan's words trailed off, as if he were thinking several sentences ahead of what he was saying. "Mike Edgeware always said he didn't believe in coincidence when working on an investigation…"

The shock swept through Taylor's body. "Are you saying that you think I had something to do with—"

"No. I'm saying that perhaps some of the things that happened were a result of your arrival, not that you had anything to do with them. Maybe whoever is behind this changed his…or *her*…plans because of your presence. You admitted your identity to Jeremy Edwards, and the next night he's murdered. You told Byron Treadwell who you were, and that night he was murdered."

"But Donovan…the murders of the man and woman at the lodge house. I never saw them and they certainly couldn't have known anything about me. In fact, as near as I can tell, they didn't know anyone or anything connected to this."

A sigh of resignation escaped his throat. "That's true. Maybe the timing of your arrival on the scene really is nothing more than a coincidence."

"I wish Inspector Edgeware believed that. He seems to have me pegged as his number-one suspect." Taylor brushed away the uneasy feeling. "What else did you find in the sketches. Anything that relates to a subterranean level beneath the known cellar?"

"I think so. The sketch of the lower level contains an indication of stairs that do not show on the blueprint. There's also the same indication of stairs on the other sketch of the subterranean level. When the one sketch is placed on top of the other sketch, the indications are in an identical place. However, that place is not indicated on the blueprint. It must be a hidden door of some type."

"That means we're going to have to search for it. We can start by checking out the other entrances from the house to the lower level and that secret passage from the greenhouse to the manor house."

Donovan reached into the bag, withdrew a bottle of water and unscrewed the cap. He took a long drink, then replaced the cap. "We have our work cut out for us. We'll start tonight. My guess is that we'll be up all night, so perhaps a little nap this afternoon might be a good idea."

He pulled her into his arms. The feeling surrounding them consisted of equal parts anxiety, apprehension, elation and relief. Pieces of the puzzle were coming together. Things were beginning to make sense. Yet nothing had been resolved. But the answer was very close at hand.

And was the ultimate danger—a life-threatening danger—also close at hand and closing in on them?

He placed a tender kiss on her lips. "I need to track down Alex. We have a little *business* to discuss. One of his cronies was here while you were gone, wanting money. It looks like Alex might be running up some gambling debts again. I thought I had made it clear to him last time that I wouldn't be bailing him out anymore. I guess I didn't make it as clear as I thought."

"I'll gather up your old toiletries and hide them in my room. I wouldn't want anyone to see that you had thrown them out and wonder why. That will also preserve them in case we want to have anything analyzed later." Taylor set about completing her task.

Donovan reached for his cell phone. He didn't know where Alex was, but he did know Alex would have his cell phone with him. He dialed the number. The moment Alex answered, Donovan stated his purpose without bothering with any pleasantries. His voice was all business. "We need to have a discussion—now!"

There was a moment's hesitation before Alex responded. "Uh, certainly. How about tomorrow morning after breakfast?"

"No, Alex. I said now."

"Could you give me a hint as to why you seem so upset?"

"Does the name Robert Fontaine sound familiar?"

There was a long pause followed by a heavy sigh. "I'll be there in fifteen minutes."

Donovan disconnected the call, then turned to Taylor. "Did you find everything?"

"Yes, I have it all here in the bag."

His smile was a bit wary, but sincere all the same. "One thing is for sure. Once a man has allowed a woman to search his private bathroom and inspect his toiletries, he no longer has any secrets."

She responded with a soft and loving chuckle. "You're safe. I didn't find anything that scared me."

He brushed a quick kiss across her lips. "I'll see you later."

As soon as Taylor left, Donovan set about putting away the items she had purchased. He paused as a thought occurred to him. If someone had been tampering with his personal things, what would stop whoever it was from tampering with the replacements? He felt a little foolish, but decided to lock his toothpaste and soap in a cabinet rather than leave them in the bathroom.

A few minutes later there was a familiar knock at his door. Alex had arrived. Donovan opened the door and ushered his cousin into the sitting room.

Alex eyed him curiously, an unmistakable look of concern on his face. Donovan didn't say anything, preferring to see where Alex's guilty conscience would lead him. It didn't take long.

Alex nervously cleared his throat. "You mentioned Robert Fontaine…."

"Yes. He came to see me today."

"Bobby came here to see you? What on earth could he want with you?" Alex attempted an amused chuckle, but it didn't work.

"I think you know."

"You mean that little matter with the check?" Alex stuck

his hands in his pockets as he nervously paced back and forth. "He had no business doing that. I told him I'd take care of it."

"And how did you propose 'to take care of it'?"

"The deal is going through, it's just going to take a few days longer than I anticipated."

"Explain the details of this deal to me. Since you've involved me in it, whether on purpose or inadvertently, I think I have a right to know why a stranger came to my door wanting me to redeem a bad check you wrote."

"I told you. I'm buying a vacation cottage." Alex reached for a glass and filled it with water from the faucet. He turned toward Donovan. "You have any aspirin around here? I have a headache."

"No, you might try the kitchen. Ask Mrs. Bradley."

"Never mind." Alex downed the glass of water, then set the empty glass on the counter next to the sink. He sucked in an audible breath as if trying to collect his composure before continuing. He wandered around the sitting room, looking at things he had seen hundreds of times. He finally came to a halt and faced Donovan.

"It was a terrific plan. I found out that a developer wanted the land. I could buy an old cottage in bad need of repair and then resell it one week later for more than double what I paid for it without spending any money on repairs. All I had to do was get Bobby to hold on to that check for a few more days until the rest of the deal went through, then I could redeem it plus pay him interest for holding it for me. Apparently he decided he didn't want to wait a few more days, and came to you for the money."

Alex shifted his weight from one foot to the other in an awkward manner. "Did you...uh, did you pay him?"

"No. I told him I wanted to see the check, and he said he didn't have it with him. That terminated our conversation."

A quick look of relief darted across Alex's face. "I see. That's good. I didn't want you bothered. There was no reason for Bobby to have come here. I told him he'd have his money in a few more days."

Donovan fixed his cousin with a hard stare. "Are you lying to me, Alex? Is this really a gambling debt? I told you I wouldn't stand good for any more of your gambling losses. Is this your way of getting the money without it appearing to be a gambling debt?"

"Honestly, it's just what I said."

"All right." He could see that Alex was going to stick to his story. Nothing would be gained by continuing to pursue it.

Alex flashed his perfected impish grin. "Am I dismissed? I was supposed to meet with Constance this morning. We're arranging for delivery of the children's carnival rides. The people want to inspect the location this afternoon to make sure everything is acceptable."

Constance Smythe—Donovan turned the name over in his mind. Would Alex know anything about the animosity and secret dealings between her and Bradley? No, there was no reason to assume that Constance would take Alex into her confidence. He would save that line of discussion for some other time. Perhaps tomorrow, depending on what he and Taylor found on their search that night.

"Yes, you're dismissed."

"See you later." Alex whistled an upbeat tune as he strolled out of Donovan's private living quarters.

Donovan watched him leave. He replayed their conversation in his mind. Regardless of Alex's assurances, Donovan did not believe his story about the cottage. He gave it a few more minutes' thought, then reached for the phone. He wanted to believe Alex, but experience had taught him otherwise. He dialed the number of Alex's solicitor. It wouldn't take long to check on the story about the property.

It was a short conversation. "So he did purchase a cottage in the Lake District and there's a viable contract pending to sell that same cottage to a land developer?"

He listened to the reply as the tension eased out of his body. Alex hadn't lied to him. "It sounds a bit unorthodox, but if you say everything is legal I'll not concern myself with it any longer."

Donovan finished the phone call, but a nervous tickle continued to plague him. The solicitor seemed satisfied, so why did he still feel uneasy about the situation? What kind of scheme did Alex have him involved in, and what would it end up costing him?

Chapter Thirteen

Donovan opened the door to his living quarters in response to Taylor's soft knock. He checked his watch. She was right on time. They had agreed to meet at eleven o'clock, after everyone else had gone to bed. A nervous energy churned in the pit of his stomach, feeding the restless anxiety that coursed through his veins.

"Are you ready to go exploring?" He attempted to keep his manner light and upbeat, but it was far removed from the way he felt.

She held up her flashlight. "Yep. I even put in fresh batteries."

He stared at the flashlight for a moment. "I think you should put that little thing in your pocket as an emergency backup." He handed her a large flashlight. "Here…take this heavy-duty light. It's much brighter and has a stronger beam that will reach farther." He picked up the other heavy-duty light. "These are the battery-powered lights we use for emergencies on the estate and when the power goes out here in the house during bad storms."

Taylor took the light from him and clicked the switch on and off. "Have you determined a starting point for our search? My first thought was to start with the known entrance to the lower level, then search for the hidden stairs to the subterranean level. Then I thought it might be better to start at the greenhouse, locate the entrance there and then follow the passageway to the lower level of the house. That would give us the advantage of knowing what a secret door in the lower level looks like, how it's hidden from sight, and maybe make it easier for us to find the others. What do you think?"

"I was thinking along the same lines. Since we know we're looking for a hidden entrance to an underground tunnel, the greenhouse would most likely present an easier search. With a lot of the structure being glass walls, that limits the places it could be."

They left the house by Donovan's private side entrance. They walked along the path using the outside illumination to find their way rather than take a chance of drawing attention to their presence by turning on the bright flashlights.

Donovan held her hand as they walked. A loving warmth flowed through the physical connection, providing Taylor with a sense of security, as if all the menacing feelings of the past had been banished. But her feeling of safety was short-lived.

The large greenhouse loomed ahead—dark, foreboding and ominous. As they drew closer a tingle of anxiety made itself known, increasing in intensity with each step she took. She held on to Donovan's hand, drawing comfort from his strength.

Donovan stopped walking. "Are you all right?"

"Yes, of course. Why do you ask?"

"You're squeezing my hand so hard that you're starting to cut off the circulation to my fingers. I just thought something might be bothering you."

She immediately released his hand as a wave of embarrassment swept through her. "I'm sorry. I didn't realize I was doing it."

He placed his hands on her shoulders as he looked in her eyes. His soft voice conveyed his genuine concern. "Do you want to turn back?"

She took a steadying breath. "No. We have to do this, to see it through. I guess I was just feeling a little apprehensive—"

They both whirled around in the direction of the greenhouse as a sharp sound pierced the silence of the night. He immediately clicked on his flashlight and shined it into the darkness—first toward the glass structure, then the surrounding area. Nothing seemed to be out of place. For the first time he realized that the lavish landscaping was more than merely beautiful surroundings. It also provided an excellent hiding place.

An uneasy sensation rose inside Donovan. Was the sound nothing more than an animal or a bird going about its normal routine? The wind in the trees? Or was someone watching them? Following their every move? Stalking them from the shadows?

He dismissed the speculation as he steeled himself. It was nothing more than his imagination running away with his sense of reason.

He gave Taylor's hand a reassuring squeeze. "It's just one of the normal sounds of the night, nothing to worry about."

They entered the greenhouse and made their way through the many rows of plants toward the back storage area. It was the only part of the structure that didn't have glass walls.

It didn't take long before they located a trapdoor in the bottom of an old storage closet. Taylor stood by as Donovan pulled it open. A tingle of excitement ran through her body. Her gaze followed the beam of his flashlight as he pointed it along the ladder descending into the dark depths.

"Very interesting." He shone the beam around the edge of the trapdoor.

She peered over his shoulder. "What's interesting?"

"Hundreds of years old, yet not a cobweb in sight. This entrance has definitely been used recently. Someone has been using this greenhouse to enter and exit the manor house."

He turned to Taylor. "Shine your flashlight down the ladder to light my way. After I'm down there and determine that it's safe, I'll light the way for you to come down."

They worked together quickly and efficiently. Soon they were both in the well-constructed tunnel—not a crawl space that led underground to the lower level of the house, but a stand-up, fortified tunnel. When they reached the dead end, they searched for something that would open a hidden door. They pushed on numerous protruding stones in the rock walls without success. They attempted to twist the wall sconces designed to hold candles and pulled on the two torch holders without any success.

Taylor leaned back against the end wall and emitted a sigh of resignation. "What's left? It seems like we've pushed, twisted and pulled on everything in sight. What are we missing?"

"I don't know. There must be something else. The age of everything would pretty much preclude anything sophisticated or some method that relied on current technology." He placed his hand on the wall next to her head and leaned forward, his intention being to give her a reassuring kiss. Before his mouth came in contact with hers, the wall gave way and began to swivel. A moment later there was an opening large enough for them to walk through.

"So that's it! Between you leaning back against the wall and me leaning forward against the same place, we were able to exert enough pressure to open this. I kept looking for something that would slide to one side, not something that swiveled from a center post."

They cautiously passed through the opening to the other side of the stone wall and found themselves at the foot of the stairs leading up to a recognizable door. Donovan shone his light at the top of the stairs. "These are the stairs from the entry hall. It's the entrance to this lower level that I knew about."

He shoved on the swivel door until it swung shut. "Okay...I have my bearings with regard to the blueprints and sketches. Let's take a few minutes and see where we need to go."

They sat on the bottom step and he focused the beam of light on the sketch of the lower level, then compared it to the blueprint. "We're here—" he indicated the spot "—and according to the sketch we want to go here, where there appears to be an indication of more stairs." He focused on the blueprint again. "That should be about there." He indicated a stretch of passageway that ran behind and parallel to the one where they were.

Donovan put his arm around her shoulder and pulled her close to him. "Now that we know about the swivel door from the tunnel, we have a better idea of what to look for in trying to find a hidden set of stairs going to a subterranean level."

The cold air clung to the stone floor of the passageway, sending a shiver across Taylor's skin. The menacing atmosphere once again assaulted her senses. An uneasy feeling rose inside her. She wanted to find the answer as much as she wanted to escape from the old dark passageway and return to the light and relative safety of her room.

She rose to her feet, took a calming breath, then shone her light into the darkness in front of her. "Let's get started."

They made their way down the passageway. There were several rooms on either side, some with closed doors and others without doors. Taylor took a moment to shine her light into some of the open rooms. Two of them contained a jumble of items such as pieces of furniture and suits of armor similar to the things she had seen on the third floor of the house. The other open rooms were empty. They did not stop to inspect any of the rooms thoroughly, nor did they open any of the closed doors.

With single-minded determination they continued their quest. They reached a connecting passageway and took it to the parallel one indicated on the blueprints. They followed the parallel corridor for a distance of about thirty feet, then Donovan came to a halt.

He shone his light on the sketch. "Somewhere along here is where we'll find the hidden door leading down to the subterranean level. It's not very clear on this sketch whether it's along this section of wall or around the corner in what appears here to be an alcove." He paused for a moment, as if trying to determine how to say what was on his mind. "I think it would be quicker if we split up. You can go one way and I'll go the other way."

A sinking feeling of trepidation accompanied the shiver of fear she tried to control. Logically she understood about it being quicker if they looked in different areas, but emotionally she couldn't get comfortable with the idea of pursuing the dark corridor on her own.

She shone the beam of light around the stone walls and along the floor. Her breathing quickened in an attempt to overcome the sudden feeling that all the oxygen had been sucked away. A cold, clammy blanket of anxiety settled over her. Everything seemed to be closing in around her. It was the house again, centuries of evil deeds buried in the memory of the structure—the intimidating sensation of being watched, of having her every move followed.

"You search this area and I'll go on down the hall and look for the alcove." He placed a tender kiss on her lips. "Good luck. Call to me if you find anything."

Taylor watched as Donovan disappeared into the darkness, then she turned her attention to the stone wall. She shone the beam of light slowly along the bottom of the wall at the floor in hopes of seeing something to indicate a swivel door—scrapes on the floor, a crevasse between stones in the wall or an area of the wall where the stones didn't seem to fit together properly. She moved along slowly, one foot at a time.

A cold draft shivered across the surface of her skin. A hard jolt of panic lodged inside her. It wasn't simply the cold air of the lower level, it was moving air. The sudden movement of air meant that something had been opened… something like an outside door. Was there someone in the lower level with them? Someone who had just entered through some other hidden entrance?

She quickly turned her back to the wall, shining her flashlight upward, then looked up and down the now dimly lit corridor. Nothing moved, nothing seemed out of place. She attempted to call out to Donovan, to seek the reassurance of his presence. She opened her mouth, but her throat closed off. She tried to force a sound, but nothing happened.

The cold air pushed against the back of her neck, sending another shiver down her spine. She reached her free hand to her nape in an attempt to still the tremor. The draft threaded its way around her fingers.

The shock of realization raced through her. Her pulse increased, and her heart beat a little harder. The movement of air was seeping through the wall. That meant an opening of some sort. The excitement of discovery swirled around her, partially obscuring her rampaging anxiety. She ran her hand along the seam between the stones, following the path of the moving air. The swivel door had to be where she was standing, but on which side of the seam of air?

She pushed hard against the stone wall. Disappointment crashed inside her. Nothing happened. She renewed her efforts by moving a couple of feet to the left on the other side of the air seam. She pushed again. Every nerve ending in her body jumped to attention as the wall gave way and silently pivoted on a center pole. Her heart pounded in her chest as the tingle of anticipation danced inside her.

She shone the light inside the opening. It appeared to be a large floor area like a landing with a small alcove to one side and straight ahead were stairs leading down into the blackness. She cautiously stepped through the doorway. The beam of her flashlight picked up a desk and chair in the alcove. How long had they been there? Years? Centuries?

She shoved down the apprehension lodged in her throat, then ventured farther into the room. As she approached the desk her gaze settled on the book on top of it. The book was a journal, and just like the top of the desk it was free of any signs of dust. Her breath caught in her lungs. She stared at the journal, almost afraid to move. Was this the final answer to the puzzle? Her hand trembled as she reached for it. A sharp jolt of fear shot through her. She hesitated, then withdrew her hand.

Donovan…she needed to get Donovan and show him

what she had found. She reached for the journal again. Should she take it with her or leave it undisturbed where she found it?

HE WATCHED from the shadows, from one of his many hiding places. His intense gaze remained riveted on her. *What are you doing, Emily? Why are you searching my lair? You don't need to seek me out. I will come to you. We'll be together…for eternity. Just as it should have been one hundred years ago.*

His breathing grew labored. His heart pounded in his chest. She was as desirable now as she had been then. The fire of passion burned hot inside him and had not diminished with the passing of time. He could not wait until the night before the festival. Before the sun rose she would belong to him for eternity.

A COLD CHILL darted up Taylor's spine, setting her nerves on edge. She jumped up from the chair, the bright beam of her light sweeping back and forth across the empty space. Once again she sensed the menacing presence, someone unseen and unheard watching her—tracking her every step, following her every move. Her heartbeat increased as the hair stood on the back of her neck. Another shiver assaulted her senses. Her insides trembled almost uncontrollably as she directed the beam of her flashlight along the ancient stone walls, into the dark corners and across the floor toward the stairs leading down into the subterranean level—into the total unknown.

"Taylor—"

The voice broke the oppressive silence. Her heartbeat jumped into her throat, cutting off her ability to say anything. She whirled around, the beam of her light landing on Donovan's face. A moment of relief settled her shattered nerves as she blurted out the first thing that came to her mind.

"You just scared the hell out of me!"

"I'm sorry. I didn't mean to startle you." He stepped through the swivel door and onto the landing, did a quick survey of the surroundings, then proceeded toward her.

"I see you've found the entrance. What have you discovered?"

She indicated the furniture. "There's this desk with a journal on top of it. Neither of them show signs of any dust so they must be in current use. I was about to take the journal and go looking for you."

He approached the desk, reached toward the journal, then paused without touching it. A myriad of sensations swirled around inside him, running the gamut from excitement to trepidation. An underlying current of apprehension wove its way through his reality, affecting every thought and feeling.

He sucked in a calming breath and reached for the journal again. He opened the cover and stared at the neat printing. He swallowed hard as the flash of realization swept through him. He scanned the first few pages, then quickly turned to the last page containing an entry. He read it, alarmed at the words and horrified as he saw the neat printing change over to the flowery handwriting of his great-grandfather—the same as the note left at the lodge house where the man and woman were murdered.

It couldn't be...it couldn't—

Total panic grabbed Donovan. He shoved the journal inside his jacket, then grabbed Taylor's arm. "Come on... we're getting out of here."

"But—"

"Now!" It was a shouted command.

A hard stab of terror hit Taylor when she saw the way Donovan's features had contorted into hard lines. Confusion ran rampant through her. She didn't understand what had happened, why his entire demeanor had suddenly changed so radically. For the first time since her arrival at the estate, Lord Donovan Sedgwick truly frightened her.

The sinister presence surrounded her, then settled over her like a suffocating blanket. She tried to ease her arm out of Donovan's grasp. He responded by increasing his hold on her. A moment later she found herself being pulled hurriedly along the passageway toward the steps leading up inside the house.

"Where are you taking me?" She heard it in her voice in the same way as she felt it in her body—her ever-increasing level of alarm with each passing second. She struggled against his iron grip as the fear coursed through her veins. What had come over him? What had suddenly prompted such bizarre behavior?

"Donovan…please, let go of me. Tell me what's wrong."

Her pleading went unheeded as he charged up the stairs and into the entry hall of the manor house with her in tow. He turned toward the hallway leading to his private living quarters.

Got to get to safety…. The words kept repeating over and over in his mind. The pain throbbed at his temples. He reinforced his determination to fight off the darkness threatening him. Images and thoughts that had been nothing more than dark swirling confusion started to congeal into a cohesive picture. Only the pure adrenaline surge kept him on his feet and moving. *Got to get to safety….*

The journal slipped from his jacket. He stopped and turned back to where it had fallen on the floor. *Can't leave it there…have to get it…the pages tell it all….* He let go of her arm as he stooped to pick it up. The moment he released his hold on her she bolted toward the staircase. He watched in agony as she took the steps two at a time toward the second floor. He fought against the darkness, desperate to remain conscious, alert and in control of his thoughts and actions. He saw her pause halfway up the staircase and look back at him.

Taylor turned just in time to see him stagger backward and bump into the wall. What had happened? She was torn between trying to find someplace where she felt safe and wanting to help Donovan. She watched him stagger toward the front door, then out into the night. Her head swirled in confusion. She didn't understand what was happening or what she should do.

Then one vital moment of the confusion cleared away. She loved him. Whatever was wrong, whatever had happened to make Donovan behave so strangely—he needed her help. She had to do everything she could to see that he was all right. She gathered her determination, turned and headed back down the stairs.

She sucked in a steadying breath, then stepped through the open door to the front porch. She scanned the surrounding area, but Donovan was nowhere in sight. Which direction would he have gone? She felt a nearly overwhelming sense of foreboding. Her heart pounded so hard she feared it might burst through her chest.

Her concerns had dramatically shifted from her own safety to his. She had to find him. There wasn't time for her to stand on the porch wondering what to do or what had happened.

The logical place for him to have gone would be around the side of the house to the private entrance of his living quarters. That was the direction he had been headed when she had broken free of his grasp. They could sort out what happened and why at a later time, but right now she had to make sure he was safe.

She still had the powerful flashlight he had given her. She clicked it on and jumped into action, leaving the porch and moving quickly along the path through the gardens and around the house. She rounded the far corner, his private terrace coming into sight. She left the path and started to cut across the lawn.

"Taylor—"

The voice came at her from out of the dark, startling her even though she recognized it as Alex. She whirled around to face him.

"Alex…what are you doing out here?"

"I spotted you from the window and came to warn you."

"Warn me?" An uneasy feeling welled inside her. "Warn me about what?"

He moved closer to her. "It's Donovan. I think he finally lost it. He seems totally deranged. It's not safe to stay in the house tonight. We need to leave before something happens."

There was a very compelling magnetism emanating from Alex, a forceful energy that had not been there before. It seemed to be reaching out to her, almost as if it was taking control of her free will.

"I don't know, Alex…I think we should help him. If he needs a doctor—"

"No, we have to leave." He grabbed hold of her arm. "We have to go now, before it's too late."

"Let go of me, Alex." A new level of panic welled inside her. "I'm not going anywhere with you."

He looked at her, the expression on his face far from the carefree flirty one she had come to expect. "We have to leave now. We can't take a chance on waiting any longer. It's not safe to stay here tonight. We have to go now."

He started toward the path that led to the front of the house, pulling her along behind him. She struggled against his hold but to no avail. When they arrived at the driveway, he ignored his car and continued on foot toward the front gates.

A cold chill of fear spread through her body. She knew at that moment that she was in serious trouble. Her fingers tightened around the handle of the large flashlight she still held. It was as if the flashlight Donovan had given her was her only hold on reality.

Chapter Fourteen

Alex kicked open the door to the lodge house and pulled her inside. A new fear swept through Taylor, settling on top of the fear already there. It was no longer an unseen presence, an ominous feeling, an unknown danger that filled the air. This was not the Alex she had come to know, the good-natured flirt who seemed to make having fun his number-one priority. His entire countenance had taken on a frightening dark malevolence.

"I've waited a long time for this. You belong to me now, just as you should have one hundred years ago. Only, this time there won't be any husband coming to your rescue..." His hard, cruel laugh filled the air. "Not that it did him any good."

He dragged her across the room. "I saw you looking at the journal. What did you do with my journal, Emily?"

Cold terror ran through her body. "I...my name isn't Emily. You have me confused with someone else. Please, Alex...let me go." She desperately struggled against his hold. "Alex...it's me. Taylor MacKenzie...remember?" She tried to make her voice as calm and soothing as possible, something far removed from what she felt. "I'm writing the book about the British country festivals?"

She could see it in his eyes. Nothing she said had registered with him. At that moment all the pieces fit together. Alex was responsible for everything that had been happening—charming, affable, easygoing Alex. In his mind he had somehow become William Sedgwick. Had he inherited the madness of his great-grandfather? Had the curse come to fruition, making Alex its pawn?

Would William's final crime against Taylor's ancestors repeat itself?

Then a new fear gripped her. Donovan…what had Alex done with Donovan?

A moment later Alex shoved her roughly to the floor, knocking the flashlight from her hand. The words hissed from his throat as his face contorted in rage. "Now, Emily…you are mine for eternity."

DONOVAN FOUGHT the horrible pain throbbing inside his head. He had seen Alex drag Taylor off across the lawn. He had to get to her before Alex could hurt her. He had to save her. Alex's neat writing had jumped off the page of the journal at him, then a fear more devastating than anything he had ever known gripped him when he saw Alex's writing morph into that of his great-grandfather.

He had to maintain control, to fight off the pain and blackness. Taylor was in danger—life-threatening danger. He could not allow anything to happen to her. He focused his concentration, drawing on every bit of strength and determination that existed within him. He loved Taylor very much and he had never told her. Nothing was more important to him than her safety. He forced the darkness from his mind, a driving willpower giving him the strength he needed. Where would Alex have taken her?

The veil of confusion parted. The blinding headache subsided. The lodge house…where his great-grandfather had dragged Emily Kincaid one hundred years ago—right before he raped then killed her.

Pure adrenaline pumped through Donovan's veins, spurring him into action. He raced toward the lodge house, his feet digging into the soft lawn as he forced his legs to move faster and faster. Every muscle in his body strained to achieve more momentum. He gave a fleeting thought to calling the police, but knew he didn't dare take the time. Every second counted. The time it took him to make a phone call could literally be the difference between life and death.

A moment of relief tempered his panic when he saw the lodge house door standing open. He had been right about where Alex had taken her. The panic returned full force. Would he get there in time? He barged through the door, then came to a horrified halt at the sight of Alex pinning Taylor's body to the floor as he tore at her clothes.

Donovan lunged toward Alex and pulled him off Taylor. It was only then that he saw Alex's knife. Even though he was an inch taller than Alex and weighed twenty pounds more, Alex seemed to possess a physical strength far beyond anything Donovan had ever associated with him. It seemed almost effortless for Alex when he tossed Donovan across the room and against the wall.

The pain seared through Donovan's shoulder, but his determination to save Taylor far outweighed his personal discomfort. He charged Alex, tackling him and knocking him to the floor. Alex leaped to his feet brandishing the knife. He advanced toward Donovan, knife raised and a look of total madness glowing in the depths of his eyes.

Donovan frantically sought out something to use as a weapon or at the least something to defend himself with. His father had long ago stripped the lodge house of all its furnishings, leaving it vacant and bare. He tasted the fear racing through his veins. The searing pain shot through his shoulder and throbbed deep inside his body. Alex's superhuman strength was too much for him, especially with his injured shoulder, but he knew he had to do something and do it very quickly. He backed toward the door. If he could lure Alex outside, then Taylor would have an opportunity to get away.

He shoved all the command into his voice that he could muster, then barked out an order. "Back off, Alex!"

Alex took another step toward Donovan. "You think you can save Emily? You foolish peasant. You'll never have her. No one will have her except me."

Alex let out a bloodcurdling scream as the knife sliced through the air seeking its target. Donovan's quick reflexes kicked in. He dodged the main thrust of the strike, but not fast enough to avoid having the sharp blade catch the edge of his forearm. His attempt to escape the knife had put his back against the wall without a clear path to the door. Alex raised the knife again, poised to administer the deadly blow. Before the knife could slice through the air, Alex let out a groan and sank to the floor. A trickle of blood oozed from the nasty gash on his head.

Taylor stood behind Alex's crumpled body, the heavy-duty flashlight in her hand. Her chest heaved with her ragged breathing. A sick sensation churned in the pit of her stomach and her legs felt weak. Her body trembled as the adrenaline subsided and the fear began to lessen. She stared at Donovan, her gaze riveted on the blood running down his arm.

She reached toward his wounded arm. She tried to speak, finally managing to force out some words. "Oh, Donovan...I was so frightened. All I could see was Alex striking at you with that knife. I've never hit anyone before in my entire life." A flood of emotional tears welled in her eyes. She loved Donovan so much. The thought of him being harmed, especially because of her…

A shudder swept through her body. "Are…are you all right?" She helped him as he struggled to his feet.

Donovan winced in pain as he twisted his shoulder. He managed to put his arms around her, oblivious to the blood and ignoring the discomfort. "You're safe. Nothing else matters."

The first calm he had experienced in quite a while finally settled over him. He placed a loving kiss on her lips. "You are all right, aren't you?"

"Shaken up but unharmed."

He held her body against his, allowing her warmth to flow to him. His words came out in an emotional whisper. "I don't think I would have been able to go on if anything had happened to you." The emotion nearly overwhelmed him as he continued to caress her. His words were barely audible, almost as if he had not intended to say them out loud. "This isn't the right time or place, but I can't keep it inside me any longer. You are the most important person in my life. I love you, Taylor. I love you so much."

Had she heard him correctly? A moment of joy flooded through Taylor, filling her heart. Nothing had ever sounded as good. "I think I started falling in love with you the night I arrived." She felt his arms tighten around her.

Then her gaze fell on Alex's body sprawled out on the floor. Her moment of elation was short-lived. She shook her head, not sure what to think or feel. There was so much that still needed to be sorted out. "To think that all of this horror was Alex's doing."

Donovan looked over at Alex's body and drew in a

calming breath. "We're not done here, yet. I'm sure that blow you landed to his head won't incapacitate him for long. I'll stay here to make sure he doesn't go anywhere. I want you to run back to the house, wake Bradley and have him call Inspector Edgeware and also request medical help, then get some rope to tie up Alex—some *strong* rope."

"Will you be okay here if he comes to while I'm gone?"

"I'll be fine." He gave her a confident smile. "I have the knife, and if all else fails, I'll follow your lead and hit him again with the flashlight." The smile faded and his expression turned serious. He placed a tender kiss on her lips. "Now get going…and hurry."

DONOVAN EASED HIMSELF into the corner of the sofa in the sitting room of his private living quarters. His shoulder wasn't broken, but it had been badly wrenched. The cut on his forearm had required twelve stitches. Fortunately the knife blade missed anything important.

Taylor hovered nearby, trying to be helpful. "Are you in much pain? Is there anything I can get for you?"

He pulled Taylor down next to him. "A couple of weeks and I'll be good as new."

Inspector Edgeware seated himself in a chair across from the sofa and directed his question to Donovan. "Now that you've had a couple of days to rest and collect your wits, I need some answers."

"How about Alex? Is he still in the coma?"

"Yes. The doctor says there's no change from the night he attacked you and Miss MacKenzie. He's in the psychiatric section of the hospital, and I have a guard on his door in case he regains consciousness and becomes violent."

Donovan picked up the journal from the end table. "It's

all in here. Some of it is straightforward and some of it needs to be interpreted."

The inspector cocked his head as he stared questioningly at Donovan. "What is that?"

"It's Alex's journal. He kept it hidden away in a secret room below the house—it accesses a subterranean area I didn't even know existed that dates back to the original structure from the late 1300s."

"If there is anything in it that relates to this case—to the four murders as well as this attack on the two of you—then it's material evidence and I need to take possession of it."

Donovan handed him the journal. "It clearly states that he committed the murders…at least it was his physical persona that did it, but the mind behind the crimes wasn't Alex."

Mike Edgeware's eyes narrowed as he leveled a hard stare at Donovan. His voice carried a hint of sarcasm. "You're not going to try to tell me some sort of ghost story, are you? Something about your cousin being possessed by the evil spirit of your great-grandfather? That the explosion happened right on schedule just as the curse said it would and your great-grandfather just sort of floated out of the crypt and entered Alex's body?"

"No, that's not what I'm saying. I've studied Alex's journal very carefully over the past couple of days—" he touched his fingertips to the dressing covering the stitches in his arm "—ever since I returned home from emergency medical treatment. It's far more complex than that. It's…"

Donovan looked toward Taylor. She saw the anguish in his eyes and knew it was too emotionally painful for him to continue to talk about it. Her voice was soft and caring. "Is it okay with you if I tell the inspector about the journal entries?"

He gave her hand a squeeze, then leaned his head back

and closed his eyes. She turned her attention toward Mike Edgeware.

"To put it as simply as possible, there were only two people between Alex and the title of Lord Sedgwick along with the accompanying estate and fortune—Alex's uncle, Lord James Sedgwick, and James's son, Donovan Sedgwick. Since Donovan was not married and had no children, that made Alex next in line after Donovan for the inheritance. And he wanted it."

Inspector Edgeware registered his disbelief. "Are you trying to tell me that these murders and an assumed elaborate scheme all comes down to money? Nothing more than basic greed?"

"That's how it started, before it took a very bizarre turn. Alex's initial plan had to do with title and money. He had devised an elaborate plan and set it into motion. It began with him methodically drugging and poisoning Donovan's father, James. Everyone seemed to forget that at one time Alex had decided on a career as a doctor before dropping out of school to pursue other things. Before that he had studied to be a scientist. He knew chemicals and drugs. He chose an obscure concoction to give James that brought on the blinding headaches and memory lapses. It was the same thing he later used on Donovan.

"This produced the desired result in that James believed he had inherited William Sedgwick's madness. That he would be the one to fulfill the curse. Toward the end he began to suspect what was happening, but didn't know how or who or why. He explored the lower level beneath the house and found the hidden subterranean level. He made notes and secreted them away in the false bottom of the trunk he left to Donovan. James did not commit suicide. He was murdered. That makes five murders that Alex committed, not four, plus two more attempted murders with Donovan and me."

Shock registered on the inspector's face as he shook his head in disbelief. "You're sure? That's all here in Alex's journal?"

"Part of it is and part of it is in the journal James hid in the trunk. You put the two writings together, and that's the story they tell. Alex had practiced for months to duplicate his uncle's handwriting. He forged the suicide note that Donovan found. He also spent quite a bit of time copying William Sedgwick's handwriting. It first started as a lark. He had intended to produce some journals which he would *discover* after he had James and Donovan out of the way. He intended to claim that the journals were his great-grand-fathers and sell them. He had even speculated about being able to sell the book and movie rights to the story of his great-grandfather and the Sedgwick Curse."

Donovan's voice broke into Taylor's explanation. His tone conveyed a combination of bitter resentment of what had happened and resignation about what couldn't be changed. "Yes…Alex certainly had some elaborate plans for his future. I wouldn't be surprised if he had also mastered my handwriting and was ready to produce my suicide note at the appropriate time—you know, my un-bearable grief over my father's death and so on. The doc-tor took a blood sample from me to send for analysis to see what kind of chemicals and drugs are in my system. I've also provided him with my personal items to test." He glanced at Taylor. "Miss MacKenzie insisted that I replace those products with new ones, then she gathered up the old and stored them in her room."

Taylor directed her comments to Inspector Edgeware. "As you can imagine, the discovery of the truth and its implications has been far more upsetting for Donovan than his physical injuries."

"I think it was while Alex was developing his forgery skills with our great-grandfather's handwriting and formulating what he would write in the phony journals that he started developing the personality traits of William Sedgwick. It will probably take a psychologist studying the journals to come up with some definitive answers, but it seemed to me that the more he immersed himself in the past and his created fantasy, the more it became a part of him until he couldn't tell where Alex stopped and William started. It wouldn't surprise me to find out that in the end he had become William pretending to be Alex."

Mike Edgeware directed his question to Taylor. "And just how are you involved in this? Why would Alex have chosen a complete stranger, an outsider as his victim in apparently repeating the crimes of a hundred years ago? Did you have any connection with Alex before arriving at the estate? Perhaps some communication with him during the time you were corresponding with James Sedgwick?"

"Well…there was an initial deception on my part. Donovan has known about this since shortly after my arrival, but no one else in the house knew, including Alex. Emily Kincaid was my great-grandmother. My grandmother was the toddler sent to safety in Canada following the murder of her parents by William Sedgwick. My real purpose in coming here was to find out about my family background. I had no idea what Emily Kincaid looked like. It wasn't until Donovan showed me a picture of my great-grandmother that I saw the striking physical resemblance between us."

Donovan handed the inspector a copy of the photograph of Emily Kincaid. "See for yourself, Mike. They could be twins."

Mike studied the picture for a moment before handing it back to Donovan. "I see what you mean."

"According to what I could decipher from Alex's journal, he was aware of the photograph and it was seeing Taylor the night she arrived that finally pushed him over the edge of the thin line he had been treading between Alex and William. In his mind she was Emily. She became his obsession just as Emily had been William's."

The inspector's cell phone rang. He concluded a very quick conversation, then turned toward Donovan. "That was the doctor. We'll never be able to find out what was going on inside Alex's head. He just died without regaining consciousness."

A quick jolt of alarm shot through Taylor. She turned a questioning look at the inspector. "Alex died?" She heard the quaver in her voice, but couldn't control it. "As a result of my hitting him with that flashlight?" Her gaze darted frantically between Donovan and the Inspector.

Donovan took control of the conversation, addressing his comments to Inspector Edgeware. He may have phrased it as a question, but there was no doubt that it was intended as a statement of fact. "Am I correct in assuming that there will not be any charges brought against Miss MacKenzie in this matter?"

"No, there won't be any charges. We had already discussed the matter. It was determined that she acted in self-defense, her actions were justified."

A rush of relief flooded through her body. "Thank you."

"I'll be going over all the journals and other physical information in detail during the next few days. I'll also request that the doctor send me a copy of the analysis of your blood. Is there anything else at this time that you'd like to add?"

Donovan glanced at Taylor, then returned his attention

to Mike Edgeware. "I can't think of anything at the moment. If something occurs to either of us, I'll call."

"I'll require a formal, signed statement from each of you, but for now I believe this takes care of the situation." Mike paused as if he wanted to say something but wasn't sure how to word his thoughts. "I...uh, your father and I had our differences, but he was a good man. I was truly shocked when I heard he had committed suicide. It didn't make any sense to me. And now I'm equally shocked to find that he was murdered. I'm very sorry about what happened to him."

Donovan extended a gracious and sincere smile. "Thank you, Mike. I know my father would have appreciated your sentiments."

General conversation continued for a few more minutes, then the inspector left.

Donovan pulled Taylor into his embrace. "There's one more pertinent matter to handle. I've called Constance Smythe and asked her to come here at two o'clock this afternoon," he glanced at the clock on the fireplace mantel, "which is in about ten minutes. We'll get this blackmail business with Bradley out into the open and have a showdown once and for all about any bloodline connection between her and William Sedgwick. I discussed the matter with Bradley a couple of hours ago and believe that his only concern was to protect the family name and avoid a scandal. I've also spoken to my solicitor about the implications if Constance does have a DNA link."

"And speaking of Constance, what about the festival? Are you going to allow it to go on in the face of everything that's happened?"

"Two hundred and fifty years of history, including world wars, could not disrupt the festival. Not even the original crimes of William Sedgwick on the very eve of the festival could cancel the proceedings. The villagers, the people from town and even visitors from as far away as London enjoy the festival. Many people have been planning for months to participate in various areas—vendors selling their wares, children competing in the games, artisans displaying their crafts. The festival will go on as tradition dictates."

Bradley knocked at the door, then entered the private area. "Constance Smythe is here for her appointment."

Taylor grasped Donovan's hand as she rose to her feet. "Would you prefer that I leave?"

"No, there's no need."

"Then I'll just sit over here out of the way." She settled into a chair by the terrace door.

Donovan immediately noted the nervousness that surrounded Bradley. His usually expressionless mask showed his uneasiness. "Don't worry, Bradley. As I told you earlier, I don't hold you in a position of blame. I will ask you one more time if you're interested in seeing criminal charges brought against her for blackmail or extortion, whichever is appropriate. Please consider the situation without concerning yourself with public opinion or gossip. Don't worry about it reflecting on the Sedgwick name. What do *you* want?"

"Thank you, sir. That's most generous, but as I said earlier I don't wish to pursue the matter. It's been a terrible burden on my conscience which is why I finally brought it to your attention. I prefer to consider it closed."

"Okay, Bradley." Donovan took a steadying breath. One last hurdle to tackle. "Send Constance in."

A moment later a bubbly Constance entered the room and rushed to Donovan's side. Her words gushed out, almost as if she were a teenager. "I was shocked when I heard about what happened. I've been so worried about you." She threw her arms around his neck as if she were going to kiss and hug him. "I'm happy you're all right."

Donovan winced in pain as she embraced him and immediately shoved her away. "Be careful of my shoulder and arm. It will be a while before they've healed."

She seemed genuinely shocked by his brusque manner. "Oh…I'm terribly sorry. I should have realized—"

"I didn't call you here to engage in casual conversation."

"Yes, I'm sure you want a final report on the festival."

"No, Constance, that's not what I want."

The twinkle in her eyes clearly showed her misinterpretation of his comment. "Donovan…this is so unexpected. I'm thrilled that the truth is finally out in the open." She snuggled next to him on the sofa. "You and I both want the same thing, darling."

Donovan rose to his feet, crossed the room and stood next to Taylor's chair. Constance's eyes widened in shock when she saw Taylor, then a wariness flashed across her face. "Exactly why did you ask me here if not about festival business?"

"I want to talk about the money you extorted from Bradley. He has told me that you claim to have evidence that you are in fact an illegitimate heir of my great-grandfather."

The wariness on her face quickly turned to panic. "I don't know what you're talking about."

"Bradley told me everything—"

"This is outrageous! You're going to take the word of a servant over mine? Bradley obviously has some sort of agenda of his own and is trying to implicate me in his wrong doing."

"Before you become even more indignant, let me continue. I went to Bradley to ask him about his clandestine payments to you. He didn't come to me." Donovan held up his hand to stop whatever it was she was about to say. "And I have an eye witness to the payment that occurred in the greenhouse a few nights ago."

"An eyewitness?" The confidence and bravado Constance had earlier displayed quickly faded.

"I've also consulted my solicitor. Let me tell you what I am prepared to do. If you can show undeniable proof of a DNA link between you and me, then I'm willing to offer you a settlement as your claim against the estate. If not," he leaned forward and leveled a stern look at her, "I think you might be happier living somewhere else."

"But the festival—"

"Will go on this year just as always. Next year's festival will be coordinated by the new lady of the manor." He shot a quick sideways glance toward Taylor, his expression questioning, then returned his attention to the matter at hand. "So, Constance...what is your decision? Oh, there's one more thing. I will take it as a gesture of good faith if you return the money you took from Bradley."

Constance Smythe glared at Donovan, shot an angry look in Taylor's direction, then whirled around and stomped out of the room.

Donovan pulled Taylor up out of the chair and into his arms. "I guess that answers the question about her lineage."

"So it would seem."

"That leaves only one question."

"And that would be...?" She held her breath, hoping against hope that he was going to say what she wanted to hear.

"Taylor MacKenzie...would you do me the honor of becoming my wife and the lady of the manor?"

She slipped her arms around his neck. "I love you, Lord Donovan Sedgwick. I would be honored to be your wife."

Taylor's body stiffened when the sound reached her ears…the same sound that had so frightened her on two other occasions. "Uh, maybe there's one more question. That noise…"

Donovan emitted a soft chuckle. "Oh, that. We're so accustomed to it that we don't really hear it anymore. It's the backup generator that provides basic emergency power during storms when we sometimes lose electricity. The noise is a self-testing readiness check that the system periodically performs."

Taylor smiled at him. "I feel very foolish. When I heard it before, I thought it was something sinister." She brushed a loving kiss across his lips. "I'll be honored to live with that sound, too."

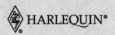

SPOTLIGHT

National bestselling author

JOANNA WAYNE

The Gentlemen's Club

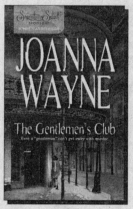

A homicide in the French Quarter of New Orleans has attorney Rachel Powers obsessed with finding the killer. As she investigates, she is shocked to discover that some of the Big Easy's most respected gentlemen will go to any lengths to satisfy their darkest sexual desires. Even murder.

A gripping new novel... coming in June.

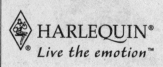

HARLEQUIN®

Live the emotion™

If you enjoyed what you just read,
then we've got an offer you can't resist!

Take 2 bestselling love stories FREE!

Plus get a FREE surprise gift!

SPOTLIGHT

A NEW 12-book series featuring the reader-favorite Fortune family launches in June 2005!

THE FORTUNES OF TEXAS: Reunion

Cowboy at Midnight

by *USA TODAY* bestselling author

ANN MAJOR

Rancher Steven Fortune considered himself lucky. He had a successful ranch, good looks and many female companions. But when the contented bachelor meets events planner Amy Burke-Sinclair, he finds himself bitten by the love bug!

The Fortunes of Texas: Reunion—
The power of family.

> **Exclusive Extras!**
> **Family Tree...**
> **Character Profiles...**
> **Sneak Peek**

Silhouette®
Where love comes alive™

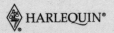
HARLEQUIN®

INTRIGUE®

Return to

M^CCALLS' MONTANA

this spring
with

B.J. DANIELS

Their land stretched for miles across
the Big Sky state…all of it hard-earned—
none of it negotiable. Could family ties
withstand the weight of lasting legacy?

AMBUSHED!
May

HIGH-CALIBER COWBOY
June

SHOTGUN SURRENDER
July

Available wherever Harlequin Books are sold.